Night Walker

BY

Lisa Kessler

Entangled Publishing, LLC
2614 South Timberline Road
Suite 109
Fort Collins, CO 80525

Visit our website at www.entangledpublishing.com.

Entangled Publishing is a subsidiary of Savvy Media Services, LLC.

Edited by Kerri-Leigh Grady
Cover design by Heather Howland

eBook ISBN   978-1-937044-12-1
Print ISBN   978-1-937044-13-8

Manufactured in the United States of America

To Ken and Ally,
who read Night Walker *in all its*
incarnations and never lost hope
in the book or me...

Prologue

Kate couldn't remember the drive home or walking from her car to her front door. Her mind kept replaying Tom's surprised face, the way he jerked his hands free of the woman's tight sweater, and the flushed cheeks of his grad student. Her knuckles ached from clenching her fists, struggling to control her emotions. Blood smeared across the palm of her hand where her fingernail broke the skin.

She could still hear his footsteps echoing behind her in the desolate parking lot and the pleading in his voice. *"Please, can't we talk about this?"* His desperation made her nauseous.

What could he possibly explain?

After three tries, she finally managed to calm her trembling hands and unlock her apartment door. Forcing a deep breath into her lungs, she steeled herself for what awaited. The eight-by-ten engagement photo smiled at her from the side table. Her knees threatened to buckle under the weight of betrayal.

Leaning against the door, she struggled to understand. Their wedding was less than a month away. All their plans, their dreams, tossed away for a pair of most-likely-fake double Ds.

How could she have been so blind? She almost married him.

For the third time since she'd sped away from the university, her cell phone buzzed. She powered it off and tossed it aside. The bastard could call all night, send flowers, beg on his knees, but nothing would change the fact that she'd never walk down the aisle in the designer gown that *he* insisted she buy. She'd never move into the new condo they'd had their eye on. And she would never trust him again.

It was over.

She wiped her nose and glared at the photo on the table. Shouldn't she be jealous? Did she even care if he'd slept with this woman? Was she devastated because she would miss Tom, or because her life wasn't turning out the way she thought it should?

Puzzled, she pushed away from the door and turned the frame facedown on the table. Her gaze locked onto her parents' photo. Nearly two years had slipped by since the accident. She'd worked so hard to distance herself from the pain of their loss that she'd avoided dealing with the remainder of their estate. She still hadn't sold their house.

Instead, she'd pushed her relationship with Tom forward, avoiding her emotions by planning a wedding to a man she wasn't certain she loved.

Gripping the frame, she tilted the photo to cut the glare from the overhead light. Her mother's warm smile brought a swell of heartache—real heartache, not this shock of betrayal and sudden change that Tom had delivered.

"I wish you were here, Mom." She wiped a tear from her cheek. "You probably would've seen right through his sexy, crooked smile."

She waited, half-expecting to hear her mother's voice telling her she deserved better.

Because she did.

"I think it's time for me to go back home. I'm through hiding, Mom."

Once she returned the photo to the table, the tightness in her chest loosened its grip. This wasn't the end of the world. In fact, it was a chance at a new beginning.

She'd call her school in the morning and let them know she needed a leave of absence. Then she'd get in touch with the caterers and the perky wedding planner.

She could be on the road by the afternoon. She lifted her chin a notch and dropped her engagement photo in the trashcan. Tomorrow, she would take control of her life and her future, and this time she wouldn't rush into anything.

CHAPTER ONE

When they parked at the Mission de Alcala, Kate stared up at the bells. Although she grew up in San Diego, she'd never played tourist and visited this famous landmark, which she admitted now was a shame. The white arched bell tower of the first Spanish mission in the New World stretched toward the heavens, oblivious to the changing landscape around it. For a moment, she felt like she'd been transported back in time.

Edie hefted her camera bag over her shoulder. "Hurry up! We don't want to end up standing for the service."

"I'm coming." Kate ran up the uneven tile steps after her friends.

When they entered the white adobe sanctuary, her breath caught in her throat. The natural pine ceiling arched high above them, voices echoed in the cavernous space, and soft chords from the pipe organ at the rear of the hall floated down. The music washed over the congregation, filling the church with its somber peace.

Her mother would have loved this place.

Lori grabbed Kate's hand and pulled her across the sanctuary to a pew by the opposite door. Candlelight filled the chamber with a warm glow, and soon the only sounds were the soft chants from the priests. Images of Christ's crucifixion lined the walls, and the quiet hymns from the choir added to the poignancy of the Mass. Bittersweet sorrow swelled in her heart. This would be her second holiday season without her parents, and her first without Tom. The Mass felt like a solemn reminder she was alone in the world.

The room blurred behind a wave of tears.

"I need some air. I'll be right outside," Kate whispered to Edie.

Edie gave her an *are you all right* look, and Kate managed to smile and nod before slipping out the door. As the heavy wooden door clicked shut behind her, she stepped into a lush courtyard with centuries-old adobe crosses rising through thick ferns that threatened to swallow them. More candles flickered around the garden. Shadows moved across the surrounding walls, mingling with the darkness that gathered in the corners and alcoves.

The cool night air filled her lungs, calming the storm brewing inside her. Seeing the families and couples in the sanctuary stirred up heartache. She had erected protective walls around the spaces her parents and her ex-fiancé used to fill, but now they crumbled. Kate took another deep breath and stared at the pale moon. She could almost hear her mother's voice telling her to stay strong. Keep moving forward.

Just as she'd promised herself she'd do.

Clearing her throat, Kate focused on her surroundings and followed a worn tile path to a weathered sign. The courtyard, and the crosses within it, honored the Native American neophytes who worked at the mission in its early years. Kate scanned the garden again, finding even more of the half-hidden handmade crosses peering at her from a thicket of ferns. Most of them now leaned to the side, weathered from years of exposure to the sun and rain.

The once-strong angles of the markers now drooped as though they wept.

She followed the path deeper into the garden and found another cross nearly engulfed by the foliage and flowers that grew around it. Though the path here was unkempt and the aging monument covered in moss, a simple floral wreath adorned the neck of the cross.

How many Native Americans died at the mission in its early

years? She wondered if anyone really knew. She learned about the missions in elementary school, but her teachers never discussed the relationship between the missionaries and the local tribes. Was neophyte a fancy word for slave? She didn't know, but whatever their role might have been, it was encouraging to see the indigenous people who had lived at the mission had not been forgotten.

When the service concluded, the murmur of soft conversation broke through her solitude. Mass was over already? Kate frowned. How long had she been outside?

Car engines started and brakes squeaked, the headlights drowning out the candlelit shadows. Beyond the black wrought iron gates, small groups of people departed together until finally the floodlights over the parking lot blinked off. She would have worried about Lori and Edie's absence, but she knew they had plans with their digital cameras after the mass.

According to her friends, Dia de los Muertos was the perfect night for ghost hunting. Lori and Edie always enjoyed ghost stories when they were kids, and their fondness grew until they considered themselves amateur paranormal investigators. What better place to find them than in the oldest building in San Diego on the one night a year reserved for the dead?

Kate didn't share their zeal for spirits, but she had no problem waiting for them to have their fun. She was happy to have a few minutes to herself anyway.

The candlelight glimmered around her, the flickering flames left to burn out sometime before morning. The warm glow made for eerie light, casting long shadows of the weeping crosses over the garden. It was exquisite and melancholy in the same moment.

She caught a sudden chill. The longer she lingered, the more her sadness mutated into unease.

The back of her neck prickled. Kate crossed her arms and walked toward the sanctuary doors. She suddenly felt exposed and alone. Before she reached the doors, Lori and Edie came up the path at the other end of the courtyard, snapping pictures as they walked, until Lori disappeared from view.

When Edie saw Kate approach, she grinned. "Oh, you should see some of the great shots we got tonight. We had lots of orbs in a couple of pictures of the bell tower. There might be even more when we can look at them on a larger screen."

"You'll have to show me once you get them on the computer." Kate glanced around the courtyard. "Where'd Lori go?"

Edie turned around. "She was right behind... "

"Edie... Kate." Lori's voice, a loud and insistent whisper, emanated from the shadows.

Kate flinched when she heard her name. She had no idea why she was so jumpy tonight. They tracked down Lori and found her kneeling by one of the crosses. She beckoned them closer.

Edie rushed over with an eager grin, camera at the ready. "Wow. Look at this." She squatted beside Lori.

The cross was smaller than most of the others, weather-beaten and canted. There was a single letter in the center, a T, and a single candle burned beside a bundle of large white blossoms.

"Who do you think left those?" Lori whispered.

Kate shrugged. None of the other crosses had fresh offerings. "Probably the priests, right?"

"I don't know." Lori glanced at the other crosses. "Maybe this person's relatives still visit every year."

"Can you imagine?" Edie whispered. "Being remembered like that? I hope someone's still bringing me flowers after I've been dead a couple hundred years."

Kate thought about correcting them, telling them these crosses were memorials to the Native Americans. But she didn't. Something about the cross held her rapt. The conversation around her faded away as Kate moved in closer to the fragrant blossoms.

She'd never seen flowers like these with huge, beautiful blooms of white, silky petals and a center like pure sunshine. And the scent. It was the primrose-like perfume that made her reach out to touch them, entranced by their spell.

Had she seen these flowers before?

"Kate? Are you okay?"

Kate looked up at Lori, her brow furrowed and mouth pinched in concern. "I'm fine," she said, yanking her hand away from the flowers. "Just a little tired, I guess."

"We're almost done. We need a couple more pictures around the front by the steps," Edie said.

"All right." Kate straightened, still unable to pull her attention away from the cross and its bouquet. "I'll wait for you here, okay?"

Lori continued to frown, but Edie said, "No problem. We'll be right back."

Kate watched them wander off before kneeling closer to the cross. Unable to stop herself, she traced her finger along the T in the center.

Behind her, someone cleared his throat. Kate jerked her hand away and shot to her feet. When she turned around she found a tall, dark-haired man staring at her.

Her cheeks flushed with heat. She hoped he hadn't witnessed her touching the relic. She waited for some kind of admonishment, but he didn't say anything.

Not with words.

Something in his dark eyes captured her. His gaze wandered over her face like a tender caress, and strangely, instead of screaming for Lori and Edie, she caught herself imagining his touch on her skin.

"I hope I did not frighten you," he said.

His deep voice resonated through the empty courtyard, and the intimate tone weakened her knees. The hint of a Spanish accent didn't hurt, either. Nervous laughter escaped her before she could contain it.

Her face warmed all over again. "Just a little startled. I didn't see anyone else out here."

He stepped closer without encroaching on her personal space, his eyes locked with hers from beneath thick lashes. "Forgive me."

She swallowed hard and prayed she wasn't blushing. "No problem." She looked away before she embarrassed herself even further, focusing on the cross. "It's beautiful isn't it?"

"*Sí*." He nodded slowly. "Yes, it is." His barely there smile made her think he wasn't referring to the flowers or the cross. "I am Calisto.

Calisto Terana."

Expectation hung as heavy as the scent of eucalyptus, as if he waited to hear something more than just her name.

"I'm Kate." Instead of offering to shake his hand, she tucked a stray lock of hair behind her ear. "It's nice to meet you."

"The honor is mine, Kate... " His accent colored the vowel in her name. It had never sounded more beautiful. She reminded herself to breathe.

When he hesitated for a moment waiting for her to speak, she realized she hadn't shared her last name as he had. She flipped through a rapid pro and con mental checklist, and decided it couldn't hurt. Maybe they *would* meet again.

"Bradley," she said.

A sexy smile curved at the corners of his lips. "I hope this will not be our last meeting."

She glanced around the shadowed courtyard, feeling vulnerable, and almost gave in to her first instinct—to run. But she remembered her promise to herself. Be strong. Take action. She lifted her chin and said, "I guess you never know."

With a smile that said he had every intention of seeing her again, he tipped his head. "*Buenos noches*, Kate Bradley."

Her heart raced and her palms sweated when she realized he meant to leave. No man made her palms sweat. Ever.

His gaze held hers for a moment, full of unspoken promises she didn't understand. Without another word, he walked away.

Kate willed him to turn toward her one last time. It would be easy to get addicted to the way his gaze caressed her, entrancing her with his full attention. She wet her lips and shook her head slowly, struggling to break the spell.

A strange man had flirted with her in a dark courtyard. *Hello!* Huge danger signal for a woman alone.

But she never felt threatened. As if she'd met him before.

"Who was that?" Lori tucked her camera inside her bag.

"He said his name was Calisto Terana."

"He looked sexy from where I stood. Yum!" Edie grinned.

Lori nudged her with her elbow. "Looks can be deceiving. Why was he loitering after Mass and hitting on Kate?"

There went Lori, being overprotective, like Kate was her younger sister instead of a peer. Kate rolled her eyes. "He wasn't hitting on me. He was a complete gentleman." She paused, glancing in the direction he'd gone. "Old fashioned."

Lori hooked her camera bag over her shoulder. "You didn't give him your number, did you? Old fashioned or not, you don't know anything about this guy."

"Yes, Mom! I've been a single adult just as long as you have, remember?"

Lori hooked her arm through Kate's. "I still worry about you. You've been through a lot lately. I don't want anyone to take advantage of you."

Kate relaxed, though she still chafed at being treated like a child. "Believe me, I don't want that either."

Part of her was shocked she even considered looking at another man. A couple of weeks ago she wanted to wipe all the bastards off the face of the earth, and then tonight a gorgeous guy with an accent and a healthy dose of manners suddenly had her heart racing. Go figure.

They started toward the car. Kate peeked over her shoulder, wondering where Calisto had gone. No doubt it was for the best that he walked away when he did.

But secretly she wished he *had* asked for her number.

Edie unlocked the car. "What kind of name is Calisto anyway? It doesn't sound Mexican."

"Maybe Spanish?" Lori said.

Kate replayed the way he said her name. "He did have an accent. Not quite Mexican though. Maybe he is from Spain."

"Oh, I love accents." Edie pretended to shiver. "Why don't I ever meet handsome foreign men in dark courtyards?"

"Get in the car already." Lori smiled.

Their banter continued as Lori pulled out of the mission's parking lot toward Old Town, but Kate wasn't listening anymore. At the other end of the lot she saw him standing in the moonlight.

Calisto.

He stared right into her eyes. Even at this distance, the heat of his gaze flushed her skin, and her breath caught in her throat.

What if she never saw him again? A knot of panic tightened in her stomach.

He watched them roll down the driveway, bowing his head before turning to walk back into the shadows. Kate sighed and finally faced forward, chastising herself for acting like a love-struck teenager. The last thing she needed right now was a relationship. She'd just been burned so badly that she took a leave of absence from her teaching job and left the state of Nevada.

How could she stomach even looking at another man?

She stared out the window and smiled in spite of herself. Calisto didn't seem like any other man she'd ever met. Against her better judgment, she caught herself hoping they would meet again.

§

1775

She was dead.

Part of him still could not, or would not, believe it. Even now as he covered her body with dirt, he imagined this was a foul dream. Still clothed in his missionary robes, Father Gregorio Salvador prayed he would awaken to the sound of her laughter, or see her dark eyes sparkle with shared humor again. Tala had the most beautiful dark brown eyes with a tiny hazel crescent at the bottom of her right iris.

She used to smile at him every time he told her she had the moon in her eyes.

His jaw clenched. He would have his vengeance.

As he laid the bundle of large, white Romneya flowers over her grave, his tears fell onto the freshly turned soil covering her body, like raindrops darkening the sandy dirt. The sight brought him to his knees.

He knelt at her grave, silently begging the God he once served for answers. Was it wrong to love her? Was God so unforgiving of their sin that He sought to take her life and damn his soul? They had hurt no one. He had broken his covenant with God, yet she was forced to pay his penance with her life? Why punish her?

But he already knew. What greater punishment could he suffer than to go on living without her? He was certain no deeper pain existed.

Surely God knew he had been no more than a naive boy when he took his vows in Spain.

He buried Tala at the edge of the cliff where they met in secret during the warm summer evenings to watch the sun set over the water and color the sky. He hoped her soul would find peace there. Taking the rosary beads from his neck, he laid them over the flowers covering her final resting place. He would never touch another rosary. God had forsaken him, punished him for loving her, and he wouldn't serve Him any longer.

Kissing his fingertips and touching the flowers, he whispered, "My love forever."

He tugged at his collar, and then stripped off his robe. Clothed only in his black wool pants and sandals, Father Salvador walked into the darkness of the hills. He couldn't bear to look back.

§

Calisto watched her until the car faded away into the night. The Old One's promise had finally come true. With his heightened vision, he had seen the lighter crescent of color in the lower corner of her iris. He recognized her in an instant. She had the moon in her eyes.

Tala, his love, lived again.

Her features were familiar, but not exactly as she had once been. Her skin was lighter now and the angle of her jaw softer, but her long black hair and her eyes had not changed. Hearing her voice, seeing her smile, brought back memories of a life they once shared.

The sound of her laughter was like a burst of sunlight in his endless night.

But Kate Bradley wasn't Tala. She had no memory of him. It was a bittersweet moment to see her face again, yet be unable to touch her. Although she didn't seem to fear him as a stranger, she also didn't recognize him as a lover.

He knew nothing about her life now.

The desire to touch her had overwhelmed him. He yearned to taste her lips and hold her in his arms. There would be time for that later, he promised himself.

It would have been simple to reach for her thoughts and learn her secrets, to become exactly the man she desired, but he denied himself the intrusion. He vowed not to use his preternatural power to entrance her or to listen to her private thoughts. He'd given up his mortality, his soul, for this moment, this second chance, and if she fell in love with him again, he needed to know it was real. No other person had ever touched his life like she had. Though she was no longer Tala, surely a piece of the soul he once loved lived inside of her.

Calisto walked into the shadows, wondering if she still sang with a voice that rivaled the angels. Would she dance with him in the waves of the Pacific as they had centuries before?

He was anxious to find out. How long had it been since he'd been eager for anything? A smile tugged at the corner of his mouth. Kate Bradley.

He would see her again. Soon.

Clearing his thoughts, Calisto opened himself to his animal spirit, allowing the raven to take shape in his mind. Gradually, the air around him sparked with energy as his body shifted and changed from a tall, dark-haired man into a large, jet-black raven. Fully changed, he shook his body and stretched out his wings before launching himself into the air. Silently, he soared with the wind and winged his way through the night sky.

CHAPTER TWO

Blood marred the stone wall of his modest dorm room. His knuckles stung each time his fist slammed into the rough rock. Pain cloaked the bitterness and rage that festered inside him.

The monsignor had passed him over. Denied his chance at his destiny.

Again.

It would be Brother Cardina who would fly across the Atlantic Ocean to San Diego. Brother Cardina would watch over the Night Walker and witness immortality with his own eyes.

Grinding his teeth together, he struck the wall once more, imagining it was Brother Cardina's pious face, but he held back, careful not to hit too hard. Bruised and bloodied flesh could go unnoticed within the ancient walls of the Fraternidad Del Fuego Santo, but broken bones would not help his cause.

Pain burned up his arm, calming him. He stepped back and basked in the ache.

Brother Cardina was no match for an immortal blood drinker.

He moved closer to the wall, drinking in the earthy scent of his blood. He would get his chance. Staring at the fresh crimson stain, he stuck out his tongue and allowed himself a long, slow lick. He closed his eyes and smiled, resting his cheek against the wall. For now, he would be patient.

Clenching his raw fists, he opened his eyes and stared at his pencil sketches of ravens. His chance would come.

Soon.

§

"Go with God," Calisto whispered as he tossed the lifeless body into the ocean far from the shore. Although he had forsaken religion centuries before, his victims might still find a merciful afterlife in spite of their many sins. He hoped, for their sakes, they would.

The Pacific waves lapped at the Southern California beach. The ocean was a perfect disposal for his meals. The sea drank them into itself, and the bloodless corpses sank to the depths of the ocean, food for the marine life. In the cold waters, it took weeks for the bodies, or what remained of the bodies, to float to the surface. If they did wash ashore, the decomposition made it virtually impossible to determine the exact cause of death.

Not that it mattered. If pathologists did discover the true cause of death, he doubted they would link the deaths to someone with no boat and no records of accessing one. And how would they explain bloodless victims with no discernable wound?

No one spoke of Night Walkers anymore except as merely folk tales.

Blood drinkers in Europe had called themselves vampires years before Calisto ever heard the word, but they knew nothing of what it meant to be a true Night Walker. He despised the glamour that went with the ridiculous name they adopted. He found very little romance in death, even less in immortality.

As the years passed his strength and power grew, making him less of a man and more of a monster. He'd slowly changed into a hunter stalking his prey. He fed on the refuse of humanity, killers, drug lords, and child abusers, then gave his victims' bodies to the sea.

Vampires were for movie screens and romance novels. And he would never think of himself as one of them. He was a Night Walker. But it didn't matter what he called himself in this modern world. No one believed in his kind, regardless of the label they used.

He wouldn't believe it himself if he weren't already living in endless night.

But tonight his existence changed forever. After over 200 years of waiting, he saw Tala smile again, heard her laughter. He felt more human than he had in centuries. Though newfound hope lightened his spirit, he had to remain patient and proceed with care and caution.

He needed to get to know her again, and for her to know him.

But what if she didn't fall in love with him this time?

He stopped walking to look at the moonlight shimmering on the waves. Could fate be so cruel to show him her face again, to let him know she lived once more, only to have her push him away? As many times as he had dreamed of this day, it never occurred to him she might not want him.

His jaw tightened. She smiled at him tonight. She'd seen him watching her as she drove away. Something inside of her remembered him. He felt it.

Or was he blinded by hope?

Calisto continued down the sand until he reached his home. He wanted to see her again. Surely after waiting lifetimes for her to return, he had been patient enough. He didn't want to endure one more night without her.

Music blared, interrupting his thoughts. Through the windows of his home, charity patrons mingled and laughed. He'd hoped the benefit party would be over before he got back. He was in no mood to entertain a room full of wealthy mortals. Not tonight.

Tonight he wanted to relive the moment Tala smiled at him. He had forgotten the way the moon sparkled in her dark eyes, and the way her full lips curved in a welcoming smile. If only he could have touched her.

With a determined sigh, he closed his eyes and focused his thoughts. As he approached his front door, he straightened his clothes. Certain no traces of his victim's blood stained him, he pulled open the door.

"Calisto! What a wonderful surprise." Betty took his newly

warmed hand as he entered. "I was afraid you might not make it. The party has been a huge success. Come, I'll introduce you around."

"No. Forgive me, Bettina." He raised her hand to press a kiss to the back of her fingers. She enjoyed hearing her full name with his Spanish accent. Flattery came easily for an immortal with the power to persuade and years of practice. Although he regretted toying with her, tonight it was a necessary evil. "I do not mean to be rude, but I am too weary from my business trip to entertain guests. Please continue to make use of my home, but I must retire to my room and rest."

"Oh, I understand completely," she said with an almost giddy smile. "I'll start wrapping up the party down here. Don't worry about a thing."

"I never do." He went upstairs to his room, and closed the door behind him.

Within a half hour Betty's heels clicked against the Spanish tile foyer floor, echoing through the empty house. She had cleared the guests, proving again the wisdom of his decision to elevate her to Director of Foundation Arts. Not only was she intelligent, loyal and hardworking, but her infatuation with him also made it easier to hide his true nature from her. She rarely questioned him, and for an immortal to live among mortals, it was imperative they take him at his word.

However false it might be.

"Calisto?" Betty knocked on the door.

He already knew what she would say. Her thoughts were an open book to him, but he thought it best to keep up appearances. "Come in, Bettina."

His dark hair hung loosely around his face, freed from the band he used to keep it tied back. He sat on the edge of his king-sized bed as she opened the door. Betty was the only person to ever see him in such a casual state.

She tried to hold back a smile. "The house is all yours again. Everyone's gone."

"Thank you. I wish I had been a better host for you tonight."

She smiled and shrugged a bare shoulder. "No problem. Everyone was thrilled to be inside your home. We raised close to one hundred thousand dollars tonight."

"You did a wonderful job."

Her expression said she hoped for more from him, but he couldn't focus on small talk.

Leaving flowers at the mission in memory of Tala usually left him feeling despondent, but tonight had been the opposite. Tonight, he wrestled against hope instead of bitterness. Fate finally offered him a second chance at love and happiness.

"Well, I guess I'll go then," she said. "I'll be in the office in the morning."

"I will be out of town again, but perhaps we can set a meeting for Tuesday night? You can update me on anything needing my attention."

She pursed her lips for one brief second and then assumed her usual professional expression. When he hired Betty, he explained she would probably not work with him often. Even so, he knew she didn't expect his frequent trips, but she kept her opinions to herself. Working for an influential philanthropist, she expected some eccentricities. He paid her well, and it wasn't her place to inquire of his whereabouts. Every once in a while, he mentioned details about trips abroad to his homeland in Spain, and she seemed satisfied with his explanation.

"Tuesday night is fine," she said. "How about six o'clock? We could meet somewhere for dinner."

"Perfect. Just leave a note to let me know where I am to meet you." He loathed computers and e-mail.

"I will."

He stood and worked at the buttons on his shirt. "Good night, Bettina, and thank you."

Her all-business nod indicated she realized he wasn't in the mood for conversation. "Goodnight. I'll see you Tuesday."

And then she was gone.

He waited until he heard the front door close and the lock turn before leaving his bedroom. He had trained her well.

When the soft purr of her car's engine faded into the distance, Calisto went downstairs and sat down at his grand piano. Playing was one of the few activities of late that helped ease the loneliness plaguing him. The music surrounded him in a calming embrace, like a child wrapped in his mother's arms.

Over the years, he had become a virtuoso, a product of having centuries to practice. In that time, he had memorized countless masterpieces by Chopin, Mozart, and Beethoven, but right now Rachmaninoff's "Vocalise" poured from his soul, through his fingertips, making the grand piano ring with emotion.

The music spoke words he couldn't recite, and he played with fervor and accuracy only an immortal being could achieve. Tonight the piano sang, not with the bitter ache of emptiness but with hope and the promise of love. Passion built in the melody, and in his mind he saw her eyes shining as he bent to kiss her lips. He closed his eyes as he played, envisioning her body pressed against his, her warm skin enticing him to hold her tighter.

At the final cadence, his hands remained frozen over the keys, suspending the final chord as it echoed through his empty house. When silence crept around him, Calisto rose from the keyboard and made his way to the secret chamber buried deep within the cliff of his beachfront home.

He would find her again. Tomorrow night he would search for Kate Bradley. For the first time in decades, he was anxious for another night.

As the dawning sun warmed the earth above him, he settled into the cold depths below. Closing his eyes, his ancient heart quieted and his lungs let out a final breath.

§

1775

Blood trickled down her arms and legs, but she couldn't stop to nurse her wounds. Not now.

She ran, breaking through the bushes as they tore at her flesh, never slowing her pace. Thorns stabbed her bare feet, and the pungent smell of sagebrush filled her lungs as she forced herself to move faster.

Deafening wind tugged at her buckskin dress and pushed her back, but she continued to run. Her life depended on it.

Scrambling through the brush and over the rocks, she ignored the pain as the rough terrain ripped at the bloody soles of her feet. With a glance over her shoulder, she saw him closing in, his face veiled in shadows.

She ran faster, her lungs aching with pain. Her heart raced as erratically as the rabbits that darted in front of her. Blood from her split lip burned the back of her throat.

How much longer could she stay ahead of him?

"Tala," he yelled, his voice loud enough to startle her. He had drawn closer. *"Hay en ninguna parte funcionar."*

She didn't agree. Escape was still an option. If she reached the boulders, her pursuer would have to abandon his horse or risk the animal losing its footing. If the Spanish guard were on foot she would have the advantage. He didn't know the terrain as well as she did.

The pendant around her neck thumped against her chest with every stride. Her arms and legs felt weighted with stones as sweat rolled down her face and stung her eyes. Clinging to hope, she pushed herself, pounding her aching heels into the rough dirt and pumping her arms faster.

Until her foot tangled in an exposed root.

She hit the ground hard, knocking the air from her lungs. Gasping, she scrambled on her belly, her fingernails scratching into the dry granite soil as she tried to drag herself away.

The thump of his boots on the dirt spurred her on.

She had to get away.

Before she could struggle to her feet, he grabbed her ankle. She kicked his wrist with her free foot, but he didn't loosen his grip.

When he flipped her over, she screamed until he covered her mouth with a dirty, calloused hand. Tala stared at him in shock. She recognized the guard from the Mission de Alcala, but the lustful hunger in his eyes was new and turned her stomach.

She slid her bloodied fingers over her slightly rounded abdomen and murmured a soft apology to her unborn child.

He pressed a knife to her throat and tore at her dress with frenzied, rough hands. She struggled to break free, but his weight pinned her to the ground. When she scraped her broken nails across his cheek, he grasped her wrists with one hand and held her prone. And then he violated her.

She closed her eyes, praying for the spirits of her Kumeyaay ancestors to guide her soul.

§

Kate screamed, waking herself from the dream. Her nightshirt stuck to her sweat-drenched body. Coming to San Diego brought back the nightmare that had haunted her since childhood. She shuddered, pushing her hair back from her face. She thought by now it wouldn't terrify her so much, but the dream felt real, the scent of sagebrush, the ache in her feet, the panic.

Too real.

Shaking off the dream, she got up and did her best to get a jump on the last few items on her to-do list. Since the renters moved out, she had the perfect opportunity to get her parents' home ready to sell. But instead of making calls to carpet cleaners and painters, she surfed the web on her laptop, searching for Calisto Terana in San Diego.

The search engine's hourglass turned over and over like it used a hamster running in a wheel as its only power source.

"Oh come on." She clicked the refresh button again. Maybe he wasn't from San Diego. He might've been a tourist visiting from Europe or something.

Finally the screen shifted, and she stared at the page in shock.

All of the search results showed a Calisto Terana, philanthropist and founder of Foundation Arts, the same charity her mother had supported. The same charity slated to inherit her mother's piano. Kate glanced at the baby grand sitting in the corner and sighed. She'd tried to take care of everything last year. As the only child, no one else stood beside her to help with the loss, the loneliness, and the demands. In the end, it was too much too soon.

Losing both parents at once, without warning, left her bereft and barely functioning. Lori and Edie helped her box up most of their things and put them into storage, but Kate fell apart at the thought of selling the house. She didn't make arrangements to donate her mother's piano and sheet music, or many of the things her mother requested in the will.

In the end, she left the house furnished, rented it out, and left Point Loma for her new life in Reno. She'd deal with the rest of the estate later when her emotions weren't so raw, she'd told herself.

It was definitely time to finish up her parents' trust.

She set the laptop on the table, deciding to walk off some of her excess energy. It was a small world. What were the chances the founder of her mother's favorite charity would be at the Mission de Alcala at the same time as her? What were the chances he'd be at the Mission at all?

And what were the chances he'd be gorgeous?

She sighed, remembering the way he approached her with the confidence and stealth of a jungle cat. He'd worn khaki slacks and a sage button-down shirt with the sleeves rolled up loosely, exposing his muscular forearms.

It seemed plain to her that he was successful and professional, but there was something more she couldn't put her finger on.

She reached up behind her neck, rubbing at a tight muscle. If she closed her eyes, she could still see him staring at her with dark, brooding eyes that warmed when his lips hinted at a smile. His broad shoulders and narrow waist made his athletic build impossible to ignore.

He had a European air about him, and even discounting his accent, Calisto didn't strike her as a San Diegan. He wore his dark hair just past his shoulders, but rather than allowing it to hang in his face like a La Jolla surfer, he tied it back. And despite his olive skin, he didn't seem particularly tanned.

The way he looked at her still haunted her thoughts and sent a shiver down her spine. Somehow Calisto had made her feel like a priceless treasure without ever saying a word. He hadn't even touched her. And when he said her name...

She shook her head. Snap out of it.

In the den, she sat down at her father's empty desk. She pulled her mother's worn address book from her backpack and dug through it for the Foundation Arts phone number. Her mother wanted this, she told herself. She was fulfilling her mother's wishes, not concocting a ploy to run into Calisto again.

Not much of one anyway.

What would be the harm if she happened to see him again? He was sexy eye candy. It wasn't like she was going to marry him.

Now she sounded like a moonstruck fifth-grader. Great.

Kate rolled her eyes at her excuses and flipped pages in search of the number for Foundation Arts.

Her mother supported the arts around San Diego for most of her life. Kate hadn't been shocked to discover she left her baby grand piano and collection of rare sheet music to her favorite charity. On some level, it did hurt a little that her mother didn't leave it to her. She was by no means a virtuoso, but she knew how to play, and a piano would have been handy for her job as a choir director. She could've used it to plan the music for her classes and student choirs.

It didn't surprise her, though.

Her mother lived to support the foundation, to support "The Arts." As if Kate's work was less than art. Her mother had her own set of goals for Kate's future. *You have miles of potential,* she'd tell her. She really wanted her daughter to be a performer of some kind. Although Kate aced her vocal performance juries in college, teaching was her true passion.

The disappointment was plain in her mother's eyes the day Kate turned down an offer for graduate school to study voice. Instead she entered the teaching credential program. She'd found her calling. She wouldn't live her mother's dream, but she wished her mom could've seen her work.

If she had been able to witness the joy on the teens' faces when they sang together on stage for the first time, maybe then she might have realized Kate hadn't settled. She might have understood Kate *was* an artist, and better yet, her work ensured an ongoing love of music in the next generation of art lovers.

If only.

Finding the number, she went to the phone and made the call.

"Foundation Arts, this is Betty."

"Hi, I'm Kate Bradley. My mother left her piano to the Foundation—"

"Oh Kate, I'm sorry for your loss," Betty said. "Martha was a wonderful woman. We all miss her. She spoke highly of you."

Kate was more than a little surprised. "She did?"

"Of course," Betty said, a smile coming through in her voice. "You're a choir director in Nevada, right?"

Kate's surprise morphed into shock. "Yes. I teach middle school chorus."

"I'm sure it takes a lot of patience."

"Yes, it does." Kate collected her thoughts. "Um, the reason I called though… My mother left her baby grand piano and her sheet music collection to your foundation. I just wanted to find out who to call about the piano moving."

"I can handle all of it for you. I'll need your signature on a few documents, and I'll take care of everything else."

Kate raised a brow. "You'll handle finding piano movers?"

"Sure thing."

"Great. How soon can we get this going?" Kate asked.

"Well…" Kate heard pages flipping on Betty's end of the call. "I have a meeting at six o'clock tomorrow night. I can be a little early. How about five-thirty at The Fish Market? It's the one near Seaport Village, on the bay."

"Sounds great. I'll see you then." Kate placed the phone back on the receiver with a little smile. Maybe her mother respected her work more than she ever realized. Too bad it was too late to tell her how much it meant to her.

§

1775

Gregorio lived with the tribe for nearly three months before they took him to the Old One. He still mourned Tala's death, unable to move past the pain and emptiness weighing down his soul. He drank very little and ate only when someone reminded him.

The pain of her loss became his only reality. Shadows and loss colored every part of his world.

Every time he saw the Romneya bloom in the valleys, he ached with memories of Tala, of the way she wore them in her hair and how they perfumed her skin. The sight of the ocean waves where they learned each other's customs now tore him apart.

As the weeks passed, he found some solace in the tribal beliefs and eventually became involved in spiritual discussions with the Shaman about death, spirits of the dead, and the belief they might one day live again.

The night of the full moon, after the tribal ceremonies ended and embers were all that remained of their community fire, the Shaman told him stories of the Old One. The white-haired man lived on the cliffs overlooking the ocean. They believed he could delve into the minds and hearts of men. If the Old One found Gregorio worthy, he would bestow on him a new title, and Gregorio would become a member of the tribe.

The Shaman honored him with his invitation to meet the wise old man and make Gregorio a part of their tribe. But it did little to raise his spirits. A new name, a new life, it didn't matter. Tala would not be part of it, and his soul would still be empty.

Each night when he slept, he saw her, held her, tasted her lips, and drank in the sound of her laughter, and each morning when he woke, his loss felt raw.

He began to hate the sun.

CHAPTER THREE

Calisto's eyes fluttered, and he knew the sun had set. His chest rose and fell, breathing even though his body no longer needed the oxygen. His heart beat in a slow rhythm once more.

After a hot shower, he dressed in jeans and a black, button-down shirt, checking his reflection before heading upstairs to his office. Kate's face haunted him, making it difficult to focus. Sitting behind his large oak desk, Calisto thumbed through the mail Betty left for him, paying more attention to the voices he heard in the night than the envelopes that bore his name.

The name he used in this lifetime.

He hadn't used his real name in centuries. Every few decades, when it became apparent he was not aging, he would drop from sight, usually staging some sort of horrific death that made identifying his body impossible. No one suspected the charred remains weren't his. But with the advancements in crime forensics, his next demise would probably be at sea without a body to recover.

After a few months away, he would re-establish himself with his new identity, purchase a new home, and begin again. But this time could be different.

He had remained in San Diego anticipating Tala's eventual

return. Now that he had found her again, they could move away together. He had been Calisto Terana for nearly twenty years now, and he would probably be able to keep this identity even longer if they moved to a new city. If things remained quiet.

But it was not always quiet. Over the centuries there were people who sought to prove he was not what he seemed. The Fraternidad Del Fuego Santo, the Brotherhood of Holy Fire, still confronted him from time to time. The monks were part of a rogue sect of the Roman Catholic Church, living in the same monastery where he had trained lifetimes ago.

For decades they attempted to end his immortal existence. Righteous fanatical fire burned in their eyes when they confronted him, seeking to kill what they considered an abomination before God. He still bore a scar from one of their encounters. His right forearm had an indentation where one of the monks sliced off a chunk of his flesh. As a Night Walker, he healed rapidly, but flesh torn from his body would not regenerate.

The scar was the closest the Fraternidad had ever come to wounding him. During the last century, their physical attacks were rare, but they still watched him. He sensed their presence at times, heard their thoughts and prayers. While most of the monks kept their distance, unsure how to kill him, every few years an especially righteous warrior would show himself and force an inevitable battle.

There were times Calisto welcomed the challenge. Anything to break the monotony of an unchanging existence.

He straightened in his chair, holding a single parchment envelope. His name and address were written in a scratched script only achieved through use of a quill, and a single red wax signet sealed the contents inside.

A signet he had not seen in over 200 years.

He ran his fingers over the entwined flames of the ancient seal, his brow furrowed. He hesitated to open it and sat back in his black leather chair, quietly spinning his own signet ring around his finger with his thumb. He fought to make sense of the envelope he now held in his hands.

The envelope had no postmark. It must have been hand-delivered. But seeing the signet told him enough about the sender. Fraternidad del Fuego Santo.

He knew *where* the letter came from even if he wasn't sure from *whom*.

With a sigh of frustration, he broke the seal and carefully removed the letter inside. It read simply:

We know where you sleep.

Calisto crumbled the letter with a scowl. He slammed his fist on his desk, and then shot from his chair.

They had no right to judge him. In fact, he still held them responsible for helping to create him. And they dared come to his home and threaten him. Did they have any idea of his power? It didn't matter. He would put a stop to this.

The monk came to his home while he slept. This messenger had gone too far. It would end now.

Calisto raked his fingers back through his thick hair, snagged his black leather jacket free from the coat hook, and stormed into the night.

Tala lived again, and he would not let the church come between them. Not this time.

§

Kate had spent the entire day shopping for something appropriate to wear to her meeting with Betty. She told herself that was the reason anyway. It wasn't because she secretly hoped Calisto Terana might show up, too. No, it wasn't that she wanted to see him again. Not at all.

Ok, maybe just a little.

It was dark by the time she got back to her parents' house. She dropped her Macy's bags and collapsed onto her dad's overstuffed easy chair. She looked down the hall at the office. She should at least check her e-mail. But exhaustion weighed heavy on her shoulders. Instead, she reclined the chair and let her eyes drift closed. She just needed a little rest.

Her breathing deepened, and gradually the landscape took shape.

Her body tensed, her mind already anticipating the chase, the fear. But instead she saw... water?

Waves lapped at her ankles, and a man walked beside her. His face was lost in the shadow of the bright sun that warmed her skin.

She held a flower, studying it, twisting it with her fingertips. It wasn't a rose. The petals were larger and more delicate. Then she recognized it. The same flower she'd seen at the mission in the courtyard. The scenery around her gradually shifted, fading and growing darker as the dream changed. The woman ran through dry brush, fighting for breath, for life.

The sound of her own scream woke her.

Kate sat up, sweating and shivering all at once. Her mind raced with receding terror and confusion. The dream had always been the same—until tonight.

Why would it change now, after all this time?

She struggled to keep the details fresh, fighting to remember. There was a man. Could he be the same man who chased the woman in her nightmare? She wasn't sure, and the more she thought about it, she realized she didn't want to know. She hoped she would never see that man's face.

Finally Kate managed to stand, then wandered into the dark kitchen for a glass of water. It was probably just her pent-up emotions about being back at her parents' house, combined with her anger at Tom's betrayal, that changed her dream. Either way, she couldn't go back to sleep.

The clock on the stove read 2:33 a.m. The sun would be up in a few hours, and she felt like she hadn't slept at all yet. She dug through one of the plastic shopping bags on the kitchen counter and pulled out a box of instant hot chocolate. Maybe if she had something warm and soothing to drink, she might be able to sleep.

It didn't hurt that hot chocolate was her go-to comfort food.

She dumped the packet into the cup, filled it with water, and after ninety seconds in the microwave, she had a steaming mug of hot chocolate. Leaning against the sink, she took a cautious sip in an effort to keep from scalding her tongue. She caught herself thinking about the man on the beach as she stared into the darkness. Kate wasn't sure why the man had suddenly appeared in her nightmare but it was a relief to think about something other than the woman running for her life.

She carried her drink back to the living room and set it on the side table as she sat on the piano bench. Kate tentatively touched the keys. She wished she had been a better student. She took lessons and managed to pass her requirement to complete her degree in music, but she never truly mastered the art of this instrument.

When she played, it sounded methodical and choppy, not like concert pianists who had the ability to make the piano sing, cry, laugh, and scream with intensity. But right now her labored attempt at Beethoven's "Für Elise" would have to suffice—anything to cover the deafening silence of the dark, empty house. She would have preferred something by Mozart, since most of his pieces made her smile, but his intricate sonatas were too difficult for her to play.

Beethoven's classic was one of the most demanding piano pieces she ever learned to play. The slow, almost liquid beginning never left her memory, or her fingers. Grateful for the company of the music, even if it was slightly labored, the melody eased her fears and gradually released her from the hold of her nightmare. Finally, with a hint of a smile on her lips, she gave up Beethoven and instead banged out a gorgeous rendition of "Chopsticks," grinning as she held the final chord. She could almost hear her mother now, rolling her eyes and telling Kate that playing "Chopsticks" with two fingers was a waste of a piano.

It felt good to smile when she remembered her parents.

She took her mug back to the kitchen. Rinsing out the cup, she stared at the predawn darkness, lost in thought. What would happen to her mother's piano? Would Calisto ever sit on that same bench, or touch the keys? She shook her head and turned off the water. She didn't even know if Calisto played the piano.

Settling back into her father's easy chair, she hoped for a little more sleep. The warm beverage helped calm her nerves, and with luck her nightmare wouldn't interrupt her again tonight. With a yawn, she curled up and closed her eyes. This time there was no running and no thundering hooves. No, this time a scent like sweet jasmine and a white flower that looked like crushed silk filled her dreams. And in her sleep, Kate smiled.

§

1775

The full moon glowed above the warriors whose pace Gregorio struggled to match. He wiped sweat from his brow though the cool, crisp air stung his lungs. They neared the cliffs and the treacherous climb to the opening of the Old One's cave. Not only was the terrain steep, but instead of firm rock footing, hard sand formed the cliff. The farther they climbed, the more he slipped, scraping his hands until the skin was raw and bloodied. Never had he been so grateful for the sandals protecting the soles of his feet.

By the time he reached the mouth of the cave, his heart raced. The warriors stopped, leaving him to enter alone. Torches rested inside carved holes in the side of the cave and lit a narrow pathway.

Once his eyes adjusted to the dim light, he moved deeper into the cliff, his shadow flickering on the walls around him. The sight of the Old One beyond the final curve of the tunnel did nothing to ease his apprehension. In fact, the closer he came to the man sitting cross-legged on the other side of the fire, the more his anxiety grew.

The Old One's long, white hair fell past his tanned shoulders, and although the firelight was not bright, the old man's dark eyes seemed to glow crimson for a moment. A cold chill slid down Gregorio's spine, and he squeezed his eyes closed to clear his vision.

He bowed his head. "Greetings," he said in the tribal language of the Kumeyaay. "I am Father—" He corrected himself. "I am Gregorio Salva— "

"I know who you are." The Old One didn't speak in his tribe's tongue, but in Spanish.

"You know the language of my country?" The fire snapped, echoing through the cave.

"I know many languages," the Old One said. "Why have you come?"

Hot, stagnant air choked him and sweat trickled down his back. "To become a member of the tribe."

"No. You came for answers that might heal the pain in your heart." He stoked the fire without making eye contact.

Gregorio frowned. "How do you know this?"

The Old One's gaze rose from the flames to meet his, and a strange realization formed in his mind. Deep in the old man's eyes, he saw wisdom that appeared far older than the man. Only his pure white hair betrayed his age. His face bore no lines or wrinkles. It made no sense. Gregorio rubbed at his eyes, sure he was mistaken, but the man's youthful face remained a contradiction.

The Old One ignored his question. "You seek vengeance. But vengeance will not bring you the peace you seek. Only love will heal your wounds."

Gregorio bit back the pain and loss that were his constant companions. "I will never love again."

"You will. When she lives again."

Gregorio's gaze shot up to meet the old man's. "I will never live to see that day."

"You seem certain." The Old One ceased poking the fire, resting the long stick against the side of the cave. "Are you so sure of the world around you that you would give up a chance to see her again?"

"I would have offered my life to save hers, but I did not get that chance," Gregorio said.

"And now you would kill those who took her from you."

"They deserve no better."

"Perhaps not." The old man tossed another log into the flames. "You were once one of them, an outsider. You came on a ship to this land and laid claim to something which did not belong to you. What makes you a better man than them?"

"I was naive. My intentions were only to help these people. The warriors tell me you can look into a man's heart. Surely you can see I speak the truth."

The Old One went silent, and his eyes seemed to glow in the dim firelight, as though the old man wasn't simply looking *at* him but rather *through* him.

"You loved Tala," the Old One whispered.

"With all my soul." He wondered how the old man knew her name, but perhaps the Shaman from the tribe informed the Old One of her death.

"Enough to wait for her to walk this earth again?"

"You believe she will?" Gregorio struggled to keep his voice controlled when everything in his body wanted to beg this medicine man for any kind of magic to bring her back.

"Do you always answer with more questions?"

"Forgive me, but I have been raised to believe when a soul is laid to rest, her spirit dwells with the Lord in Heaven. How can you be certain this is not true?"

"How can *you* be certain this Heaven you speak of exists?"

Gregorio clenched his fists to keep from shaking the white-haired man. "Now it is you who answers with questions."

A small smile curled on the Old One's lips, briefly giving his face the lines of an older man. "I have given no answers. Not yet." His stare mesmerized Gregorio until he was lost in the Old One's eyes. "First you must answer my question. Is your love for her strong enough to see you through the years until her soul finds you again?"

"It makes no difference." Gregorio met his eyes, his voice dropping to a whisper. "No man lives forever."

The Old One's laughter echoed through the cave. He shook his head. "You know nothing, Father Salvador."

"Father Salvador no longer exists. Only Gregorio remains."

"Is that so?" The Old One's eyes twinkled in the firelight. "A man can change his name, his title, but he is still the same man, no?"

"No. I will never be that man again."

The Old One rose from the fire with ease seldom seen in one so aged. Gregorio watched as he retreated into the shadows and returned with a pipe and clay goblet. "We will make a trade this night. I will give your body the strength to face the centuries. You will be ageless. Immortal."

"If that were truly possible, what would you take from me in exchange?"

"You will give up the sun, and you will help these people regain their land and their culture. These priests baptize them and take away their names and their beliefs. You will help them to free themselves from the bonds of a God they do not understand."

Gregorio wanted to refuse. Both sides of this trade were impossible. No man lived forever. Only God was immortal. And how could he honor his end of the bargain? He was no warrior. How could he help the native people to reclaim the land the Mission now declared its own? He wouldn't know where to begin.

Seeming to sense his reluctance, the Old One sat beside him, placing the smoking pipe in Gregorio's hands. "Look into the fire. What do you see?"

He stared at the flames and puffed the pipe, letting the peyote smoke fill his lungs.

"I see her," Gregorio said. "Her long black hair is falling down her back. She has the Romneya I gave her tucked behind her ear, and the moon is in her eyes." His voice shook with emotion as his jaw clenched, fighting to hold back tears. "She is laughing, splashing through the waves on the shore."

"You can see her again," the Old One whispered. "Love her again."

Was the fire getting hotter? The flames grew, and the peyote smoke filled the cavern. His head spun and his eyesight blurred. He could no longer distinguish reality from illusion.

The Old One danced around the fire, his shadow circling the walls of the cave. Everything spun like a whirlwind, each image blending into the next. Nothing made sense, and he wondered if he might be dreaming. The Old One lifted him to his feet with one hand. A sudden burning pain shot through him, and his heart raced.

He saw a lush jungle and triangular stone structures. And blood, so much blood. Chants echoed through his mind in a language he had never heard. His legs crumpled under him, but he didn't fall. The Old One brought a clay goblet to his lips, and he drank until the cup was empty.

Somewhere deep within, Gregorio's soul cried out in warning, and the last remnants of his faith clutched at his mind. For a moment he hesitated, but then he saw Tala smiling up at him and heard an echo of her laughter. He needed to see her again. To love her again.

Gregorio took the cup once more, but instead of quenching his thirst, the lust for more grew. The Old One filled the cup again and again, and Gregorio drank until he fell to the ground.

"Live forever," the Old One whispered. And the shadows swallowed him in their suffocating embrace.

CHAPTER FOUR

Calisto rushed toward the Mission de Alcala with preternatural speed. He listened intently, not only to the night sounds around him, but to the mortals he passed. Long ago, he learned to close his mind to the internal feelings of men and women, shielding himself from their intrusion, but tonight he *wanted* to hear them.

Tonight he hunted.

The Fraternidad had violated his home while he slept. Calisto ground his teeth. They would pay for their intrusion.

He didn't know how they had masked their presence from him. He hid his true nature from the mortals, but somehow the Fraternidad learned to hide from him as well. But this time, they had come too close while he lay defenseless beneath the earth.

Calisto rolled his shoulders back, loosening the knot of fury building within his muscles. They wouldn't threaten him again. He would see to that. The zealots would respect his power, or they would die. He didn't care which. He'd finally found Tala again, and he wouldn't let their intrusion come between them.

As he approached the mission, his chest tightened with bitterness. He hated this place, these walls that he helped to build. The church annihilated a beautiful culture and replaced it with the beliefs of another. He tried to stop them once, but he was a different man back then.

Calisto jumped over the fence with ease and searched for the thoughts of the man who delivered the threat to his home. He stayed in the shadows, concentrating on each of the inhabitants. He listened to the thoughts of the mortals around him, allowing them to whisper into his mind. One priest was consumed with his dinner choice, while an employee in the gift shop tallied the days' total receipts. He dug deeper, searching for thoughts regarding a monk visiting from Spain. After a few more minutes, he growled in frustration.

The monk from the Fraternidad del Fuego Santo was not at the mission. None of the priests knew much about why the monk traveled to San Diego or where he slept, only that he arrived two weeks earlier and would be in San Diego indefinitely.

Calisto hadn't seen the man's face yet, but he now had his name. Tomas. Father Tomas De Cardina.

Calisto disappeared into the darkness. He had no time to waste. The Gaslamp Quarter nestled in the middle of the high-rise downtown buildings would be his next stop. Allowing his mortal façade to fall away, he focused his immortal abilities, stalking the streets of downtown, searching the memories of the mortals around him.

Surely someone had crossed paths with Father De Cardina by now.

Face after face passed him by, one man worried about his job, a woman concerned for her sick mother, and another wondering if her date stood her up. Endless human babble intruded on his consciousness, but still he found no one who had been to the mission.

Frustration burned like indigestion. He wanted to find Kate again, not waste precious time searching for another fanatic from the Fraternidad. While at times he enjoyed hunting them, now that she lived again, his priorities had changed.

They killed her once. He wouldn't take the chance they might hurt her again.

Valuable minutes slipped away, but no simple solution presented itself. The monk would not be mentioned on the Internet, nor would he rent a hotel room. The Fraternidad would forbid such publicity.

Calisto searched until his preternatural senses were overloaded. The scent of beer and sweat overpowered him as men and women gyrated against each other to heavy, thumping music inside the nightclubs. He heard their insecurities, the yearning, and the few who hoped they might have finally found love.

Love. He clenched his fists, fighting to control his emotions. He loved once, but it was gone far too soon, stolen from him. Worse yet, now that he had a chance at love again, the same faction who ordered her death centuries before threatened to keep them apart.

His rage was getting him nowhere.

In an effort to calm his mind, he ventured downstairs into the dimly lit Café Sevilla, lured by the familiar sound of his native tongue. Flamenco dancers clapped to the rapid beat of the Spanish music, drowning out the voices of the bar patrons. The club below the restaurant was warm, making his body feel even more inhuman and cold.

Stepping up to the bar, he ordered a brandy and swirled it in his glass as he settled in a dark corner. The flamenco show ended and one of the performers smiled in his direction from the edge of the stage as if she recognized him. Calisto returned the gesture with a polite nod. He often came to the café to watch them dance. The sound of the rhythmic clapping to traditional Spanish folk songs spoke to him.

They reminded him of a place and time he had once called home.

Tonight, he visited for a different reason. His gaze moved over the patrons, studying their faces until he spotted a woman who wore a gold crucifix around her neck. He opened his mind to hers and saw the mission bells and candles. His fingers tightened around his glass. She had been at the Dia De Los Muertos mass.

Calisto watched her sip a margarita. Thick, dark hair framed her fair skin, and her large brown eyes met his from across the room. He placed his untouched drink on the bar and approached her.

"Good evening." He allowed the hypnotic tone he usually reserved for his victims to color his voice, making his lies more believable. "I think we met at the Mission de Alcala last night. For the mass?"

"Oh." She nodded, accepting his mental suggestion as fact. "I thought you looked familiar."

When she offered her hand, he placed a polite kiss on the back. The scent of her blood enticed his heightened senses, tempting him. Hunger gnawed at him. He wouldn't be able to stay much longer.

He straightened, releasing her hand as he spoke. "My name is Calisto, and you are?"

"Gina," she answered.

Flirtation filled her gaze as she wet her lips, but he wasn't interested in a lover. He indulged in human pleasures of the flesh a few times over the centuries, but sex left him feeling more alone and isolated.

Without love, it was an empty act, and eventually he lost interest.

He didn't want her body. He wanted her memories. Encouraging idle conversation, he studied her mind, searching.

His interest was piqued when he saw the sanctuary of the mission in her mind. "You speak Spanish, yes?"

She nodded. "My family is from Mexico. Why?"

"There was a priest at the Mission from Spain—"

"Father Tomas! I met him, too."

"This world is indeed a small one, no?" He smiled, letting his eyes hold hers. He saw the monk's face in her mind and gathered all of the information he needed from her. His gaze burned into hers, mesmerizing her until he could reshape her memories. It drained him mentally, but trivial, non-traumatic memories could be altered. He erased his face from her mind as a teacher might erase a chalkboard. And then he was gone.

Gina had indeed met Father Tomas. Moreover, her family offered to house him during his stay in America, but the priest declined. He told them he had church business to attend to in Point Loma.

Father Tomas already made it plain that he knew where Calisto lived. Point Loma was nowhere near his home. Odd...

So what *business* did Father Tomas have in Point Loma?

§

1775

Buried alive.

Clawing in a panicked frenzy, Gregorio shot up from the earth with a strength he'd never possessed before. When he broke free of the soil, he gasped deep breaths driven by fear rather than need. He turned back to see the shallow grave he escaped. What had the Old One done to him?

His body reeked, and he was sickened to realize he was covered by dirt, blood, vomit, and excrement. And he was thirsty.

Dear God, he had never been so thirsty in all his life.

"You must wash."

Gregorio spun around to find the Old One placing a large Spanish barrel full of fresh water on the ground before him. A barrel much too large for any man to carry alone.

"You buried me alive," Gregorio shouted.

"You first must die in order to live as I do." The old man dipped his hands in the water, rinsing them.

Gregorio frowned. "You speak in riddles."

"Wash," the Old One said. "We will speak at the fire, and then you must feed."

Gregorio nodded, although he still didn't understand. Had the old man tried to kill him? The Old One walked away, but something about the way he moved confused Gregorio, and he rubbed his eyes. The farther the old man walked down the beach, the more difficult it became to see him clearly. His body appeared to mutate, shifting into a bird. No, not a bird. A white-headed eagle.

And without a sound, he took flight.

Flight? Gregorio's jaw went slack. Impossible. Unable to believe what he'd just witnessed, he stared out at the troubled ocean. Although darkness surrounded him, he saw the landscape as if it were daylight.

Then he noticed the night alive all around him. Tiny crabs burrowed under the sand, escaping from the tide that sought to wash them away. Each tiny leg scuttled against the grains of sand.

And he could hear—everything.

The soft beat of a nearby owl's wings, the song of the crickets in the sagebrush, and the warning rattle of a snake combined into a twilight symphony. How was this possible? What had the Old One done to him?

Pain and need jolted through him, silencing the night. Thirst overpowered his senses. He stumbled toward the barrel and leaned far inside, drinking huge gulps of water. The moment it slid down his parched throat, his body rejected it. He coughed violently until he purged the water from his body. Moaning, he fell to his knees, still aching. And still thirsty.

Gregorio knelt on the sand, catching his breath. He needed answers. But first he needed to rid himself of the stench of death.

He stripped off his soiled clothes and washed himself. The rough sponge and cool water soothed his skin.

Behind the barrel, draped over a fallen tree, he found a leather loincloth similar to the ones worn by the native warriors. Accustomed to having his entire body covered by the robes of a priest, the loincloth left him feeling exposed to the night, but he had nothing else.

He walked down the beach, searching the night for the Old One. He caught the scent of rabbits and even heard the disembodied voices of men in the distance. Impossible, like a strange dream, and yet he was awake.

Walking farther down the shoreline, he looked up at the cliffs, searching for the cave he entered the night before. Finally, he saw the opening in the rocks and climbed up the sandy cliff, surprised at how simple the task seemed now. His body felt stronger and more agile, like one of the native bobcats of the area.

He reached the opening to the Old One's cave in half the time it took him the previous night, and he made the climb tonight without any abrasions to his hands or feet in spite of scaling the cliff face without sandals.

He moved to the back of the cave, and his head filled with questions for the Old One. What had happened to him? He felt changed, but how?

Before he could ask anything, the Old One stood in front of him. "Come. You are a Night Walker now, and you must feed."

Without waiting for a reply, the Old One passed him, walking toward the mouth of the cave. When they reached a clearing, the old man whispered, "Listen to the night, and call the deer to us."

He looked at the Old One with a questioning stare. "I do not—"

"No questions. Use your mind."

Gregorio closed his eyes and listened, soon hearing the soft calls of a doe. Envisioning the deer in his mind, he found he could connect with the animal and see the night through the animal's eyes. Gradually, he guided her into the clearing, and when he opened his eyes the deer stood before them.

Chanting low and steady, the Old One approached the animal and beckoned Gregorio forward. He tilted the doe's head back, exposing its soft throat.

"Drink."

"What?" Gregorio frowned. "I cannot. Not while the beast lives."

"You must. Come."

His disgust grew, as did his thirst, with each step he took. The doe's heartbeat called to him, a temptation too strong to resist.

The Old One drew a small dagger from his belt, piercing the doe's throat, and the scent of blood made Gregorio's hands tremble with the ache of hunger.

"Drink, young one. Do as your new body commands."

Unable to fight his thirst any longer, he knelt at the animal's throat, moaning with a mixture of revulsion and rapture. He drank voraciously, enjoying the taste of the warm blood that filled his mouth. When the animal's veins emptied and the doe collapsed, what remained of the man inside of him was repulsed.

Yet the monster yearned for more.

The Old One picked up the doe and started back toward the cave. Gregorio fell to his knees and stared up at the sky. He wanted to scream, to cry to God to save his soul, but he had no tears left. He was numb and empty.

"Why do you despair?"

Gregorio turned, surprised to see the Old One staring at him.

"Because I am cursed."

"No," the Old One said with a crooked smile. "You are blessed. I have chosen you as my descendant. You will be a great healer and lead these people against the Spanish outsiders. Come, you have much to learn."

And learn he did.

For the following month, he acted as an apprentice to the Old One, learning the ancient healing secrets of the Night Walkers. Gradually mastering his powers, he became one with the night around him and found a new purpose for his existence.

He was a healer, a Night Walker.

The Kumeyaay tribes called him *Kuseyaay*, and he became their most respected Shaman and protector. With his help, they would regain their freedom from the mission. For that purpose, the Old One chose him to receive his power.

Then one night, the cave sat empty, the cinders within the inner chamber cold, the walls free of their designs.

The Old One was gone.

§

Just after three in the morning, Calisto reached Point Loma. With so few people awake and on the streets, he opened his mind without a mental overload from the humans around him.

He could not court Kate with the specter of the Fraternidad haunting him. The monks needed to remember whom they were dealing with. Hunger gnawed at his veins, reminding him that he hadn't fed. He needed blood to keep his strength from waning. Hoping to find sustenance, he walked toward a well-lit corner in the distance. When he reached the convenience store, he lowered his mental shields, listening to the humans around him. Before he sorted through the entire fog of information, he found something interesting.

An ancient Latin chant.

His brow furrowed as he quietly walked through the parking lot, his mind fully focused on the chant, letting his Night Walker instincts draw him closer to his prey. When he reached the shadowed corner of the lot, he saw the face he'd searched for. Calisto smiled.

Father Tomas sat behind the wheel of a silver sedan. The chant he repeated shielded his thoughts, keeping Calisto locked out of his mind. Calisto clenched his fists and sucked in a deep breath. Apparently the Fraternidad knew more about his kind than he realized.

How long had they blocked his mental probes?

He burst into the passenger seat of the car, taking pleasure in the terrified gasp of the driver.

"Father Tomas De Cardina, I presume?"

The monk recovered from his shock and quickly thrust the cross that hung around his neck into Calisto's face. "Stay back, creature of Satan."

Calisto laughed. "Is that what you think I am?" He reached out to clasp the crucifix, and with a jerk of his wrist, snapped the gold chain from the monk's neck. "If you know so much about me, then surely you know the church helped to make me what I am."

He shook his head. "Lies! You sold your soul to Satan himself, and now you are his apprentice. You are an abomination before God."

Calisto smirked. He heard the blood coursing through Father Tomas' veins at an alarming rate, tempting him, calling to him.

"What you believe is of no consequence to me. I will not be threatened, least of all by the Fraternidad, and never at my own home."

Surprise filled the monk's gaze, and his mental chant faltered.

"I have not forgotten the signet of the Fraternidad." He held up his left hand, showing his own ring. His personal signet bore the holy fire of the Fraternidad, but it also included a finely carved bird soaring across the top. Lifetimes ago, it symbolized the dove of peace, but now Calisto considered it a raven, his Night Walker spirit animal.

A bead of sweat made its way down Father Tomas' forehead. "We know what you are, and we will do what we must in the name of God to insure that you make no others."

Calisto frowned at the unexpected answer. "Why would I make

another?"

Father Tomas kept silent, staring at the crucifix in Calisto's hand. Again Calisto attempted to reach the monk's mind, only to find the same repeated chant shielding the monk's true thoughts.

He grabbed Tomas' robe and yanked him closer. "Answer me!"

Frustration burned through Calisto. He felt his eyes glow crimson with rage.

"Santa Maria!" Father Tomas gasped and jammed a knife into Calisto's abdomen, stabbing up underneath his ribcage.

Calisto's eyes widened as pain seared through his chest. Blood spilled from the gaping wound, but his body tingled, healing from the inside out. He let go of the monk with one hand and plucked the knife from his torso, wrenching it free from the fanatic's clutched hand.

Father Tomas struggled like a wild animal in the presence of a predator. Calisto dropped the knife to the floor of the car and clutched the monk with both hands. He drew Father Tomas closer. His fangs grazed the monk's skin just below his ear. The priest fought to break away, but Calisto's grip was inescapable. The more the monk struggled, the stronger his pulse became. The scent of blood combined with fear intoxicated Calisto. His thirst clawed to the surface, threatening to seize control.

"Let me go! In the name of God, let me go!"

Calisto's voice was no more than a cold whisper. "I have no God. Not anymore."

He sank his fangs into the monk's neck and drank. The man's life flashed through his mind, visions of Spain and the monastery where he trained centuries ago. He lost himself in the images, so modern and yet still the home he remembered.

His lips pulled at the monk's throat, drawing more blood. But then one of the visions made his heart stutter, an image he never expected, and one that changed everything. Calisto jerked back, but the monk's eyes were vacant.

"No!"

It was too late. Father Tomas was dead.

Calisto released him, growling in disgust at his lack of control. He was left with more questions than answers.

Kate's face loomed in Father Tomas' mind. The Fraternidad knew she lived again.

And they watched her, too.

CHAPTER FIVE

Kate stretched as sunlight poured through the window into the living room. Heading into the kitchen, she made a cup of coffee and a piece of toast and shook her head in disbelief at the beautiful November day. Back in Reno the days had already cooled as winter moved in, but here in San Diego, she could wear shorts into December. Though the climate here was familiar, she still found it amazing.

She popped open her laptop and glanced over the top local news stories on her homepage. Years ago, her father read the newspaper at this same countertop every morning. The memory brought a smile to her lips.

Settled in with her breakfast, she scanned headlines. One caught her eye: *Spanish monk slain, body dumped at the doors of the Mission de Alcala.*

Kate frowned. The priest, Father Tomas De Cardina, was visiting from a remote monastery in Spain. The police didn't have a motive for the killing, and they hadn't yet released the cause of death.

What kind of person would murder a monk? Kate sipped her coffee and considered what would drive a person to then treat the monk's body with such disrespect.

Shaking her head, she finished her toast and set her laptop aside. The last thing she wanted to read about was bad news. She grabbed her Macy's bags and poked through her wardrobe purchases.

Before her appointment at The Fish Market, she had lunch plans at Horton Plaza with Edie, so she headed upstairs to clean up and get ready to go. Kate looked forward to spending a little more time with Edie. Being back with her friends again definitely helped lift her spirits. Except when they hovered and lectured. She hoped to show them she didn't need their mothering anymore. She would be strong. She would be confident. She would find her way.

After a quick shower, Kate dressed, grabbed her purse, and headed into the sunshine.

§

Betty rushed into her office, dropping the mail on her desk in an effort to save her coffee before it slipped completely out of the crook of her arm. Yes, she could've made two trips, but she hated going all the way back to her car for one item. It was an inefficient use of her time.

She set her coffee on the coaster and moved around her desk to settle in her executive chair. She loved the feel of the cool leather soaking through her linen suit. It made her feel powerful, all business. As a girl, she dreamed of being an attorney, but not because she longed to fight for justice or truth. A lawyer commanded respect. They were women that even rich, influential men feared.

Of course, she never became an attorney. College wasn't all it was cracked up to be. In the end, she didn't need a diploma to hang on the wall. She possessed an abundant amount of determination and organizational skills that college graduates would kill for.

And it was finally paying off.

Sipping her coffee, she quickly sorted the envelopes into stacks. Betty opened the drawer, retrieving her gold-plated letter opener. She started out as a personal assistant by accident. Three years ago she answered an ad for a receptionist at a talent agency in Los Angeles. While she waited in the lobby for her interview, she struck up a conversation with a guitarist from some rock band she had never heard of. Before she knew it, she had a job working for him.

Even though she was the best personal assistant her employer ever had, the job hadn't lasted long. On a trip to San Diego to represent him at a dinner party, she met Calisto Terana, founder of a charity that raised money for performing arts in schools and colleges as well as promoting the arts to rural schools on the reservations.

After an enjoyable evening of small talk and cocktails, he asked her to move to San Diego and work for the foundation. She never looked back. Calisto offered her a six-figure salary and an office in La Jolla with a view of the ocean. Not to mention he was one of the most reclusive and sexy eligible bachelors in Southern California. She'd be nuts to refuse.

But she'd soon discovered reclusive was putting it mildly—more like virtually nonexistent most of the time. He rarely came into the office, and when he did, it was usually after hours and at the tail end of another trip. Although she'd hoped for more interaction with him, she grew to love the independence of running the office herself. For the most part, he let her have complete control of the foundation's operations, as long as she kept him up-to-date on her activities, and Betty enjoyed every minute of it. Within a year, Calisto named her director.

The title suited her just fine.

Betty had the mail opened and sorted in no time. She glanced at her calendar and smiled when she saw her meeting with Calisto tonight. Her steel-gray business suit was tailored for a perfect fit, but she decided she'd have to run back to her condo before the meeting to change into something less… uptight. Calisto kept a very professional distance with her, but deep down she wished he would open up so they could get to know each other better.

He represented everything she wanted in a man: tall, dark, handsome, intelligent, cultured, and extremely wealthy. Her pulse raced just thinking about him, and every evening meeting with him offered another potential opportunity to expand their relationship.

Betty prided herself on not allowing opportunities slip by.

Although she'd worked for him for a few years now, she really didn't know anything about his past, except that he was originally from Spain. Calisto didn't like to talk about himself and even when she asked direct questions, usually he found some way to get around them.

She discovered he was an accomplished pianist purely by chance one evening when she walked in on him playing after work. Her employer remained a mystery to her, but that made him even more desirable in her mind. Betty loved a good mystery, especially when it came wrapped in a six-foot-two-inch chiseled body with dark eyes that could melt you where you stood.

She worked quickly to get their donor list updated. If she worked through lunch, she could leave with plenty of time to change and let her hair down.

If tonight went according to plan, Calisto would be the one melting. She could hardly wait.

§

1775

The Old One was gone.

Gregorio struggled to grow into his new role within the tribe. He settled disputes, reading each party's thoughts to discover the truth, and healed the injured, closing their wounds with his own blood. The local tribes admired his abilities and judgment. They treated him with honor and awed reverence, but deep inside, his soul still burned with rage and hungered for revenge.

Tonight, he would hunger no more. The Kumeyaay people were not neophytes, as the priests so often labeled them. They were a proud people, rich with tradition, but the Church sought to change that, to change them, by whatever means necessary.

The Spanish, his own people, would pay for taking Tala from him and enslaving the Kumeyaay tribes. The priests would not go unpunished.

The moon shone brightly above them, casting light on the silent mission as the tribes banded together to fight for their freedom. Over 600 warriors silently surrounded the structure. The Spanish would call this the day of the Alcala Massacre, but for Gregorio, the Night

Walker, it marked the night of judgment for a man he once called friend.

He had prepared the warriors for this fight, drawing pictures of the muskets and explaining how they were used. Warriors gathered from many tribes, each sharing a common fear of the white men who sought to steal their identity and way of life.

Tala's death at the hand of a Spaniard provided further proof the white men were a threat to *all* of the tribes. Even their women and children were not safe.

With the warriors in place, a single battle cry broke the evening's stillness. In seconds, the wooden planks of the mission's roof blazed. At the same time, another band of warriors smashed the clay flumes that brought fresh water into the mission, making it impossible to extinguish the fire.

Gregorio remained hidden in the darkness, watching the fire feed on the buildings he helped erect only a year earlier. Father Jayme insisted they move the mission from the coast to the inland valley, closer to the native workers. Gregorio helped them move one plank at a time and rebuild one adobe wall at a time.

He looked up at the bell tower now engulfed in flames. So much had changed in such a short time. A few musket blasts erupted as the Spanish guards made a feeble attempt to defend the mission, but it was already too late. They soon realized the futility of their efforts and sought to escape with the priests and servants.

Kumeyaay women and men scrambled out of the burning mission, taking whatever food and trinkets they could carry. But Gregorio didn't move.

It wasn't long until he saw the man he waited for.

"*Amar a Dios, hijos!*" Father Luis Jayme called as he ran toward the natives.

Gregorio rushed forward before the priest uttered another word and yanked him close. They stared at one another, eye to eye. The depth of his hatred for this man stunned him. Until Tala's murder, Gregorio had never hated anyone, but this man had introduced a bitter emptiness into his soul that slowly poisoned him.

They were once close friends. Brothers. But again, so much had changed. Too much.

Father Jayme's face brightened with a smile. "Brother Salvador! Thank our Lord you are safe. We feared you were dead."

The priest opened his arms to embrace him, but Gregorio stepped back, meeting his gaze with a cold stare. He tasted bile in the back of his throat. Every muscle in his body tensed. "You betrayed me."

Father Jayme shook his head, his eyes pleading. "No, Brother Salvador. I saved you. Satan himself made you love her and caused you to stray from your faith. She tempted you until you broke your vows. I protected you when you could no longer protect yourself—"

Gregorio's fist connected with Father Jayme's face before he realized he intended to hit him. When the robed man fell, Gregorio grabbed his arms and yanked him up.

"I gave you my confession, and you used it against me. Did you know the soldier you paid to kill her also raped her?" He shook him like a rag doll. "Did you?"

The priest sobbed as blood trickled from his misshapen nose. "I do not know what you are talking about."

Gregorio threw him to the ground. The priest cried out in pain.

"Once I called you my brother, and now you lie to my face? I saw him running away from her dead body, Luis! He took my ring that hung around her neck." He grabbed the priest's hand and twisted his finger. "This ring that is now around *your* finger! Tell me the truth."

Father Jayme stammered his response. "You should not have given it to her. I corrected a mistake that you never should have made."

Gregorio leaned in close and spoke with clenched teeth. "By killing an innocent woman?"

"A heathen! Satan in the form of a dark-skinned woman stole you from your true calling. Stealing you from God. I saved you."

He stared into the priest's eyes, fighting the urge to rip the man's head from his body and sickened at how the scent of the priest's blood tempted him.

"If Satan exists, Luis, then I am looking at him right now."

He removed his signet ring from Father Jayme's finger and slid it back onto his own. "You broke your vows by using my confession to harm another, and God Himself will judge you for that sin."

Unable to bear the temptation of being so near Father Jayme's bloody face, he turned away from the priest. With a nod from him, the native warriors moved in. As Gregorio walked away, short screams punctuated the thuds of sticks and knives as the natives beat and stabbed Father Luis Jayme to death.

It would not bring Tala back, but it felt justified. A life for a life. But the guilt he felt for trusting Father Jayme with his confession would linger forever.

He and Tala met secretly for months before he finally made that fateful confession. He made a fatal error to confess his secret love and his desire to give up the priesthood. Why had he done it?

But he already knew.

From the first moment he kissed her, he had known he loved her. After they lay together, guilt weighed on him until he could no longer bear it. He wanted to give up his missionary robes forever. When he learned Tala carried his child in her womb, he took it as a sign from God that he would become a husband and father. He actually believed Father Jayme would absolve him of his sin and bless their union.

How wrong he had been.

Gregorio moved on through the thick smoke, his revenge not yet complete. He needed to find one more man. Within minutes, three guards stumbled away from the inferno that devoured the mission. He recognized Tala's killer instantly as the man he'd seen riding away from her body, clutching Gregorio's signet ring. Fury lit through him. Using his heightened speed, Gregorio knocked the man to the ground and roared in anger.

The guard gasped, struggling to escape. The terror in his eyes reflected the fire in Gregorio's. The Old One warned him not to allow others to see his sharpened teeth, which now resembled fangs. They should only be used to feed on animals and heal mortal wounds, not to strike fear or inflict harm.

But as he looked into the guard's mind he saw Tala, her long hair tangled with brambles, her legs bleeding as this man chased after her on horseback. He watched the dog tear at her dress and rape her, holding his dagger to her throat.

In that moment, his rage was primal and all-consuming.

The man's blood sang to him, his pulse raced, and without hesitation, Gregorio yanked him close and buried his fangs into the other man's neck. Until now, he'd only fed on animals. He was unprepared for the power and pleasure of human blood.

Vaguely, he realized the guard fought to break free, screaming for help, but Gregorio's grasp remained firm and unbreakable. He drank, overwhelmed by the images that sifted through his mind, his victim's memories playing out before him.

He saw Spain, faces of men and women he did not recognize, and then he saw Tala running, her cheeks covered in tears, and he bit harder, pulling at the guard's veins until the man went limp and his heart ceased beating.

Gregorio dropped the body in sudden disgust. What had he done?

But he knew, and worse yet, he enjoyed it. He was truly a monster, a blood-drinking demon. Scanning the smoke-filled clearing, relieved to see no one witnessed his atrocity against humanity, Gregorio ran.

CHAPTER SIX

Calisto woke as the sun dipped behind the horizon. With a sigh, he rubbed his hands over his face, still shaken by seeing Kate in the priest's mind the night before.

The Fraternidad knew where she lived, and he did not. How could he protect her from them if he couldn't find her?

But he would find her. He had to find her.

Stepping out of a hot shower, Calisto quickly towel-dried his hair and stared at his face in the mirror. He would find Kate tonight after his business meeting. With Betty's help searching on the computer, he would find her. If necessary, he would hire a private detective to locate her during the daylight hours.

Before the Fraternidad sent a replacement for Father Cardina.

Perhaps after they received his message at the mission's doors, they would finally leave him alone.

He dressed in a pair of black slacks with a dark green turtleneck and the tweed sports coat Betty gave him for Christmas. Seeing him wear it would make her smile, and he owed her at least that much.

Her obvious infatuation with him made reading her thoughts unnecessary. He tried not to exploit her feelings. He cared for her as best he could, and never gave her false hope of a relationship between them. She was the closest thing he had to a friend in this world, but he learned long ago having mortal friends made it far too painful to leave when the time came.

Calisto didn't allow himself to care for or love anyone, not ever.

He did strive to treat the mortals around him with respect, and if he made them happy in the process, so much the better. As long as he didn't become too attached, or entangled in their lives. He remained ever watchful not to cross that line.

Upstairs in the main house, he settled behind his desk and found the address for the restaurant to meet Betty. The scent of her perfume still lingered on her stationery. He smiled at the personal touch as he folded the paper and tucked it into his coat pocket.

He stepped out of the house and glanced at the stars. The sight of the moon reminded him of Kate. He wondered when they would meet again. For the first time in centuries he remembered what it felt like to carry hope in his heart.

It was a dangerous thought.

Shaking his head, Calisto pushed the feeling from his mind. Tonight he would focus on business. First, he needed to feed or his skin would be too cold and far too pale. He had an hour before his meeting with Betty, not much time. Walking down the beach, he vanished into the darkness.

§

Kate signed the final paper documenting her mother's donation of the piano and sheet music to the foundation and couldn't help but notice Betty glanced at her watch several times.

"Sorry I'm so slow. I like to know what I'm signing."

Betty shook her head with a smile. "Not a problem. I'm expecting the founder any minute, and I'm starting to worry he might have lost the address or something. He's not usually late."

"Calisto's coming here?" When she saw Betty's perfectly plucked eyebrow arch, Kate struggled to rein in her excitement. "My mom mentioned him to me before…. He's Spanish, right?"

"Yes." Betty's smile brightened as she watched the door open. "And it looks like he just got here."

§

Calisto followed the hostess back to the table Betty reserved, surprised to find she wasn't alone. Another woman sat with her back to him.

"Calisto!" Betty rose from the table to greet him, the picture of sophisticated beauty, dressed in a simple black cocktail dress that accentuated her long, shapely legs. She usually kept her blonde hair pulled into a tight French twist, but tonight it fell loosely down her back.

He smiled, taking her hand and pressing a kiss to her knuckles. "Good evening, Bettina. I apologize for my tardiness." He turned to acknowledge the other woman at the table. "I didn't realize you invited anyone else to our—"

His words caught in his throat the instant he saw the other woman. Her large eyes were dark as midnight, except for the tiny crescent, and the sight of her smile as she stood to offer her hand felt like a summer breeze warming his cold heart.

He took the chance encounter as a sign. Destiny had crossed their paths again, offering their souls another chance at love. He prayed fate would be kinder to them in this lifetime.

Betty gestured to Kate with a curt, businesslike smile. "Calisto, this is Kate Bradley. Martha Bradley's daughter."

He fought to keep from pulling her into his arms. Instead, he managed a nod. "I am sorry for your loss. Martha was a wonderful woman. She will be missed by all."

Martha Bradley. In his excitement over seeing Kate at the Mission, he hadn't recognized her last name. Martha was one of Foundation Arts' longtime donors, yet in all those years he'd never met her beautiful daughter.

Tala had been close to him all this time, yet just out of his reach. The thought caused his chest to tighten.

He watched her mouth, waiting to hear her voice again. He ached to touch her. It was the sweetest torture he'd ever known to see her alive once more, and not be able to hold her in his arms, to kiss her soft lips. Fire licked at his heart, awakening passion he had long ago forgotten.

"Thank you." Kate offered her hand in greeting. "I've heard a lot about you. I didn't realize who you were when we met at the mission the other night."

He was unprepared for the electricity that shot through him when he took her hand. Touching her again after lifetimes apart made him feel both weak with gratitude and selfish. He never wanted to let her go.

Her skin felt warm against his lips as he pressed a lingering kiss to her knuckles. "The pleasure is mine, Kate Bradley."

Clearing her throat, Betty stepped closer to Calisto and took his arm, her smile growing when he finally forced himself to relinquish Kate's hand.

"This coat looks wonderful on you. Isn't it the one I gave you for Christmas?" Betty stood nearer to him than she ever had before.

Calisto raised a brow. "I believe it is."

For the first time, Calisto wished he'd not used her infatuation to keep her pliant and unsuspecting. He'd waited so long to see Tala again, and the last thing he wanted to stand in his way were petty jealousies.

He forced himself to shake off his irritation as Kate glanced at Betty with a momentary look of concern. Kate flashed a smile and stepped back, and Calisto casually removed Betty's hand from his arm.

"Kate signed the documents for Martha's piano so we can pick it up for her," Betty said, turning to face him more fully, using the movement to move close to him again.

Calisto nodded, putting some space between him and Betty. Kate looked stunning in her burgundy lace dress, her full lips tinted with wine-colored lipstick. The way her black hair spilled over her shoulders made him yearn to run his fingers through it. How had he survived so long without her?

"I think I've signed everything, so I guess I'd better get going." Kate smiled at Betty, and cast a brief glance in Calisto's direction. "I don't want to interrupt your business."

"Nice to finally meet you in person, Kate," Betty said with a stiff smile.

Kate returned the pleasantry as she shook Betty's hand. "I enjoyed seeing you again, Calisto."

She was leaving. He couldn't let her go, and yet he couldn't make her stay. His heart pounded. Taking her hand, he placed another tender kiss to her knuckles. "Again, the pleasure was all mine."

Kate lifted her hand from his and smiled. She picked up her purse and offered a final nod. "Good night."

With one last look over her shoulder, she walked away.

His mind raced with panic as he watched her go. He needed to see her, and soon. Nothing would keep him from her.

Visions from Father Tomas filled his mind and anger flooded through him. The Fraternidad knew she lived again. Tomas had seen her. His train of thought ground to halt. The monk told him they would not allow him to make another blood drinker.

They must believe he would make Kate a Night Walker.

Even now, after centuries had passed, the church still tried to keep them apart. But they would not succeed this time. Kate gave his empty life new meaning with a simple smile. He would not allow anyone to steal it away. Not this time.

§

Kate drove away from the bay with a dreamy smile. Why was she so stuck on this guy? Hearing him talk made her heart flip.

She shook her head as she drove back to Point Loma. Infatuation was a strong emotion when you were alone. Kate tried not to think about the way he stared at her, the way his dark eyes held her in his gaze, like he could undress her with just a look.

Her skin flushed hot thinking about it. She recalled her mother mentioning he was handsome, but geez, handsome was an understatement.

Ok, so he was incredible. It was time to move on. The last thing she needed was another man in her life. Tom's betrayal was too fresh, and trust wasn't something she was ready to try again anytime soon. Infatuation might be harmless and fun, but it needed to end there.

How could she work on a new life and a better future when she let a hot guy with a silky voice break her focus?

She didn't have the emotional fortitude for anything more than getting her life back together.

Turning up the radio, she tightened her grip on the steering wheel. Tonight turned out better than she expected. She sang along with the music and pulled off when she saw a familiar taco shop. Good Mexican food was the one thing she missed most when she moved to Reno. Nothing else measured up to the spicy flavor of a carne asada burrito from a San Diego taco shop.

Her mouth watered thinking about it.

She ordered her burrito, hold the salsa, and a large iced tea. As she waited at the window for her food, she thought about what might have happened if she'd stayed at The Fish Market with Betty and Calisto. Part of her wished she had, but it would have been awkward. Betty made it obvious they had work to do. Besides, no sense in tempting herself with some crazy infatuation for a rich Spanish bachelor who probably dated a new supermodel every week. In fact, that was the last thing she needed.

She definitely made the right decision when she left. So why couldn't she stop thinking about him?

Kate traded the cashier a few dollars in exchange for her dinner and drove home. Time to focus. She needed to shove thoughts of Calisto aside and consider her long-term plans. She still hadn't decided what to do about her teaching position in Reno. She wanted to investigate her career options in San Diego.

If she could immerse herself in a job search and dealing with her parents' estate, Calisto Terana would fade into a distant memory. She was certain of it.

Her thumb unconsciously traced over the back of her other hand where his lips brushed her skin a couple of hours earlier, and her pulse pounded at the memory of his touch. Kate rolled her eyes and sighed. *Get a grip.*

After polishing off her dinner, Kate sipped her iced tea and surfed the websites of the county's many school districts. There weren't many openings, but she had a few options, including an opening for a position on an east county reservation. When she clicked the link for more information, the page loaded a photo of Calisto and described the grant he created to fund cultural music and art teachers for the school. She stared too long at the photo, thinking about how he looked at her. With a start, she realized she'd lost track of time again.

Really, this was getting ridiculous.

She stabbed at the keyboard to shut down the computer. Tomorrow, she would polish her resume and research local private schools. For now, she wanted to play the piano, possibly for the last time. Maybe if she played something, she'd be able to think about something other than Calisto.

But the longer she played, the more she wondered what he would do with her mother's instrument. Betty told her he was an accomplished pianist. Would his fingers touch these keys?

It was hopeless. Kate closed the cover over the keyboard and grabbed her purse. She was going to a movie. It didn't matter what was showing, as long as it gave her something else to think about.

§

Word of Father De Cardina's death traveled quickly back to Spain. The monsignor let out a sigh, crumbling the courier's letter. He had hoped to avoid more bloodshed.

For centuries, the Fraternidad Del Fuego Santo kept a quiet watch over the Night Walker, a monster who had once been one of their own.

During the Alcala Massacre, a lone monk had watched the carnage from the shadows. He witnessed the Night Walker feeding, drinking the blood of one of the guards, and rewrote history. Father Jayme was named the first Catholic martyr in the New World, and Father Salvador, along with his lover, Tala, were erased from all written records in the Catholic Church, but not forgotten.

The Fraternidad del Fuego Santo hid the story of the native woman with the moon in the iris of her right eye and the creature with a thirst for blood.

They still hadn't found a way to kill the unholy abomination. In recent years they resigned to keeping a sentinel on the Pacific coast to observe his movements and be certain he did not spread his curse.

The truth behind the Mission de Alcala uprising had been buried for centuries. They could not risk allowing the world to discover what the Church had unknowingly unleashed. From Brother Cardina's communications, they learned the Night Walker had met a woman with a strange marking in her right eye. Brother Cardina seemed convinced the abomination believed the woman to be the reincarnation of his Native American lover.

Of course she would have no memories of Father Gregorio Salvador. Reincarnation was a fallacy. But if the Night Walker believed she lived again and sought to make her immortal, the consequences would be dire. The Night Walker was formidable enough alone, but if Satan took the woman's soul, too, the threat to the flock would be mighty. If only they understood the unholy races better.

Over the years, the Fraternidad collected files of research on the Night Walkers, but the creatures had remained secretive. The Church still had more questions than avenues for answers. Most people remained unaware of their existence, and that was the best the Fraternidad had managed.

They still weren't sure if his life could be ended, and the moral implications of the Church ordering such an action were endless.

Murder, though justified, had been the catalyst that brought them to their present dilemma.

However, they would not sit idly by and watch the Night Walker unleash another unholy blood drinker into this world. Surely if the abomination believed his lover lived again, he would seek to make her an immortal like him. They had to control the situation.

His office door creaked open.

"You sent for me, Father?"

The monsignor looked up to see the young monk enter his chamber, shutting the heavy door behind him. "Yes, Brother Mentigo. I have received word from San Diego. Brother De Cardina has gone to the Lord's arms."

The color drained from the younger monk's face as he made the sign of the cross. "God rest his soul. Was it the—"

"Yes." The monsignor handed him a crumbled slip of paper. "The priests at the Mission de Alcala found this message pinned to his robe."

Do not start a war you cannot win.

"Is this blood?" Mentigo asked. His brow creased, and he rubbed his thumb across the paper as if to test the words.

"It is."

The monk wet his lips. "He wrote this?"

"*Si.*" The monsignor gestured to the seal on the back. "That is his signet. He still has it after all of these years."

Brother Mentigo nodded. It seemed he caressed the seal, his fingers brushing over the script on the front once more. The monsignor cleared his throat, and the monk lifted his gaze, returning the note.

"Our mission falls on your shoulders now," the monsignor continued as he tucked the note into his robes.

"What would you have me do, Father?"

"Keep your distance from the Night Walker, and be certain the woman has no contact with him. And pray, my son. Pray she stays away from him. We must keep this world safe from another blood drinker, and we will use whatever means we must."

"You believe he will make her a Night Walker?"

The monsignor pressed his lips together, quiet for a moment before answering. "I cannot say, but we must not take that risk. Remember, no one else can know. Stay in contact with me alone. "

"I will, Father." He turned away, and the monsignor thought he saw the younger man slide his tongue along the edge of his teeth, burying an eager smile.

Once he was alone, the monsignor clasped his hands together, wondering if he had just sent another young priest to his death. He hoped not. He already saw the stain of Brother De Cardina's blood on his hands each time he closed his eyes. He did not want to lose another priest to the Night Walker's appetite.

Sadly, it was a chance he would have to take. Although they did not know how to end the Night Walker's life, the woman still remained mortal, and if they needed to kill her in order to save the world from the plague of another blood drinker, they would do what must be done. God help them.

CHAPTER SEVEN

Calisto watched from the sidewalk as Betty drove out of the restaurant parking lot. He didn't need to look into her mind to know she was disappointed their meeting ended early, her tight shoulders, aloof chin, and death grip on her steering wheel gave away her state of mind. It couldn't be helped. His thoughts revolved around Kate, the sound of her voice and the feel of her soft hand in his. He couldn't concentrate on the business he needed to discuss with Betty.

Usually, he buried his emotions without a second thought, but this newfound hope growing inside of him was impossible to hide. Deep within, icy fear stabbed him. The Fraternidad's focus on Kate did not bode well under any circumstance, but he couldn't forget the image of Kate in the priest's mind, holding a small child in her arms, drinking its blood. The image, hazy and incomplete, had the telltale markers of a fear or dream, not a real memory, but it told him absolutely why they had targeted her.

Their belief he would turn her into a Night Walker was preposterous. If they understood the price she would pay for immortality, they would know he could never steal her humanity. Unfortunately, their foolishness made them dangerous. This same group of zealots had ordered her death once before. He didn't doubt that they would do it again.

This time he would be ready for them.

He walked toward the water's edge and closed his eyes, letting his mind reach outside of his body, searching for hers. When the person he sought was not nearby, locating them mentally became almost impossible. Many years ago, when his Night Walker abilities grew in power, he learned to bind his spirit to another raven, connecting them over great distances. Seeing the world through the bird's eyes, he sometimes found who or what he was looking for.

But without a raven to aid his search, he was forced to sift through the deluge of mortal thoughts pouring in. When he could tolerate no more, he shielded his mind, and his spirit grounded once more. Kate wasn't nearby. Without a phone number or an address, he had little information to locate her.

She'd left the restaurant less than two hours ago. Perhaps she was still in downtown San Diego. Hidden in the darkness, he made a running start while the air around him charged with electricity. With each stride, his body transformed and feathers black as night covered him. His final step became an easy leap, and he took to the air.

Soaring over the coast of San Diego, he batted his wings against gusts of ocean wind. He much preferred to fly as a raven than to ride in a car. The feel of the wind and the scent of the salt air brought him peace. He never mastered driving automobiles. He loathed being trapped inside a metal prison hurdling along the busy freeways. Although a car might travel faster from place to place, in the air as a lone raven, he had complete control and freedom.

Calisto landed in a dark, empty alleyway behind a nightclub in the downtown Gaslamp Quarter. Willing himself back to his human form, he straightened his clothes and walked into the masses of mortals on the sidewalk.

At the corner, he prepared to lower his mental shields to search for her. Before the onslaught of thoughts hit him, Calisto noticed a familiar face across the street. He stopped and stared. Perhaps fate would lend him a hand in this lifetime. When the light changed, he followed in her direction.

Kate hurried inside a movie theater, and Calisto smiled. A movie sounded like a great idea.

§

Kate bought her ticket and found a seat on the aisle in the middle of the empty theater. Tuesday night was obviously not the most popular night of the week for moviegoers, which suited her fine. She wasn't looking for company right now anyway. She ate her popcorn, watched the slides for local businesses flash across the large screen, and incorrectly answered movie trivia questions that kept her mind off Calisto.

Sipping her soda, Kate shifted in her seat. She had the odd feeling she was being watched. After a moment, she glanced toward the bottom of the theater. Her heart leapt when she saw who stood below.

Calisto looked up at her, and the moment their eyes met, Kate wasn't sure she could breathe. He climbed the stairs to her row, his eyes never straying from hers, and her pulse quickened.

"Is this seat taken?"

She swiped her buttered fingers against the napkin in her lap and cursed the crumbs she knew had fallen all over her blouse. With a smile she hoped would distract him, she said, "No. It's all yours."

He returned her smile and removed his coat while she had a field day taking in all the muscular curves that lurked under his fitted knit shirt. Kate snapped her gaze to the movie screen the second he turned to take his seat.

God, she hoped he didn't see her staring.

"It is nice to see you again, Kate." The overhead lights dimmed.

Kate nodded, finally allowing herself to glance at him again. "It's strange that we keep bumping into each other."

"Perhaps it is fate," he said.

Kate hoped the dim lights hid her flush as the previews flashed on the screen. Neither one of them touched or said another word during the movie, although she wanted to, desperately. The romantic comedy should have made her laugh, but she found it impossible to concentrate. Knowing he sat beside her, catching the scent of his cologne, made her skin tingle. She ached for him to reach over and touch her.

Oh, she was in so much trouble.

§

The credits passed over the screen, but Kate didn't move. She wasn't sure she could. Half of her wanted to stay in this moment forever, and the other half wanted to protect her heart and run home to safety.

Finally, Calisto broke the silence. "It was a nice surprise to find you here, Kate. The evening is still young. Will you allow me the pleasure of buying you a cup of coffee?"

She looked at him, already losing herself in his dark eyes. "That sounds great."

An inner battle between her heart and her head raged. Her heart wanted her to be near Calisto, to learn everything about him, and her head told her to escape before she got too attached to this way-too-perfect-to-be-true man. What happened to her plan not to rush into anything? She was supposed to be taking control of her life.

Kate walked down the aisle toward the door. The feel of his hand at the small of her back shot chills through her until she finally spun around to face him.

"I'm not looking for a relationship right now."

She hadn't realized how close they were, but she didn't move away. Calisto remained quiet for a moment before his hand dropped to his side. A gentle smile came to his face, but his eyes hardened.

"Forgive me if I gave you the wrong impression. I hate sitting in a café alone, and I thought I might get to know you better."

Stupid! Did she honestly think he was interested in a romantic relationship with her? Her infatuation clouded her thinking. Why would Calisto Terana, philanthropist and longtime bachelor, give up his lifestyle for a choir director from Reno?

Wake up, Kate.

She took a step back. This close to him, the urge to touch him overwhelmed her. "I'm sorry. I've been under a lot of stress. I guess I read too much into this. I'd love to have a cup of coffee with you."

"I would be honored." Calisto offered his arm.

Placing her hand in the crook of his elbow, Kate followed his lead into the bustling nightlife of downtown. The November evening air was crisp, and the fog rolled in, embracing them in its mist.

She walked a little closer to Calisto, telling herself it was because of the cold. Billows of misty clouds made beautiful orange halos of light around the old gas lamp streetlights while their footsteps echoed along the empty sidewalk.

After they traveled two blocks, Kate smiled up at him. "I hope you know where we're going, because I haven't been down here in years."

"It is not much farther." He teased her with a smile.

"I don't mind the walk." The haze around them blurred the city lights. She could imagine they were the only two people in the world. "It's a beautiful night."

He brought his free hand to lie over her fingers on the crook of his arm. "Yes it is." He looked down, his gaze like a caress. "Incredibly beautiful."

Kate caught herself imagining what it would be like to kiss him. Not a good sign considering she came back to San Diego to get distance from a relationship, not embroil herself in another. She pulled her gaze from his and focused on walking in a straight line.

"How long have you lived in San Diego?"

Calisto paused for several seconds. "I lost count years ago. How long have you been away?"

"Nine years," Kate said.

"Why would you leave a paradise like San Diego?"

"Who says Reno isn't paradise?"

Calisto shook his head slightly. "I meant no disrespect to your new home, but I wonder why you would give up the ocean and the perfect weather."

Kate shrugged. The movement sent her fingers over a ridge of muscle in Calisto's arm. "I don't know. San Diego, especially the beach, never felt like home. Watching the waves made me lonely. I know it sounds strange, but I don't have a better way to describe it. Almost like being haunted or something."

Had she really just said that? She never told anyone how she felt when she stood on the beach, not even Tom, the man she had planned to marry. What was it about Calisto? She barely knew him.

Kate laughed, shaking her head. "Sounds crazy, doesn't it?" She smiled up at him, feeling vulnerable and most definitely not confident in that moment. He opened the glass door of a dimly lit café. "Sure you still want to have coffee with me?"

"I have never been more certain of anything in this life." Calisto grinned. His hand brushed the small of her back, an encouraging touch. She let him guide her to a corner table, reveling in the feel of his hand against her and the acceptance in his smile.

Every time he touched her, her entire body tingled in response. And even though she shouldn't, even though she needed time and room to settle into her new approach to life, she wanted more of Calisto. She yearned for it.

He took the seat across from her. Kate dreaded the awkward silence sure to come, but it didn't.

"You are a musician in Reno?"

She relaxed into her seat, enjoying the way his accent colored the name of her city. "Yes, I direct a couple of middle school choirs. How did you know that?"

"I wish I could say that I knew your mother and she told me this, but I cannot. Sadly, I am not involved with the donors at the foundation as much as I would like."

"Betty told you, huh?" Kate laughed.

"I wondered why a musician would give up a beautiful instrument like your mother's piano."

"My mother didn't give me a choice in the matter. She wanted you to have it," Kate said, surprised at how bitter she sounded.

"Do you play?"

She shrugged. "Not very well. But I get by."

"Get by?" He moved his chair back and crossed an ankle over his leg.

In this new position, Kate could enjoy the cut of his shirt over his chest. She cleared her throat. "I can plunk out melodies just fine, but

I'm a little rusty at playing the bass line with my left hand."

"Sometime, I would love to hear you play."

God, she couldn't get enough of his accent. Focus, Kate. "Oh I'd be too embarrassed. Betty told me you're a concert pianist."

He cocked his head and raised his eyebrows. "How well I play has nothing to do with it."

Kate laughed, leaning back slightly as the waitress placed their drinks in front of them. "What will happen to my Mom's piano, anyway?"

Calisto grasped the warm coffee mug and answered, but Kate didn't register the words. The café, its customers, the smell of coffee, even time faded when she noticed his hand.

"Kate?"

His ring. She couldn't take her eyes off of it. Something about it seemed… familiar. Maybe she *was* insane. She couldn't have seen it before, and yet she was sure she had. Either that or she had some vivid déjà vu.

"Kate? Are you all right?" Calisto asked.

Kate blinked and shook her head slowly, breaking the trance she felt when she noticed the ring. "I'm sorry. I saw your ring and I can't help thinking I've seen it before." She searched his face for something that might tell her why the ring seemed so familiar. "I swear I'm not usually this crazy, but it looks familiar to me."

His gaze held hers, his voice soft but commanding. "You are many things, but crazy is not one of them. Perhaps intuition told you of our meeting in a dream. Stranger things have happened in this world, no?"

Dream. The word sent a chill down her spine. "You believe in déjà vu then?"

"You do not?"

"I asked you first." She sipped her coffee, desperate to shake off the nagging anxiety that haunted her since she saw his ring. Something inside of her kept grasping for a memory that she knew didn't exist.

"Yes, you did."

His voice guided her back to the present. "Do you always answer a question with another question?"

"You are not the first to accuse me of such a thing." Calisto smiled, lifting his coffee to his full lips.

"Now that I can believe. So maybe I've seen your ring before, huh?" She glanced at his hand but, concerned the design would entrance her again, she returned her attention to his face.

"Maybe so." He placed his mug on the table. "As I said, stranger things have happened."

Kate nodded. Strange things were happening all right. She sipped her coffee, unable to take her eyes off of his. Did he feel the same attraction?

She was a choir teacher who lived out of state in a two-bedroom apartment, and he was a reclusive philanthropist. This was real life, not a fairy tale. She had to wake up. She was on the rebound here.

"We should probably get going." She set her mug down. "It's getting late."

"I suppose it is." He looked almost disappointed, but he rose from the booth and moved around to help her to her feet.

"Thank you." The second her fingers touched his, a shock of desire zipped through her. She had to force herself to let go of his hand. Keeping a clear head was difficult when her body reacted to him this way. He made her feel more alive, her senses heightened. Her heart raced just holding his hand.

Imagine if we kissed. Her skin flushed with heat and she rolled her eyes at herself.

"Where are you parked?" Kate asked.

"I am not."

"You're not? Did you take a cab or something?"

"Something… "

Kate grinned, shaking her head. "You play the man of mystery well, don't you? I'd be happy to give you a ride. It's the least I can do since you saved me from a night all alone."

"You should never be alone." Calisto offered his arm, tipping his head slightly toward her.

She placed her hand into the crook of his arm, barely resisting the urge to run her fingers along his bicep. "Are you always so charming?"

His eyes lost focus, and something shifted in his expression. For a moment, he looked as haunted as Kate felt. "Not always," he said.

She glanced at his ring again and wondered whether she had as much control over her life as she believed.

CHAPTER EIGHT

Calisto raised a brow. The small yellow car was not what he expected.

"Just a sec, I've gotta let you in from the driver's side." Kate leaned across the steering wheel and unhooked the bungee cord that held the passenger door closed.

He had no love for automobiles. They weren't from his era and since he had the ability to fly, he didn't see the purpose in learning to drive a car. That did not mean he hadn't ridden in many BMWs, Lexus, Jaguars, and Bentleys. He knew the luxury of leather seats and climate control.

This car had neither.

He schooled his features to hide his doubts about the car's viability when he tugged the door closed. The driver's door had vice grips where the window crank should be, a bungee cord held the passenger-side door closed, and duct tape covered the small tear in the corner of the convertible top. Even though it was November, she had the top of her faded VW bug folded down. He envisioned a surfboard hanging out the back like many of the college students who came to La Jolla in search of waves to ride. Kate claimed she didn't belong in California, but her car most certainly did.

"Sorry. I probably should have warned you about Bessie before you accepted my offer to take you home."

"Bessie?"

"My car. I've had her since college. When I realized I finally could afford another car, I bought her a new engine instead." She turned the key and smiled at him. "I still haven't fixed the passenger door. I've been searching for a salvaged door off the same model bug. They're tough to find now and… " Her cheeks flushed with color. "And now I'm rambling. Sorry, I do that sometimes when I get nervous."

He rested his hand over hers on the gearshift. "Did I complain about your car?" Kate shook her head slowly and he smiled. "I am grateful for your company, and here is a little-known secret." He leaned closer to her. "I have never ridden in a convertible before."

Her eyes sparkled with delight. "You're in for a treat." She put the car in gear and pulled onto the street.

Calisto usually despised riding in cars, but Kate's car, in spite of its battle scars, was far from the metal prison of the luxury vehicles he'd ridden in before.

The night air blew through his hair, caressing his skin, and he closed his eyes, drinking in the sensation. It almost felt like flying. In all his years, the wind had never gusted this way against this skin. Only his feathers had ever experienced this freedom.

The moonlight shone in the midnight of Kate's hair, and the wind brushed it back. He memorized every curve and angle of her profile, loving the way she sang with the radio under her breath.

Echoes of her native melodies filled his mind and for once it brought peace instead of bitterness and rage.

She still loved to sing.

By the time they reached the interstate, their conversation was comfortable. Within twenty minutes, they left the freeway and the thickening mist threatening to blanket the roads. They wound down the narrow road along the La Jolla cliffs and stopped in front of his house.

Kate whistled at the automatic gates that opened to reveal his winding driveway. He tried to see his home as Kate might.

His large, hacienda-style house overlooked the Pacific. On the rare occasions he stood at the arched windows on the second floor, he could see pods of dolphins jumping through the surf in the moonlight. The stucco walls were a tan shade that complemented the warm sand and ice plant that crept up the cliffs.

Kate flipped the keys to kill the engine and stared. "It's beautiful."

"I am glad you like it." He unhooked the bungee cord to open his door. "Come, I will show you around."

She seemed to consider his offer for several seconds before nodding once. "All right, but I can't stay too long. It's late and I hate driving in the fog."

He hoped she couldn't see the joy he felt. He was certain it would only scare her to know the depth of his desire and the intensity of his hopes.

Lost in his thoughts, Calisto led Kate down the limestone walkway to the front door. He wasn't ready for the night to end. She had recognized his ring, his personal signet from Spain. It bore the flames of the Fraternidad Del Fuego Santo, and a dove of peace soared above the fire. There was no other ring like it in the world.

Lifetimes ago, he gave the signet to her, a token of his devotion. She wore it like a pendant on a fine leather strap around her neck, and she treasured the ring as she treasured him. Calisto cleared his throat, struggling to bury the thoughts before they resurrected his emotions.

He wondered if she had any other memories of him. He was tempted to peer into her mind.

The weight of her hand pressed against the crook of his arm, and the urge to hold her almost overwhelmed his tenuous grip on his self-control. He still remembered how perfect she fit into his arms, the way her body molded against his. How would she feel now, changed but still so like her former self? Having her close again was a tremendous temptation.

When he opened the door, he stepped back to allow Kate to enter. "Welcome to my home."

"Thank you." When she passed by, he caught the scent of her hair and squeezed his eyes shut.

She smelled like sunshine.

§

The click of her shoes echoed against the polished Spanish
tile floor of the foyer and reverberated in the spacious great room.
The rest of the floor was covered with sand-colored carpet, and
whitewashed driftwood beams hung high above, accenting the vaulted
ceiling. A large fireplace with a raised hearth stood in the corner
with French doors on the right leading to a deck that overlooked the
beach. Light colors decorated the entire room. Yet nothing looked
touched, like no one lived there.

Kate thought maybe by seeing his home, she'd get a glimpse into
the mysterious Calisto Terana. Though the hacienda was stunning,
nothing inside revealed anything about its owner. No stacks of
unopened mail, no photos of family, not even coats draped over the
sofa.

Nothing was out of place.

He led her through the house and out the French doors without
a word. Moonlight sparkled on the waves below. They stood together,
leaning against the railing of the deck. Plumes of fog floated through
the air, glowing in the moon's haunting light, and the scent of salty sea
air filled her lungs.

"It is beautiful here, no?"

Kate nodded as the sea breeze blew through her dark hair.
Without meaning to, she leaned a little closer to him. "Yes it is."

"When I need to clear my head and think, this is where I come."
He stared at the ocean. "This is where I find my peace."

She watched the wind pull at the leather tie that held his hair
back. Why was he telling her these things? They just met, but the
feeling that they'd known each other forever pervaded her thoughts.
Did he feel the same?

Even the profile of his face made her heart flutter. The angle of
his forehead, the strength of his jaw, and the curve of his lips spoke to
her, called to her, and made her yearn for him. She wanted to untie his
hair and slide her fingers through it.

Turning toward the waves, she sighed. "I used to come to the beach as a teenager and sit for hours watching the water, wondering why I felt empty inside. The ocean never brought me any peace. The waves made me feel lonely, like a piece of me was missing. I never figured out why. I guess it was easier to move away."

"Did you fill this emptiness in Reno?" he asked without looking at her.

"I think so." Kate shrugged. "I've been happy, I guess."

Until Tom upended her world.

He nodded and shifted beside her. Carefully he caught a stray lock of her hair and brushed it back from her face.

"Do you feel empty here now?" he asked.

Kate turned, finding him much closer than she expected. Her heart pounded in her ears, and her eyes lingered on his lips before finally locking on his heated gaze.

"No," she said, surprising herself. "No, I… I like it here."

"Maybe you need new memories of the ocean to fill the emptiness." His dark eyes never strayed from hers, demanding her attention.

Kate bit back her desire and nodded, forcing herself to turn toward the water. "Maybe so."

Calisto took her hand, and Kate was surprised to find her fingers lacing together with his as if they'd been made to fit together as one.

"Walk with me?" His low voice stripped away a layer of her resolve.

Kate nodded, following him down the steps to the sand below, only stopping for a moment to leave her shoes on the landing. They walked across the cool beach without saying a word, hand in hand, and Kate watched the haze float in atop the salt water. It was eerie and beautiful all in the same moment.

"You are shivering."

Calisto's voice added to the tremors that pulsed through her body. Why did he have to be so perfect? He looked at her like she was the only woman in the world.

"Am I?"

He smiled, raising their joined hands to place a tender kiss on her knuckle, and then tugged off his coat and draped it over her shoulders.

"Is that better?"

Kate nodded, no longer able to speak. His masculine scent surrounded her, and before she could stop herself, she pulled his coat so tight, the cold lining spread gooseflesh across her skin.

He slid the backs of his cool fingers down her cheek, his lips hinting at a smile. "Good."

Kate tilted her chin up. When he bent and brushed his lips against hers, her breath caught. Her pulse raced and electricity shot through her veins. Her skin warmed. Had she ever wanted anyone this badly?

She brought her hand to his chest. His chiseled muscles responded to her touch, and a moan escaped her as he clutched her tighter. Calisto's fingers slid through her hair, and her lips parted, her tongue tasting him, tangling with his until her knees buckled.

Dear God, this man could kiss.

Gradually she drew back, softening the kiss until her forehead rested against his. She stared into his eyes, wishing she knew his thoughts. Wishing she understood what it was about this man that made passion ignite through her bloodstream like wildfire.

Her pulse throbbed in her ears, and she took a small step back. She tried to remember the list of things she still needed to finish at her parents' place, and her job back in Reno. Anything to regain control of herself.

Real life didn't involve rich, exotic bachelors on private beaches. She fought to think of the music she loved, to recall the pain she felt when she walked into Tom's office three weeks ago. She needed to protect her wounded heart and fight the growing attraction to the man who made her body ache for his attention.

He reached for her hand, and her fingers entwined with his. Traitors.

§

He watched her face as they walked down the beach together. He had to concentrate to keep from dragging her back into his arms. Until he kissed her, he hadn't understood the true depth of his loneliness, but now that he'd held her again, tasted her lips, he couldn't let her go.

For the first time in centuries, he felt content and alive.

Until Kate pulled away from him.

He wanted to understand her, but he wouldn't allow himself to look into her thoughts. Limiting himself to the speech of a mortal man proved difficult.

He was out of practice.

"You are quiet."

"Sorry. We shouldn't have done that. I... " She shook her head and watched the waves. "I have no business jumping into a relationship right now, and I have no interest in being a one-night stand either. If I gave you the wrong impression, I'm sorry about that."

"I did not mean to rush anything."

"You didn't. I kissed you back." She sighed and finally looked up at him. "I'm probably going back to Reno soon anyway. The last thing I need right now is more drama."

"Do you have anyone waiting for you there?" The question surprised him. He wasn't sure he wanted to know the answer. It hadn't occurred to him until this moment that Kate might be in love with someone else.

Jealousy curdled in his stomach while he waited for her to answer.

"Not anymore."

Her answer didn't relieve him as much as he hoped it would.

"We were going to get married until I caught him fooling around with one of his grad students. That's why I came back to San Diego. I needed time away. A change of scenery, you know?" She shook her head with a sigh. "It's been an awful month for me."

"He was a fool to let you go." He gave her hand a gentle squeeze. "I wish I had more comfort to offer than words."

The suffering he saw reflected in her gaze tore at his heart. Cold fury churned inside him. He wanted to know who hurt her, and he wanted to cause him pain.

Slow, lingering pain.

"Why are you being kind to me?" she asked, jarring him from his thoughts.

"What?"

She shook her head. "I just want to understand what's going on here. I looked you up online. I know you're one of San Diego's most eligible bachelors. You could have anyone."

He scowled. "Who I *could* have is of no importance."

"No, it's very important to me. I was naïve once, and I got burned. I'm not looking for another heartbreak."

Calisto stared into her beautiful eyes. He could never hurt her.

The ocean breeze drifted past them, tugging at her hair. Her eyes sparkled, and for a moment, the centuries that separated them vanished.

His lips brushed hers, and he whispered, "I have no intention of ever breaking your heart."

Kate stepped back from him, breaking the spell. Calisto felt like the sand shifted beneath his feet when he saw the shock in her eyes.

"I... I can't do this. It's too much." She yanked her hand free, tugged off his jacket, and thrust it against his chest. "Look, I'm sorry if I led you on, or gave you the wrong idea. I shouldn't have come here with you."

Calisto stared in shock at Kate's retreating figure. He hadn't meant to kiss her. Not yet. But the night enchanted him and dimmed the line between the past and present. Was it wrong that he wanted her? He needed to spend time with her, to win her heart, but she gave him no chance.

He gripped his jacket in a tight fist and jogged after her, careful not to let himself run too quickly. The last thing he wanted was to frighten her with his preternatural abilities.

The situation was maddening. She stood so close, yet still out of his reach.

Kate almost made it to her car, but she stopped abruptly. Turning to her right, she stared at a knoll covered with the flowers he left at Tala's cross at the mission.

"They're beautiful," she whispered.

Calisto forced a smile. "Thank you."

She bent closer, smelling one of the blooms, and then finally turned toward him. "I saw some of these the other night at the mission. What are they called?"

"Romneya."

She nodded, reaching out to touch the delicate petals. "I've never seen another flower like it."

"They were native to Southern California, although now they are hard to find here," he said, drinking in her every move.

"I love them." Kate smiled. "They're gorgeous, and they smell so good... "

You have always loved them. How he wished she remembered.

Calisto leaned forward and snapped a bloom from its stem, careful not to jostle the delicate plant. Without a word, he nestled the large, white flower behind her ear.

He wasn't prepared for the emotion that slammed into him. She was exactly the way he remembered, drenched in moonlight with her favorite flower tucked behind her ear. The stark contrast of her black hair and the white petals took his breath away. His fingertips lingered against her cheek, caressing it while his gaze held hers, and in that brief moment, she was his again.

The fog surrounded them, and the rest of the world disappeared. She gazed at him, her full lips parting until he could resist no longer. Calisto bent to claim her lips one last time. Her hand slid up his chest, but instead of deepening the kiss, Kate pushed him back.

"We have to stop. This can't work out," she whispered. "I can't. I can't do this."

She ran to her car without looking back, and within a minute her little VW disappeared into the fog.

CHAPTER NINE

The sun beat through the living room window. Kate sat up, still in her Dad's favorite recliner. Glancing at the clock, she stretched her arms and groaned. Every muscle felt drained and achy.

She'd struggled with her mixed-up emotions the entire drive home. In the end, she didn't fall asleep until almost five in the morning. Six hours wasn't enough to recover from the tempest of emotions Calisto had brought on.

In spite of her exhaustion, she had a clear understanding of what she needed to do.

She would pack and head home. Running to San Diego was supposed to help her regain her emotional footing, but now her escape was on the verge of spiraling out of control, too. She'd run from her demons in Reno, and it was time she faced them. How could she gain control of her life when she let a cheating bastard chase her from her life? Besides, she couldn't stay and let herself fall into another relationship when she'd promised herself she would take her time.

She wasn't that masochistic. Not yet, anyway.

After packing up her clothes and a couple of boxes of mementos, she called the realtor to put the house back on the rental market, and then made one last call.

"Hi Betty, it's Kate Bradley."

"Hello Kate." Did Betty sound less than happy to hear from her? "What can I do for you?"

"I'm heading back to Reno this afternoon. I won't be here when the movers come to pick up the piano. Can I give you the realtor's number? She'll come by and open the house up for you."

"Sure, that'll be fine," Betty said, her voice suddenly warm and friendly.

Kate gave her the information and chuckled to herself as she hung up the phone. Of course Betty would be happy that she was leaving. Or maybe she was just reading into it because Betty was staying here with Calisto.

She let out an exasperated sigh. How did he make such an impression on her in just one night? She was usually pretty levelheaded, not swayed by a pretty face, but if she didn't stop thinking about the dark, charming, handsome Spaniard, she was going to drive herself insane.

She stared at the cordless phone and rubbed her hands over her face. How would she explain her sudden departure to Lori and Edie? She couldn't leave without at least saying good-bye.

But her heart couldn't handle another waltz around the floor with sadness. She also didn't have the strength for questions.

"Hey Edie, it's Kate."

"Hey you! Everything okay?"

No, everything sucked. She forced herself to sound cheerful. "Everything's fine. I've got to get back to Reno. The kids need me." She sighed. She couldn't lie to Edie, but if she told her the truth Lori would go on a trash-talking rampage against Calisto. "I met up with the man I met at the mission."

Edie was quiet for a second. "What's he got to do with your work in Reno?"

"Nothing. That's the point." Kate struggled to keep her voice from wobbling. "I really like him, Edie, but less than a month ago I was engaged. I'm not ready to jump into another relationship."

She held her breath, ready for judgment.

Instead, the warmth in her friend's voice reached through the phone like a hug. "You're an amazing lady, Kate. I don't know many women who would pass up a millionaire to go teach middle school, though."

Kate laughed, and her eyes filled with tears. "When you say it like that I sound far from amazing."

After assuring Edie she'd be back to visit soon, she hung up the phone, took a deep breath, and hoped she was making the right decision.

§

1775

"*Kuseyaay! Kuseyaay!* The trader is hurt. Come quickly!"

Gregorio dropped the log onto the fire and followed the women into the night. They ran through the sagebrush and up the mountainside. He followed close behind, no longer winded by running. The torches weren't necessary for him to see in the darkness either, but they helped him hide his preternatural abilities. As far as they knew he was their *Kuseyaay*, their healer, and he was careful to keep it that way.

The Night Walker blood that coursed through his veins only gave his body life after the sun died, but it also healed the wounds of the mortals around him. His position as the tribal healer gave his strange new existence purpose. He enjoyed relieving the pain of others, reminiscent of his priesthood when he served the spiritual needs of his flock. The simple act of healing someone made it easier to believe that he wasn't cursed, but in fact blessed with a newfound gift.

Gift or curse, he kept the secrets of his new state of being well guarded, just as the Old One had taught him.

As they neared the fur trader, the man moaned in pain. The foreigner was a friend to the tribe. He had traveled far from his homeland in the north, trading skins and occasionally meat from the brown bears and mountain lions he hunted.

"Lukas?" Gregorio knelt at his side and took his trembling hand. "Lukas, can you speak?"

The man's eyes rolled back, and he wheezed, his breath fast and shallow. Gregorio bowed his head, preparing to offer a silent prayer for the man's soul, when he heard Lukas' thoughts in his mind.

A snake. My right leg. Hurts. Can't move.

Gregorio reached down and pulled at the trader's pant leg. The women gasped, pointing at the oozing wound.

"Fetch water," Gregorio said.

They vanished into the woods, and he turned his attention back to Lukas. The venom had already infected his body and organs. Gregorio could pierce his tongue and lick the wound. His blood would heal the bite, but the man would still die from the poison.

Unless.

When Gregorio heard the women's footfalls fade, he bit his own wrist, wincing as his fangs pierced his flesh. He placed his open wound over Lukas's lips, watching as his blood filled the dying man's mouth.

The seizures quieted, and a final breath bubbled up from the man's lungs. Gregorio's heart sank. He had hoped the blood might heal more than superficial injuries and symptoms of greater illnesses. He reached out to close Lukas' eyes, and the man suddenly pulled Gregorio's arm to his mouth and sucked hard at the wound. Gregorio felt the pull on his veins, but he hoped his blood would counteract the venom and heal the fur trader from the inside out.

When he yanked his hand away, Lukas coughed and sputtered. He sat up and looked down at his hands. "I feel better... much better."

Then he looked down at his snakebite.

Gregorio watched the blood flow cease. The angry red flesh lightened, and Lukas' skin wove itself back together, closing the small holes in Lukas' calf. Gregorio smiled. His plan had worked. The fur trader would live.

Before he could speak, the women returned with two clay pots of full of fresh water. The wounded man's attention snapped up, but his gaze was no longer that of a man. His eyes glowed red.

Gregorio's stomach clenched. What had he done?

"I thirst," Lukas said and then growled.

The women lowered the clay pots of water.

"So thirsty… " He sprang from the ground, and Gregorio grabbed him as the man struggled to break free.

"Run!" Gregorio shouted, shocked to see the sudden change in Lukas.

The pots smashed against the ground as the women sprinted into the darkness. The fresh water soaked into the earth. Gregorio gripped the crazed man even tighter as the trader bellowed into the darkness.

He had not healed him. He had damned him forever.

§

The wind rattled against the cloth top of her old Volkswagen bug convertible as she drove into Reno's city limits. Bessie wasn't a great car for Reno's cold winters, but Kate didn't mind.

In spite of the quick fixes she'd used to keep the car functional, her bug never failed her. She bought it with her own money the week after she graduated high school, and drove it all the way to Santa Cruz when she started college.

It was her ticket to freedom.

And she'd finish restoring it soon. She just needed to find another passenger door and a new top. No problem. Plus the more projects to keep her busy, the less time she'd have to think about men.

When she made the final turn into her apartment complex, she remembered no one would be there to greet her. Even as she opened the door to her home, she half expected to see Tom's friendly smile and open arms.

Then she remembered seeing his arms around his grad student.

And for the first time since she'd caught him in the act, it didn't sting. In fact, since she'd met Calisto, it was even more apparent that Tom wasn't the right man for her. She'd never felt the passion in his arms that she shared with Calisto on the beach, and they had only kissed.

Her bags hit the floor. She shoved her door closed and flipped on the lights. Unlike San Diego, Reno had a definite change in seasons as fall succumbed to the frosty cold of winter. She tugged her hooded sweatshirt closed and turned on the heat before she plopped onto her sofa.

Home again.

Her familiar surroundings reassured her that she made the right decision. After kicking off her shoes, she sorted through the stack of mail a friend had left on the coffee table. Doing her usual mundane tasks felt strangely surreal.

When she opened a card, she issued a surprised shout of laughter.

Hi Kate -

I'm sorry about everything. It was all a mistake. I don't know what I was thinking. We need to talk. Please call me.

I know I don't deserve it, but I still hope you'll call.

Love,

Tom

She might have felt moved or even angry a month ago by his words. Instead, she felt a little sorry for Tom. After all, she hadn't been honest with herself about him. Until she met Calisto she never realized she could feel so connected to another person. She'd spent her whole life feeling distanced from everyone. Had Tom felt the distance too?

If she had truly been in love with him, she would be devastated, not laughing at how apathetic she felt toward him. The betrayal still stung, but if he had broken off their engagement before cheating, she wasn't sure she'd feel anything more than embarrassment at the rejection.

She crumpled the card and tossed it out with all the sale flyers and junk mail. With the mail stacked and sorted, she turned to her answering machine. She got through about five messages ranging from fund-raisers for the fire department to new benefits for her Discover card. Then she heard a familiar voice.

"Hi Kate. It's Tom. I really am sorry. Call me when you get back, okay? Hope everything's all right."

The machine beeped and she sat in the silence overthinking every angle. She couldn't avoid him forever, right? But she'd just as soon start her life fresh without any complications. Tom definitely complicated things, especially if he wanted to resume their old, stagnant life.

But a tiny part of her was comforted to hear his familiar voice, the one she'd thought would greet her for the rest of her life. Funny how life didn't always turn out the way she thought it would.

Maybe funny wasn't the right word for it.

She sat on the sofa and unzipped her duffel bag, throwing the clothes and toiletries out to get to the tiny treasure hidden at the bottom. Carefully, she opened the small Ziploc bag holding the Romneya. Just the scent of the flower reminded her of Calisto.

She tucked it behind her ear as he had the night before and went into the bathroom. She stared at her reflection in the mirror. Was Calisto thinking about her, too? Probably not after the way she ran out on him.

She crossed the hall to her bedroom and collapsed on her bed with a sad sigh. She felt like a lovesick puppy. Despite her best efforts, she was falling in love with a man she hardly knew. A man who was definitely way out of her league. She was not in control, had not taken anything with Calisto slowly, and was certainly on a path that would take her right back to heartbreak and weakness.

Why was she doing this to herself?

Late-night coffee and a walk on the beach. It was amazing, but she needed to let it go.

It was a toe-curling kiss, though.

She plucked the flower from behind her ear and twirled the stem, watching the petals turn around the high golden pistil. For all she knew, Calisto and Betty were an item, and he figured he'd have a little fun with her on the side. The thought alone curdled her stomach. Calisto seemed genuine and sincere, and the way he looked at her made her knees weak. She couldn't imagine it was all an act, but could she trust herself after she'd trusted Tom?

§

Father Mentigo spun his signet ring around his finger with his thumb, wrestling with impatience to get off the airplane. He'd never flown before, and he was ready to put his feet back on the ground. The cattle on board dragged out carry-on bags, reminded children to hold hands, checked voice mails on their cell phones.

A muscle in his cheek twitched.

He clutched his duffle bag to his chest and shot forward when the row in front of him finally moved. His ears still buzzed with the change in air pressure.

"Can I help you find your terminal, sir?" The blonde he'd watched throughout the flight stood at the hatch, holding a clipboard and wearing an insincere smile.

Did she fail to notice his robe? His rosary? He was a monk, not a sir. She might be stupid, but her breasts were the perfect size for his hands. He ogled her curvy figure, imagining the treasures hidden beneath her uniform, then met her gaze.

She shifted her weight and lowered her clipboard. "Is San Diego your final destination?"

"*No hablo Ingles*," he said as he disembarked.

San Diego wasn't his destination.

It was his destiny.

CHAPTER TEN

Calisto waited outside of the downtown bus station for his next meal. It was a good place to find people who would not be missed. Husbands walking away from the responsibilities of a wife and children, angry runaway teens entrenched in gang violence and drugs, men on the run from the police. They all rode buses, and all made perfect meals.

Someone might report his victims missing. No one would ever know they met their end in San Diego. He usually sought violent criminals that the world wouldn't miss. Lately, the crime rate in this area had increased, which meant he could hunt quickly.

Tonight he was in a hurry.

He settled for a petty thug recently diagnosed with cancer. He was already near death anyway. Once he turned down a dimly lit alley, Calisto slammed the man into the wall, yanked him close, and bit into the man's jugular, drinking until his struggles ceased. After closing the wound on the man's neck, he disposed of the body and walked along the bay in quiet contemplation. He needed to see Kate again. He pushed her too hard the previous night, and he vowed not to make that mistake tonight. If she gave him another chance. Kate made herself perfectly clear when she left.

She didn't want him in her life.

But her enlarged pupils and the flush that crept up her cheeks said otherwise. Somewhere inside, deep within, she remembered him. He saw it. Her heart still recognized his, but she had no conscious memory of their love.

He was still a stranger.

He had watched her drive away, unable to stop her. Nothing had prepared him for this. To find her and fall in love with her all over again was his destiny. He sold his soul to the night in order to live long enough to love her again.

But there was no guarantee of her love in return.

Tonight, he hoped she would agree to speak to him, to give him another chance. He had located her address for the piano movers in Betty's office, and now that his skin warmed with fresh blood, he was ready to see her.

Kate.

Two running steps later, he soared through the night sky toward her home. Cutting through the crisp air, using the sea breezes to aid his flight, the raven glided over the water. The lights of the city faded, and the moonlight glittered on the waves below. Finally the cliffs of Point Loma appeared.

After landing in the darkness of her backyard, he found no sign of her, no scent, no sound. No Kate. With a shake of his body, the raven gave up its form. He straightened his clothes, walked to her back door and knocked. "Kate?"

He didn't know why he called for her. He already knew she was gone. Her scent was faint, and he couldn't hear any noise inside the house. But he still hoped.

Calisto checked the carport and found her car was gone. He peered through a couple windows. No suitcases, no shoes, no trace of her. The house was empty. A growl rumbled in his chest, and he raked his fingers through his hair.

After flying back to his home, Calisto stormed into his office, throwing the door open with enough force to bury the doorstop in the wall. He reached across his desk in frustration and ripped the cordless phone from its cradle, sending the base crashing to the floor.

"Hello, Bettina." He forced his voice to chime with hypnotic purity. "Forgive me for calling you at home at such a late hour, but this is most important."

"Calisto? What is it? Is something wrong?"

"Did you hear from Kate Bradley today? We picked up her mother's piano, no?"

"Kate went back to Reno today," Betty said with a smile in her voice. "She said she needed to get home right away. But don't worry. We did pick up the piano."

"Good." He clenched his fists, fighting to keep his emotions under control. "The foundation is lucky to have you."

"I'm glad you appreciate my work. While you're on the phone, can we reschedule our meeting that got cut short last night?"

His mind raced. He couldn't maintain rational thought much longer.

"No. I will be in touch soon. Goodnight."

§

Calisto soared through the cold night air, heading north. After the phone call, he realized he had a long distance to travel before sunrise. Following his voracious feeding on two gang members, his body pulsed with strength and power. He would need the added energy to complete his flight.

Gluttony was something he avoided, usually only drinking once per night, sometimes even less. As the decades passed, he no longer needed to feed every night in order to survive. At times if he didn't find a suitable victim, he relied on wild animals, but the blood of animals did not truly satisfy his hunger any longer.

It sustained his existence, but only human blood replenished the strength he was accustomed to.

He knew other blood-drinkers, vampires, who walked this world, were known to rob blood banks. Others indulged in taking small drinks like leeches and wiping the mortal's memory clean. Those were not choices for him. He refused to live like a shadow, a parasite on humanity, watching the mortal world from an arm's distance.

He was a Night Walker, and his life still had a purpose in this world. He read the hearts of mankind, and he fed on the lowest forms of humanity, those who would seek to injure the innocent. No longer a healer, instead he found himself a hunter.

So be it.

After hours of flight, his keen eyes made out the flickering neon brilliance that was downtown Reno. His mind opened wide, searching for Kate's. He needed to find her. Gliding silent on the night wind, the raven flew on.

Calisto sensed the sunrise nearing. It drained his strength and left him lethargic. He would have to give up his flight soon.

Landing in the shadows of a darkened alleyway, Calisto straightened, once again a man. His earlier kills no longer warmed and colored his skin. Burying his hands in his pockets, he walked close to the buildings, trying to stay out of the streetlights.

For two hours, he searched for Kate or others who might know her. He found nothing.

Daylight would cover the earth soon, and he needed to find shelter. With the last of his strength, Calisto forced himself to run toward the mountains on the outskirts of the city. Just as the sun broke over the horizon, he finished digging a hole in the icy soil with his hands. By nightfall, his raw hands would be healed, and his search would begin again.

§

Calisto awoke and punched his fists through the dirt, his lungs awake once more and hungry for air. The arid soil gave way, and he rose to dust himself off. He loathed sleeping in the earth. Although he'd been immortal for centuries, he still couldn't get used to waking up in suffocating darkness.

He enjoyed opening his eyes to the glow of his oil lanterns and the softness of Egyptian cotton sheets. Not to mention a shower a few feet away.

He raised his arms and took in a deep breath, welcoming the raven's spirit. Becoming one with the bird felt natural to him now, like breathing, but it wasn't always that way. He still recalled the pain and terror the first time his body contorted into his spirit animal. He'd fought the change, panicked to lose his human form.

Now he smiled when energy warped the air around him, and his body made a fluid transformation.

Calisto took to the air, soaring over the mountainous terrain. He navigated the wind gusts, alternating between gliding and beating his wings. He loved the freedom and weightlessness of flight while he searched the landscape below.

He'd never been to Reno before. The neon signs of the downtown area sat in direct contrast to the rugged mountain peaks right outside the city. A cold gust of wind hit his wings, and he shifted his tail to compensate. He headed toward the garish buildings and landed in a quiet alley. With a ruffle of his feathers, the bird's eyes closed and his body expanded, morphing back into a fully dressed man.

Calisto checked his clothes and then walked into the bright lights of the city. Once he found a hotel, he would shower, feed, and continue his search for Kate. He almost smiled.

Then he remembered her final words to him. *I can't do this.*

His jaw tightened at the memory, but he couldn't let her walk out of his life. If immortality had taught him anything, it was patience.

§

When Kate stepped inside Harrah's, desperate after a day of moping to feel the energy of Reno, she reveled in the lights, noise, and anonymity of the casino. The hotel was a block from the Reno arch, and it boasted some of the best karaoke in the city. Singing was always a great stress reliever for her, exactly what she needed tonight.

The brightly colored carpet and neon lights were tarnished by the scent of stale cigarette smoke, beer, and cheap cologne. Hope and desperation hung heavy in the air. She made her way through the maze of one-armed bandits and card tables toward the karaoke lounge.

She followed the sound of amateur singing through the casino. When she rounded the final corner and stepped inside, a woman on the stage belted out a pitchy version of "Hit Me with Your Best Shot." It took a moment for Kate's eyes to adjust to the dim lighting before she scanned the room for an empty booth.

"Kate?" She turned when she heard a familiar voice call her name, and her heart sank when she saw Tom walking toward her.

His blond hair, usually tamed into a typical businessman cut, was mussed with gel, and his skin looked a little more tanned. He could pass for one of the college students now, instead of one of their professors.

Pathetic.

Kate turned and headed for the door, but before she vanished into the casino, Tom caught her hand.

"Please don't go."

She stopped and gave him a direct look. "I can't stay."

"Yes, you can. You came to sing. I wouldn't want to stop you."

Kate tugged her arm free of his grasp. "Well, I don't want to sing anymore. Enjoy your night."

"Can we talk?" He gestured toward a table at the back of the karaoke bar.

She sighed and crossed her arms over her chest. "There's nothing left to say."

"I want to tell you I'm sorry. I want to tell you I still love you. I never meant to hurt you."

She scowled and fought to keep her composure. A casino was not the right venue for this discussion unless Tom only wanted to avoid a scene. "It looked like you meant to get busy with your grad student on your desk. You just didn't expect me to catch you."

"It was a mistake." His smile faded, and he reached for her hand. "I am so sorry, Kate."

She stared up at him as the lounge burst into applause. Unsure what to say and desperate for a way out of the conversation, she pulled away from him. "I've got to choose a song."

Kate walked toward the deejay, ducking through the tables and all the people. Once she was a safe distance away from her past, she opened one of the notebooks and skimmed song titles.

It only took a minute to flip through the pages before she found her choice. She gave the CD number to the deejay and prayed Tom left before she finished. After the past month's events, all she wanted was some peace.

§

Calisto stepped out of the elevator feeling refreshed after his shower and a clean change of clothes. Renting a room he would never risk sleeping in during the day made for a costly shower, but after a night in the dirt, he would have spent a thousand dollars for a wet washcloth. He planned to feed and continue his search for Kate, but he heard a voice that demanded he still himself and listen.

Her beautiful voice.

He followed the music until he stood in the doorway of a darkened lounge. His gaze locked on the stage, on Kate singing about promises in the dark. He slid through the crowd, his eyes never leaving her.

She held the audience in thrall. The casual chatting quieted so that only her song carried through the large room. She connected with the audience, giving each person near the stage a full second of her attention. When the chorus of the song swelled, she tipped her head back, closing her eyes as her voice soared from her soul. The hair on Calisto's forearms rose with the electricity of her performance.

When she opened her eyes, her gaze finally met his, and he offered her a smile and a nod. She looked surprised and quickly turned her attention elsewhere. She didn't frown or glare at him, which seemed like a good sign. The final note rang out, and the crowd erupted with applause and whistles.

Kate stepped down from the stage, and Calisto made his way to intercept her.

"Calisto? What are you doing here?" Her eyes darted away for a moment, then back to his face.

"I am in town for a business meeting." Would he ever be able to tell her the truth? He silenced his inner voice. Even if he had to live a lie, it would be worth the effort to have Kate in his life. "When I heard your voice, I had to investigate."

"I'm surprised to see you... " Her voice trailed off when another man approached them.

The man smiled at her and opened his arms, attempting to embrace her. "That was amazing, Kate. Really beautiful."

Kate stepped back and turned toward Calisto.

Who was this man? Kate's shoulders were tense, and she crossed her arms as if to shield her heart. Calisto's gaze cut to the other man. Kate was definitely not happy to see him. Therefore, Calisto wanted him gone.

He stepped close to intercept the man and offered his hand. "I do not believe we have met. I am Calisto Terana."

The man shook with a firm grip and smiled. "I'm Tom Hardy."

"Tom is my ex-fiancé," Kate said.

Calisto's eyes narrowed and his hold on the other man's hand tightened. Tom immediately yanked it back with a grimace.

"That's some grip you have there," he muttered.

Calisto touched the small of Kate's back, his eyes never leaving Tom's face.

"You must have been a fool to let Kate go." Calisto struggled to keep his voice smooth and calm. Kate moved closer to him, but he wouldn't take his eyes off the man who had broken her heart. He had no intention of allowing the man to touch her again. Ever.

Tom's chin rose slightly. "Look, I don't know who you are, but Kate and I need to talk."

"As I recall, we were already talking. It was *you* who interrupted."

Tom's smile faded, his brow furrowed. "I don't know who you are, but Kate and I were engaged until very recently, so back off." He reached for Kate, but Calisto moved forward, his muscles tight, ready to attack. Tom dropped his hand to his side. "Can we go someplace and talk, please? I never got to explain."

Kate sighed. "There's nothing to talk about, Tom. What I saw was explanation enough, okay? I'm starting to feel better. I don't want to pick at the scab."

"So that's it? You're going to throw away the past two years like they never happened?"

"Why not?" She shrugged, seeming tired and annoyed. "You did."

Without another word, Kate stormed out of the lounge.

Calisto watched her go before glaring at Tom. He opened himself to Tom's thoughts, peering into his memories until he saw the look of betrayal and hurt on Kate's face when she caught Tom with another woman.

Calisto ground his teeth together. He wanted to kill him for hurting her.

Tom turned to follow Kate, but Calisto caught his elbow and yanked him back. "You have hurt her enough."

"Who are you to judge me?"

Calisto squeezed his arm. "I am someone who cares about her."

Tom tried to pull away. "Let go of me, asshole."

Calisto opened his hand, and Tom wrenched his arm free.

"Stay out of this," Tom said. "You don't know anything about Kate. And this doesn't concern you."

He tried to go after her again, but Calisto stepped into his path. It was all he could do to keep his eyes from glowing with fury. "I know that you hurt her. That is enough for me."

Tom shoved him hard, but Calisto didn't move.

"I told you to leave her alone," Calisto said, his voice low and menacing.

Tom punched him in the jaw. His teeth cut through his lower lip, filling his mouth with blood.

Calisto smiled, grabbing Tom's shirt and yanking him close. "Remember that you started this fight." Calisto hurled him backwards.

Screams echoed through the nightclub as Tom crashed into the bar, and his body hit the ground. Calisto walked over to him and jerked him back to his feet. Tom's shirt reeked of rum and beer, and blood trickled down his chin and along his hairline.

The scent toyed with Calisto's hunger. He wet his lips, struggling to focus. Tom kicked and struggled until Calisto dropped him on the ground.

"I'm going to sue you for assault!" Tom scrambled to his feet and glanced at the crowd that gathered around them.

"Call my attorney." Calisto smirked and straightened his shirt.

"What the hell is wrong with you two?" Kate pushed her way through the onlookers and stared at the blood on Calisto's shirt and Tom's battered face.

Tom glared at Calisto and reached for Kate's hand.

"Don't touch me." She stepped back.

Tom frowned. "I wanted to apologize and talk things over." He nodded toward Calisto. "Until Zorro over here decided you were a damsel in distress."

Calisto raised a brow at the comment.

Kate looked at him with disgust. "Is that what you think? Did you think I couldn't handle this myself?"

"You made it clear you did not want to discuss the past with him. I followed through on your request."

"By beating him senseless?"

Calisto looked at Tom, then back to her. "Perhaps he never had any sense to begin with."

"That's it!" Tom yelled and lunged toward Calisto. Two men in the crowd held him back, and Kate shook her head.

"You know what? I'm done talking to both of you." She turned to Tom. "Our relationship is over." She gave Calisto her attention. The fire in her eyes made his heart pound. "You had no right to come here and get involved in my personal business. I don't need you or anyone else to fight my battles for me."

She backed away, shaking her head. "I don't want to see you again. I'm done." Her gaze lingered on Calisto for a long moment. "With both of you."

Without another word, Kate stormed out of the casino.

CHAPTER ELEVEN

Father Mentigo's palms sweated with eager anticipation in spite of the cool La Jolla breeze blowing through his car window. He sat directly across the street from the home of the Night Walker. He held his breath when the tall, dark-haired immortal stepped outside. Father Mentigo trained for years for this opportunity. Finally, he saw with his own eyes a man who defeated death itself.

Cloaking his thoughts with a mental chant, Father Mentigo watched the tall, slender blonde walk with the Night Walker to a black BMW.

He merged with traffic and followed them. The blonde didn't look anything like the description of the woman in the ancient texts at the monastery. Father Tomas had been so certain in his communications that he found her.

Kate Bradley.

Since he arrived in San Diego, Father Mentigo had watched her house, but it remained dark and empty. Maybe the woman was gone. Perhaps the Night Walker never found her. If they never met, then the threat the monsignor feared was already over.

He tightened his grip on the steering wheel and ground his teeth. He had spent most of his adult life preparing for this. He was not about to see it come to an end so soon.

Not until he got what he wanted.

§

Calisto sat in silence, taking in the view of the coast through the passenger window of Betty's BMW. After watching Kate for more than a week, he'd finally returned home with a heavy heart.

While he visited Reno, he learned all he could about her, and how she lived. He knew she woke nearly every night with terrible nightmares. He knew she liked hot chocolate with whipped cream, and even after his fight with Tom in the bar, she still saved the blossom he gave her the night she left San Diego.

But none of that changed the fact that she didn't want to see him again.

Ever since the night in the bar, he warred with himself. It seemed unthinkable that he would have to live without her. Part of him wanted to pull her into his arms and hold her until she loved him in return. He wanted to mesmerize her and make her his again.

He probably should have apologized, but Tom threw the first punch. He wasn't fighting her battle for her. He was simply punishing the bastard who hurt her.

He wouldn't apologize when he hadn't done anything wrong.

The night he sat in the back of the auditorium to hear her middle school choir perform its fall concert, he made the decision to return home without her. Kate beamed that night, full of pure magic.

The music the young people sang came alive, feeding off of her energy. When he reached for the thoughts of the choristers at random, their minds echoed the same sentiments. They trusted her. Her enthusiasm and her faith in them gave them confidence. She believed in them, and their love of music shone like a beacon in their young voices.

She was an amazing woman. Alive. What right did he have to pull her away from the life she carved out for herself? And if he didn't take her away, then how would he fit into her life?

He hadn't figured that out yet.

Until then, Calisto loved her enough to walk away. For now.

"Have you heard a word I've just said?" Betty laughed.

He turned, forcing a smile and a nod. "Yes, you were telling me about another benefit the Arboroughs have volunteered to host in their restaurant overlooking the cove." He actually hadn't been listening. The ability to read her thoughts did have its advantages. "But you believe the restaurant would be too small for the event, no?"

Betty nodded with a smile of utter disbelief. "Exactly. I'm sorry, I had no idea you were paying attention. You looked preoccupied." She paused, glancing over at him before shifting her gaze back to the highway. "You were out of town longer than usual this time. Is everything all right?"

"Yes." He looked out the window again.

"You don't look all right. You look pale. Maybe you're coming down with the flu." She reached over to touch his hand. "Are you feeling all—" Betty gasped, her brow creased with worry. "Calisto, your hands are freezing."

He'd forgotten to feed. Betty's warm skin tempted him. He cursed his carelessness and slid his hand from under hers.

"Forgive me, Bettina, but you are right. I did not wish to delay our meeting, but I cannot think clearly when I am ill. Perhaps you should take me home."

Betty nodded, already maneuvering through traffic to turn around. "Have you seen a doctor?"

"Yes," he lied. "He told me to rest and drink more fluids, which I intend to do as soon as I get home."

"You'd better. I'd hate to see you get worse." She glanced at him before the light changed, and she accelerated well beyond the speed limit.

"I will be fine." He looked out his window again. He clenched his fist, reining in his emotions. Picturing his future without Kate in it was agony. But he would endure. He had no choice.

Betty pulled into his driveway and shut off the engine. He turned to get out, but she placed her hand on his sleeve. The overwhelming warmth of her touch burned his cool flesh with a dangerous temptation as his thirst clawed its way to the surface.

"Do you need anything? I could come in and make you some tea."

"No," he blurted out with more urgency than he intended.

Pulling away from her, he sought to calm the hunger growing inside him with each beat of her heart. Her blood pulsed through her veins, calling to him.

Calisto shook his head slowly. "Thank you for your offer, but I would not want you to become ill too. I can take care of myself."

"Well, call me if you get any worse, okay? You look really pale."

He got out of the car, unable to bear the intoxicating scent of her blood any longer. Leaning down to the passenger window he managed a weak smile.

"Thank you for your concern. Drive carefully, Bettina."

She smiled, looking up at him from under her perfectly darkened lashes. "I will. And I'll check in with you soon, all right? Now, go rest."

He nodded and stepped back as she drove away. His entire body ached for blood. His flight home from Reno drained him, and he had been too overwhelmed with thoughts of Kate to consider how strongly being trapped in a confined space with Betty would affect him.

At times like this, the strength of his thirst terrified him. It was carnal, primal, and when it screamed for satisfaction, he worried that one day he might not be able to control it.

If that day ever came, he feared for all the mortals around him.

The scent of blood drifted in on the cool sea breeze, distracting him from his thoughts and teasing him with its fragrant promise. Calisto walked down the beach toward a bonfire in the distance.

Pieces of flaming ash floated into the dark night sky from the large fire. Calisto instinctively stayed in the shadows of the firelight, watching the teens drink. The scent of their blood flooded his senses until his eyes burned with hunger. He fought to keep the inhuman crimson from glowing in his gaze, but his bloodlust would not remain hidden much longer. His precarious hold over his thirst weakened with each passing minute.

The college students laughed. They were kissing, caught up in each other. They had no idea a predator watched them from the shadows.

But they were not his prey.

Instead, Calisto turned toward the sound of muffled cries by the cliffs. He moved silently across the sand until he found a man with his hand pressed over a young woman's mouth. She struggled, pinned against the sandy cliff, while her attacker fumbled with her shorts.

Calisto burned with rage, but he couldn't kill the man in front of the girl.

Using his silent voice, he reached into the attacker's mind and demanded his attention. Usually he took his time, using gentle mental suggestions, but his fury over the attack increased his urgency to feed. He called to him, hypnotizing him to his own will.

The attacker stopped grasping at her clothes and looked around. Calisto gave him a harder mental push, and he released the girl, his hands flying up to clasp his head. The woman scrambled away. Calisto coaxed his prey closer.

Come to me.

The tall, gangly man stumbled across the sand toward him. Tears shone on his cheeks as he smacked at his ears, straining to break free of the enthrallment. Calisto smiled in the darkness. He already heard the man's heartbeat, the sound like primal music. He ached for satisfaction, but he fought to hold his ground and wait. His victim finally stopped in front of him, his eyes full of fear.

Just like the woman's eyes had been.

Veiled in the dark shadows, Calisto buried his fangs deep into the man's throat. Justice.

When the would-be rapist had nothing left to give, Calisto carried the body farther down the beach into the darkness. He rolled his shoulders back, his body warming as his strength returned and his heart pumped the new blood through his veins.

He hurried down the dark pier and, using all his strength, threw the body into the ocean, beyond the tidal waters, letting the waves claim it. With his thirst appeased and his strength once again restored,

Calisto focused his energy. Reaching out, he united his mind and spirit with the raven he bound to himself back in Reno.

A Night Walker shared a unique bond with his spirit animal. This was one of the first lessons the Old One taught him years ago. Piercing his fingertip and allowing the raven to taste his blood tied the creature to him mentally, enabling Calisto to see the world through the raven's eyes, and hear through its ears across great distances.

The raven circled and finally landed outside of Kate's apartment complex. Calisto now used the raven's eyes and ears to watch over her without interfering in her life. He told himself this was for her benefit, but he knew he actually didn't have the strength to walk away without the promise of seeing her each night, even if from a distance.

With his link to the raven, he coaxed the bird closer to Kate's window. Calisto's gut twisted when he finally saw her face through the bird's eyes. She stood alone in her kitchen with tear-stained cheeks, holding the Romneya.

Calisto broke the connection. He couldn't stand to see her cry.

CHAPTER TWELVE

Kate threw herself into her work until she barely had time to breathe. Her substitute teacher did a marvelous job keeping her choir in shape, and the winter concert went off without a hitch. Even the difficult three-part a cappella piece sounded glorious. Their young voices soared like angels on the pure vowels of the Latin text.

But even though she'd settled back into her regular routine of work, it wasn't getting any easier.

No matter how busy she kept herself, thoughts of Calisto crept into her mind. Something in her nightmare was connected to him. As crazy as it sounded, she couldn't shake the idea. That night in the coffee shop, she thought she recognized his ring. Now she knew why.

In her dream, the man dancing in the water wore a ring just like Calisto's. She'd seen it more than once now. The puzzle pieces still didn't quite fit, but he had to be part of it.

She picked up the dried Romneya flower, holding it in her fingertips as she lifted the phone to her ear, but she set it back on the cradle before she dialed.

She didn't have Calisto's number. Even if she did, what would she say?

Kate sighed and looked out the window. Winter break started

next week. She'd have three weeks to figure out this mess of emotions and dreams.

She set the flower back on the counter, wondering if Calisto thought about her too.

Groaning, she shook her head. She was the one who told him she never wanted to see him again. He honored her wish. She hadn't seen him since she stormed out of the casino that night.

During her winter concert, she caught a glimpse of him, but when she followed the crowd outside he was gone. Why would he think about her at all except to consider what a horrible mistake it had been to run into her in Reno?

She could apologize. For what? She didn't ask him to meddle in her relationship with Tom. She didn't invite him to visit her in Reno in the first place.

Okay, so an apology was out.

But she still needed to see him again. Somehow. She had to follow her heart. She had distanced herself emotionally from Tom long before he cheated on her. She had run away from Tom to avoid facing complications. Then she did the same thing with Calisto when she came back to Reno. She'd spent her life distancing herself from everyone when life got messy, and where had it gotten her? How could she pursue the life she wanted when she was so busy running from the scary parts?

She could go back, try to start fresh with Calisto.

Kate looked at the calendar. Winter break.

If she did run into Calisto, would he even speak to her? And how exactly would she run into him? It wasn't like they would shop at the same grocery store. He lived in La Jolla and she lived over a half hour away in Point Loma. She didn't even know his phone number.

But it didn't matter. She'd take it one step at a time and wait to see what fate had in store. It had already thrown them together in the most unlikely places. Maybe it would give them one more chance.

She was going back to San Diego.

§

He didn't stay at the mission.

Father Mentigo hated people looking over his shoulder and constantly pummeling him with their insignificant questions. Unlike the late Father Tomas De Cardina, he would do what must be done to control the Night Walker.

But his methods would not be well received by the Fraternidad, and he decided it would be best to have a private apartment. Father Mentigo would not make the same mistakes that his predecessor made. He had no intention of ending up dead on the mission steps.

In fact, what he planned would have an entirely opposite ending.

He smirked as he removed the photos from the printer. Hurrying to the warped dining room table, he slid the photos into a parchment envelope and lit a candle. Slowly turning the red wax over the flame, it dripped onto the back of the envelope flap. He pressed his signet ring into the hot wax, then blew out the candle and slid the ring back onto his finger.

Only the inner circle of the Fraternidad Del Fuego Santo received the ancient rings. Only the chosen monks of the Fraternidad knew of the Night Walker and his immortal race. But where the other monks had failed, he would succeed because he would battle the demon for the ultimate prize.

Until that moment came, he needed to be patient and cautious.

He drove to the beachfront home of Calisto Terana, safely hidden from the Night Walker by the noonday sun. At the back of the house, Father Mentigo made his way up the steps and smiled when he found the French doors. Easy to open, even with a deadbolt. He peered through the glass to be sure the house was empty before he picked the lock and slipped inside.

The light, spacious interior surprised him. He expected the Night Walker to dwell in a dark, gothic castle, not this clean, almost stark hacienda surrounded by the sound of the ocean. Father Mentigo continued down the hall until he found the office. He stopped in the doorway, his gaze moving over every detail. This was the first room that gave any hint to the personality of its owner, the first clue to understanding his adversary.

Father Mentigo stepped inside, staring up at the oak bookshelves that covered two walls from floor to ceiling. The titles on one wall ranged from *A Tale of Two Cities*, to Shakespeare's *Romeo and Juliet*. Most of the shelves held classic literary works with bindings that appeared creased and worn.

Apparently, the Night Walker was well-read.

He turned to gaze at the shelves on the other wall and found books on classical music composers, artists, poets, and architecture. Biographies, histories of music, and art styles lined the shelves, and Father Mentigo paused.

Why would an immortal care for such inane drivel as art? The Night Walker exuded power. Father Mentigo witnessed the immortal's strength the previous evening on the beach. The Night Walker controlled a mortal man's mind until he walked willingly into the arms of death without a single whimper or scream.

Death couldn't touch him, and instead of ruling the world, forcing people to bow down in worship to him, he sat in his office reading Shakespeare and philosophical texts.

A pathetic waste.

Shaking his head, Father Mentigo went to the desk and sat in the tall-backed leather chair. He ran his fingers over the leather arms, imagining that only hours before, the Night Walker touched this very surface. He closed his eyes, drinking in the image of supremacy. Most men couldn't conceive of the battle he faced.

And he had every intention of winning.

It will end with me, Night Walker.

The desk clock chimed with the passing hour, pulling Father Mentigo out of his reverie. He shook his head in silent reprimand. It was too soon to sit back and envision his future victory. He must remain focused.

After removing his tiny camera, he snapped photos of the papers he found on the desk, looking for any phone numbers that might be useful later. Satisfied he had gathered enough information, he laid the sealed envelope on the desktop and hurried out to his car.

But he had one more stop to make before returning to his studio apartment. He would have to stay inside tonight. When Calisto discovered the envelope, he would come looking for him, and Father Mentigo had no intention of being found.

He drove down the interstate, shifting himself inside his pants. His arousal came as no surprise. Knowing he manipulated an immortal, toying with inhuman power, created the ultimate aphrodisiac, exciting him far more than any woman. He was born to meet this challenge. He knew that now. And so far he enjoyed it.

Perhaps more than he should.

§

After the sun dipped below the horizon, Calisto made his way upstairs from his hidden quarters beneath his home. Something felt different tonight upon his waking, but he couldn't place what it might be. Buttoning his dark blue shirt, he made his way down the hall to his office. What he saw lying on the center of his desk made him grind his teeth with rage.

Another envelope with the Fraternidad's seal.

A heartbeat later he sat in his chair, breaking the wax. This time there wasn't a note. Instead, he removed two photos. Calisto stared at them in disbelief, his eyes moving from one to the other.

He was looking at images of himself.

Someone else had been on the beach, watching him while he fed the previous evening. His heart quickened. The pictures could easily be written off as computer enhanced, doctored. The real danger was the face of the pale man in his arms.

If someone had reported the man missing, these photos would lead the police right to his door.

Calisto shredded them. Had he been careless? He hadn't sensed anyone else on the beach, but his thirst had overwhelmed him by then.

Maybe he had been so desperate for blood that he missed sensing the presence of another.

He stood up with such violence, his chair banged into the wall behind the desk. Growling with fury, he stormed into the night. Not only had someone watched him, but now they had proof that would link him to a missing man. For centuries he had been so confident of his own anonymity, too confident.

Calisto hunted for the monk who left the pictures behind for him to find. He had underestimated his opponent for the last time. He would not make the same mistake again.

And he would not be blackmailed, not by anyone.

Chapter Thirteen

Kate woke up in her Dad's old easy chair in a cold sweat, crying in fear. Her nightmares were getting worse, and the vivid details came into focus more every night. Tonight, she saw the shadow of a man leap from his horse, knocking the woman to the ground. She saw them struggle, and she couldn't wake up. She was forced to watch the man press a knife to the woman's throat. She heard the woman's cries, and even though her screams weren't English, somehow Kate understood. The woman was begging for her unborn child's life.

Lurching up, Kate raced for the bathroom and threw up. She winced as her stomach cramped, and she retched again and again. Her body ached. When the nausea finally passed, she sat in the corner of the bathroom, pulled her knees into her chest and wept. The emptiness inside threatened to swallow her.

She wasn't sure how long she sat, curled up on the bathroom floor. She'd never felt so alone, but dwelling on it wasn't going to make it any better. She needed to get out of the house. Time to dust herself off and move on.

Within an hour, she drove the bug with the top down toward Seaport Village and a day of retail therapy with Edie and Lori. She took a long, slow breath, trying to pull the sunshine into her lungs.

Another gorgeous San Diego day. Where else could you drive around with the top down at the beginning of December?

The wind whipped her hair around her face, and she finally smiled. Getting out was exactly what she needed. Maybe today would be a good day after all.

§

Father Mentigo couldn't take his eyes off of her. She wore a dark green t-shirt that clung to the round curves of her breasts, hypnotizing him until he had to force his gaze elsewhere. Her dark blue denim shorts were no better, teasing him as she leaned over the front of her car. She stretched up to reach the top, and he held his breath, watching the sunlight shine on her dark hair. The way she struggled to lower the worn roof on her faded yellow VW enticed him to watch her shapely legs. He shifted in his seat. Oh, he enjoyed this battle more with each day.

Not only had he eluded the Night Walker the night before, but now he had also found the woman that Father De Cardina had discussed in his communications. However, the other monk had failed to mention her beauty. Father Mentigo watched Kate drive away and smiled. He would relish every bit of contact with her for as long as he could. He was more than prepared to do whatever was necessary, even if she had to die. Her life was a very small price to pay for what he stood to gain. And he wouldn't allow anything, or anyone, to get in his way.

Once her car was out of sight, Father Mentigo got out of his rental and walked toward her house with a small brown parcel. Wearing unmarked cargo shorts with a plain, khaki, button-up shirt, he posed as a local deliveryman, hoping he would not draw attention to himself. He reached her front door, grumbling to himself when he found it locked. He couldn't pick the lock right in front of the house. After checking for the prying eyes of any neighbors, he made his way around the side of the two-story home. He found the kitchen window open, and within minutes he was safely inside. It was practically empty. He frowned. Walking through the rooms, he wondered what kind of woman lived alone in an empty house. Ironic that her home was similar to the Night Walker's. Empty.

He stopped when he found her opened duffel bag.

Kneeling down, he fondled the intimate clothes he found inside. He lifted a silk nightshirt, caressing his cheek with its softness, drowning in the scent of her skin. He forced himself to put it back and continued his exploration of her bag until his fingers hooked onto a pair of silk panties. He lifted them to his face, burying his nose in the delicate fabric. The soft, feminine scent intoxicated him with its forbidden pleasure, so he tucked them into his pocket.

Since his fingers were already there, he brushed the length of his hardened shaft, sending a chill through his entire body. He closed his eyes, treasuring the texture of her panties, every move of his hand teasing his passion higher. It was her. She was touching him, encouraging him toward his release. His hand moved faster inside his loose shorts, rubbing her underwear against his organ until it pulsed with need.

He suddenly withdrew his hand, biting back his desire. Enough. He would finish this later. Right now he had work to do. Searching through her things, he jotted down phone numbers and learned as much as he could about Kate Bradley, then retreated to his car. He needed the safety of his apartment before the sun went down. He couldn't risk running into the Night Walker.

Not yet.

§

Afternoon wore into evening, and they decided to grab an early dinner and catch a movie. Lori and Edie wrestled with their bags.

Kate tried not to laugh. "Want me to carry a couple of those?"

Lori glared at Kate's little Yankee Candle store bag and held out her bulky Bloomingdale's bag. "Yes. You're definitely not weighed down enough yet."

Edie added bags from Payless shoes and Sephora to Kate's load and gave her a once-over. "That's better."

Lori continued to glare. "I still can't believe we've tromped all over Seaport Village and Horton Plaza and all you've bought is a couple of scented candles. That's just wrong."

"You're not sick, are you?" Edie struggled with her bags to feel Kate's forehead for a fever.

Kate dodged the attempt. "I'm fine. I didn't come for the shopping today, I came for the company."

Lori glanced at Edie. "Great, now we look like a couple of materialistic bitches, don't we?"

Kate laughed and followed them up the escalator to the movie theater, where a well-reviewed drama was playing. They left the theater sniffling, drying their eyes and laughing at their own sappiness.

"I hate it when they don't get to live happily ever after," Edie said.

Kate sighed. "Me, too. I like the fairy tale endings when everyone falls in love and rides off into the sunset."

Lori glanced at Edie, then Kate. "Guess it doesn't happen that way in real life very often."

"No, it doesn't." Kate wiped her eyes. "Come on. Let's get some coffee and talk. I'll buy."

She walked a couple of blocks up Fourth Avenue before she realized where she was going. When she opened the glass door she wanted to cry again. This was the coffee shop she visited with Calisto the night her life changed.

Lori settled at a quiet table and pierced Kate with a serious look. "We've talked about everything except why you moved back. How long are we going to ignore the elephant in the room?"

"Lori!" Edie shot her a disapproving look. "She'll talk when she's ready."

"Hey guys, I'm sitting right here. And I think I'm as ready to talk as I'll ever be."

Her friends sipped coffee, and Kate struggled to tell them her story without revealing the parts of herself that she never shared with anyone.

"After I called off the wedding and came back here... " She hesitated before going on. "I met a man while I was here."

Lori opened her mouth to say something, but Kate held up a hand.

"Nothing really happened between us, but at the same time,

everything did. I know it doesn't make any sense, but I've never had a connection with someone like I did with him. I couldn't stop thinking about him no matter how hard I tried. I had to come back."

Edie smiled and patted Kate's hand. "He must be something special to turn your life upside down like that. When do we get to meet him?"

Lori interrupted. "I don't know. No man is worth giving up your job and your life for, you know? You were only with him one night, right? You can't possibly know him well enough to push your life aside for a chance with him."

Kate bristled. Typical of Lori to be the cynic, and though she was right, Kate wasn't in the mood to be lectured. "I *don't* know much about him, but that's why I waited until winter break from my job to come back. It's not like I quit my job. I don't go back to work until January. Until then, I can stay at Mom and Dad's. I took it off the market for now."

Edie grabbed Kate's sleeve and tugged. "So when are you going to see him again?"

"Hell if I know. I don't know his phone number, let alone if he wants to see me again." Kate laughed and rubbed her eyes.

Lori raised a brow. "What? You made it sound like you were in love, and now you're not even sure he feels the same way? Geez, are you sure you did the right thing?"

Kate sighed. "I'm not sure of anything anymore except that I'll go crazy if I'm always wondering about what might have been."

"Why wouldn't he want to see you again?" Edie asked. "Sounds like you guys had a great time together, right?"

"Yes, but I… " Kate grimaced. "Well, he came out to Reno on business and we bumped into each other. He and Tom ended up getting into a fistfight, and I told him I never wanted to see him again."

"So let me get this straight. You came back here for a man who probably thinks you hate him?" Lori shook her head. "Do you expect me to be happy for you?"

"Damnit, Lori, can you just be my friend? I don't need lectures.

I'm prepared for whatever might come, including consequences. I might not ever see him again, but I had to try. It's a big risk, and I'm scared. But I owe it to myself to stop running away from my feelings."

Lori stared for a few long seconds. Edie broke the silence.

"I hope everything works out for you." Edie gave her a little hug. "And I can't wait to meet him. What's his name?"

"Calisto. Calisto Terana."

"The guy you met at the mission." Lori leaned forward in her seat with newfound interest and a little caution. "He runs a charity for the arts or something, right?"

"Yes. He's the founder of Foundation Arts."

Lori nodded. "I've heard of him before. He's sort of reclusive, isn't he? And I guess he's rich, too. How in the world did you end up going out with him?" She frowned a little. "You said you didn't give him your number."

Kate scowled at Lori. "I didn't."

Lori held up a hand. "Sorry. I just... I worry."

Edie interrupted. "Oh he was handsome! How did you find him again?"

"I ran into him while I was signing the papers for the foundation to pick up Mom's piano. Later that night we ended up in the same movie theater and it went on from there."

"Sounds like you've got it bad." She reached across the little coffee table to give Kate's hand a squeeze. "I don't want you to get burned in the end. I worry, too."

"Nobody wants to get burned. But it's time I went after what I want. I'm a big girl. I can deal with it." Kate set down her coffee mug, eager to change the subject. "I guess we should get back. I have a lot of unpacking to do."

Edie stood. "I have to work early tomorrow anyway. I had fun with you guys today."

"We'll have to do it again soon," Lori said. "Maybe next time Calisto can join us... "

Kate gave Lori a quick, grateful hug. "I can only hope."

They walked through the calm night to the excellent curbside parking spot Lori scored.

"Sure you don't want a ride over to your car?" Lori asked.

"That's okay." Kate handed them their bags. "I'm just around the block. I could use the walk."

"Be careful," Edie said.

"I will. See you guys soon."

Kate watched them drive away, waving before she walked toward the end of the block. Staring up at the moon, she wondered if somewhere in the city Calisto was looking at it too. It made the world seem smaller somehow, like they were closer together, sharing a moment, even though they were probably miles apart.

She shivered and kept walking. As she rounded the corner, she suddenly had the feeling she was being watched. The hair on the back of her neck rose to stand on end, and her pulse quickened. She picked up her pace, listening to everything around her. She didn't hear another set of footsteps, but she didn't turn around to check.

She was too afraid of what she might see.

What did newscasters instruct women to do when they walked alone? Keep your head up and have your keys out and ready. Now if she could only find her keys.

Kate groped through her purse, hurrying toward her car in the parking lot with her head held high, praying the paranoia was all in her mind and no one really followed her. Finally, she found her keys and grasped them tightly. Almost there.

Her instincts screamed at her to run, but she managed to cage her fears.

Clasping her keys in her fist, she walked toward her car where it sat under the dim yellow street lamp in a parking lot. Her inner voice begged her to hurry, more than certain she was in danger, but before she could run, something sharp poked through the back of her t-shirt.

"Scream, and you're dead."

CHAPTER FOURTEEN

After he fed, Calisto wandered the dark streets of downtown San Diego, searching for the Fraternidad's new ambassador, the fool who chose to break into his home and leave behind incriminating photos. Fury churned in his gut at the thought. His pursuit of the arrogant bastard yielded no leads since he had no idea whom he was looking for.

Yet.

He'd already visited the Mission de Alcala, but he didn't find anything new. None of the priests knew of the arrival of any monks from Spain. His stalker appeared to be keeping his presence hidden from the other priests as well.

Without a face or a name, he couldn't search for mortals who might have seen the monk, which made his hunt even more futile. Only by opening to all of the mortal thoughts around him could he locate the monk who dared to expose his existence. It would be an overwhelming task in such a large city, but he had no other choice.

Closing his eyes, Calisto braced himself for the pain and lowered his mental shields, welcoming all of the silent voices around him, searching for the thoughts of a monk who trespassed inside of his home.

Entwined within the myriad of voices and thoughts, he heard a mental cry that filled his heart with terror. *Please God don't let me die...*

He knew that voice. It haunted his every waking moment.

Kate.

By the sound of her plea, she was in trouble. But where was she?

Forcing himself to remain calm, Calisto struggled to find her, his mind searching for any others who might have seen her. Before he found any mental trace of her, he heard her scream.

He followed the sound, racing toward her as fast as his body would allow. Until the night settled into an eerie silence. He waited, listening, praying for a sign. His muscles contracted, ready to launch into action as panic festered inside him.

It was too quiet.

A delicious scent teased his senses.

Blood.

He tracked it to a dimly lit parking lot behind a broken-down liquor store. But he wasn't prepared for the scene before him.

Kate lay facedown on the cracked pavement of the parking lot, struggling to break free from her attacker. The man crouched on top of her, his hand tangled in the back of her hair, pressing her face against the blacktop while his other hand held the blade of a knife against her throat.

"I told you not to scream, stupid bitch!" he said, looking around to be sure they hadn't attracted any attention.

As the mugger reached for her spilled purse, Calisto emerged from the darkness, eyes glowing crimson with pure, primal fury. He yanked the leather-clad man away from Kate and held him off the ground.

Before the man uttered a sound, Calisto hit him with all his strength, feeling the bones of the man's face shatter under the force of his blow. But his rage wasn't appeased, and hearing the man's blubbering cries wasn't enough to atone for harming Kate. He wanted to rip the man's head right off his shoulders, but Kate was too close.

Instead, he threw the mugger away in disgust, finding some solace in the hollow thump as he connected with the graffiti-covered back wall of the liquor store that bordered the parking lot. The sight of the bloody body embedded in the crumbling stucco further satisfied Calisto, bringing a smug smile to his face. The man now resembled a bug smashed on a car windshield and it seemed a fitting end.

The scent of blood instantly surrounded him, intoxicating him with its fragrant call. Streams of it trickled down the wall from the mugger's lifeless body. Such a waste—

"Calisto?"

The sound of her voice shocked him back into the moment. He turned and knelt beside her, hoping to block her view of the carnage that, only moments ago, was her attacker.

"I am here," he whispered.

She nodded and her eyes drifted closed. She lost consciousness.

His hands trembled, inspecting her wounds. He couldn't bear to lose her again. If only he had gotten here sooner. He smoothed her hair back, looking over her bruised face. Other than a split lower lip, a minor scrape on her cheek, and a bump on her forehead, she seemed otherwise unharmed. The haze of panic and rage gradually thinned.

He needed to get her far from the crime scene before the police arrived. He couldn't risk having any connection to the bizarre death they were going to find plastered against the wall of the old liquor store.

After retrieving her purse and car keys, he scooped her into his arms. Slowly, he scanned the perimeter for any sign of a security camera. The yellow streetlamp sputtered, apparently the only witness to Kate's attack. Satisfied they hadn't been seen, he carried her to the old Volkswagen convertible.

Looking down at her face in the moonlight, his gaze strayed to her mouth. Part of him was sickened by his own attraction to the blood pooling on her lower lip. The scent enticed the beast inside of him, teasing his thirst, and seeing its rich redness on her sensual lips was almost more than he could bear. It awoke the predator in him, and right now he wanted nothing more than to be a mortal man again. A man who could offer her a future she deserved. A man she could love.

He didn't have time for these thoughts, though. Not right now.

Forcing his gaze from her face, he reached to open the passenger door of her car, frowning when it only opened a couple of inches. He tugged, but the door pulled back. He bent closer to the car and found the cause of the problem. The sound of his own laughter surprised him. He forgot about the elastic band tethered to keep the door closed.

Dear God, what a mess of a car.

He almost heard her telling him again that she was "restoring" the car and it just needed a new passenger door.

Shifting her slightly, he held her in one arm and reached inside to unclasp the elastic strap from the door handle. When he took a step back, the door creaked and fell open. He carefully lowered her into the passenger seat and reattached the elastic bungee strap to hold the door closed again.

He stared down at her for a moment, wanting to heal every cut on her soft skin. But he couldn't, not yet. He needed to get her, and her car, far from this place so neither he nor Kate would be implicated in any way with the gruesome murder site.

It also meant he would have to drive.

In all his years, he had never driven an automobile. The closest he had come was watching various assistants through the years as they chauffeured him. He wasn't sure he could even remember how to start the car, but right now he had no choice.

Grudgingly, he got into the driver's seat, and finding the lever underneath, he pushed it back so he sat comfortably behind the wheel. After trying three different keys, he found one that slipped into the ignition.

From what he had seen over the past hundred years, driving was not a complex operation, and he was an immortal with reflexes far more keen than a human man.

How difficult could it be?

He turned the key and nearly jerked the wheel off the steering column when the car surprised him by lurching forward. The car went silent. The engine wasn't running. What was he doing wrong?

He stared at the gearshift, wondering if he should move it. His frustration reared up, but his agitation would not make the car drive itself. He had to keep a cool head.

Not knowing what else to try, he pushed one of the pedals at his feet to the floor and turned the key again. This time the car didn't move, and it roared to life. Grasping the gearshift, he jammed it into the first position and glanced over at Kate.

Why couldn't she have owned a car with an automatic transmission?

Shaking his head, he put some pressure on the gas pedal and slowly released the clutch. Thankfully the car rolled a few feet, but without warning it jumped forward. He pressed the clutch back to the floor before the engine lost power again.

Calisto slammed his hand against the wheel, muttering under his breath in Spanish. At this rate it would take him all night to drive her home.

The faded yellow convertible pitched forward again, threatening to stall as he continued out of the parking lot, thankful it was late. The streets were fairly empty. At least he wouldn't get into an accident with another car. Her car staggered ahead, lurching each time he tried to release the clutch, bouncing and jostling them both until Kate finally stirred and woke up.

§

"Are we out of gas or something?"

Calisto watched her with a tight smile. "Not exactly."

Kate winced in pain when she laughed. "You can't drive a stick-shift, can you?"

"Does it show?" Calisto pulled over, finally allowing the engine to stall.

She nodded her head slowly to avoid more pain. "Just a little. What happened?"

"You don't remember?"

"I remember being mugged. And I remember seeing you, but everything after that is blank." She watched his eyes as Calisto reached over to brush her hair back from her face, and his touch sent shivers through her body. This wasn't how she had hoped she would run into him, but she learned a long time ago fate didn't always work out the way you expected.

"He ran off when I found you. I tried to take you back to my house to clean up your wounds, but I am afraid your car had other plans."

"I think I can drive."

"Are you sure?" Calisto studied her. "You hit your head when he attacked you. I—"

"How did you find me?" Kate interrupted.

"I heard you scream. I got there as quickly as I could."

"Thank you." Unexpected tears filled her eyes. "I was so scared. I thought he was going to kill me… or… "

Calisto turned and pulled her into his arms, stroking her hair while she wept. She'd never been so terrified. What if Calisto hadn't heard her? What if no one had come to her aid?

Would she be in his arms right now, or in a morgue?

He whispered against her hair. "You are safe. No one will ever harm you again."

Something about the way he said it made her believe him. She felt protected in his arms, and gradually her tears faded.

"I hoped I would see you again, but this wasn't how I pictured it would happen."

Calisto smiled, drawing back to meet her eyes. "I was under the impression you wanted nothing more to do with me, no?"

"I'm not sure what I want anymore," she said.

He placed a tender kiss to her forehead and held her close. "Mercy Hospital is not far from here."

"No, we don't need to do that." Just the thought of the health insurance nightmare of going to an emergency room made her head hurt. "I'm just scraped and shaken up. I'll be all right."

"Where are you staying? We can park your car and I will call a taxi."

"No," Kate trembled, shaking her head slowly. "I'm sorry. I don't want to be alone just yet."

"Then come back to my house. I will clean your wounds and you can rest."

She winced when she pulled back to meet his eyes. "Are you a nurse?"

He tenderly brushed the backs of his fingers down her uninjured cheek.

"Do you need one?" He smiled.

Grinning, she asked, "Do you ever answer questions?"

"My answers do not please you?"

Kate rolled her eyes at him, laughing again, and flinched. "Stop it… It hurts when I laugh."

"I am sorry. I would rather see you laugh than cry."

She smiled. "Let's find a safe place to leave my car… And I better drive before you give us both whiplash."

Calisto nodded and handed her the keys. "As you wish."

CHAPTER FIFTEEN

An hour later, the cab pulled away from Calisto's driveway. He helped her inside his house and up the stairs to the master bedroom.

She looked around the room, her gaze lingering on the blank walls and undecorated furniture, as if she wondered why he hadn't bothered to make the spaces cluttered and lived-in.

"I travel quite often. Lie down and rest while I get a cool washcloth for your face."

Kate smiled. "How do you do that?"

He raised a brow. "Do what?"

"Sometimes you know exactly what I'm thinking."

Calisto smiled and walked into the bathroom without responding. What could he say? He wasn't trying to read her thoughts, but at times her mind reached out to his without any effort on his part. It had been like that for them well before he ever became a Night Walker. Tala used to tell him they shared the same heart. Lifetimes ago...

He came back with a cool, damp washcloth and laid it across her forehead.

"That feels better, thank you."

"You are most welcome." He sat on the edge of the bed, looking closer at the cuts on her lip and cheek, hating them.

Many decades had passed since he used his powers for healing, but seeing her wounded called to the *Kuseyaay* once more. He couldn't let her suffer. Thankfully, he had been careful not to give her access to a mirror. Without any visual knowledge of the severity of her wounds, waking up to find them nearly gone wouldn't be a shock.

He stroked her hair back from her face, waiting until her eyes drifted closed. Slowly he brought his fingertip to his mouth and cut the tip on his sharp fang until a bead of rich blood glistened on his skin. Leaning closer, he tenderly traced his fingertip over her bottom lip, watching his blood work its magic, repairing the open wound until her skin was once again whole.

With the tribes he used to place his mouth over their wounds, and pierce his tongue so that the secret of his blood would not be revealed to them, but he wasn't sure he trusted himself to taste the sweetness of the blood on her lips.

He stared at his already healed finger. Only her blood remained. He turned his hand, watching the blood glisten, enticing him with its rich crimson color. The alluring scent called to his thirst, and he fought to bury the desire deep within.

Disgusted with himself, he bit back the temptation and rose quickly from the bed. He disappeared into the bathroom and scrubbed his hands, watching the blood from her lip thin and finally slip down the drain.

He didn't want to yearn for her blood, only for her heart and her love. Now he realized separating himself from his bloodlust would be far more difficult than he imagined. He would never hurt her, but he also needed to remember to feed well before spending time alone with her, not only to appear more human but also to control his thirst.

From the doorway, he watched her sleeping, memorizing every feature. He lit the candles on either side of the bed and dimmed the lights while she rested. Quietly, he walked into his closet to remove his jacket.

A shrill scream brought him to full attention.

"No! Don't hurt her!"

The sound of Kate's scream stabbed through his chest and he

forgot to slow his inhuman reflexes. Instantly, he sat at her bedside. Kate sank into his arms, shaking and sobbing against his chest. Calisto frowned, stroking her hair, trying to bring her some comfort.

"No one will hurt you, Kate," he whispered. "You are safe here."

She clung to him, trembling. "I know... I have a recurring nightmare. It always happens this time of year, but now... "

He waited for her to finish. When she remained silent, he drew back to meet her eyes. "What is it, Kate?"

Time froze when their eyes met. Deep within the shadows of her tear-filled dark eyes, he saw her. Tala. Her soul was there, and the knowledge of her past life now threatened Kate. Her soul struggled to remember, while her mind fought to forget.

And once again, he found himself unable to help her.

He couldn't tell her of their past together. Even if she did eventually believe his story, would she then fear him? Would she loathe him when she learned he drank the blood of the living to sustain his own life? He couldn't take the risk. She was here now, with him. She came back by her own free will, and he loved her. He would always love her.

"Ever since I was a little girl, I've had this nightmare. It comes back in the fall and it usually stops by spring. It's always been exactly the same, but now... Since I met you it's been changing." She shook her head, trying to clear away her fear. "It's getting harder and harder for me to sleep."

"Why does it frighten you?"

"I don't know. I guess because I feel helpless. The dream feels real. I can smell the sagebrush when she runs through the bushes. I see her running, and I can feel her body aching and her terror. She knows she has no chance of survival, but she runs anyway."

"Who is she?" He wanted her to search for the name, wanted her to come closer to understanding.

"I don't know. I never see her face." Kate took his hand, her thumb brushing over his ring. "But she has a ring like this hanging around her neck. That's why it looked so familiar to me before. I see it every night in my dream, dangling from a leather necklace." She tapped her fingertips against her chest, her gaze haunted. "It hits her chest with every step when she runs."

He watched her slim fingers trace the signet. Calisto's jaw clenched, holding back the onslaught of emotion threatening to overwhelm him. Kate was being tormented by nightmares of her own death.

A death she never would have suffered if she had never loved him.

"You said the dream is changing?"

Kate nodded, holding his hand tighter. "Now I can see him jump from his horse and knock her down. She tries to get away, but he's too strong. He pulls a dagger out of his belt and holds it to her throat. I hear her crying and saying something, but I don't think it's English." She wiped away a tear and added quietly, "I'm just glad I still wake up before... "

Before he rapes and kills her, Calisto thought bitterly. At least fate protected her from that final truth. So far she hadn't seen her own face in her dream.

Hopefully, she never would.

He lifted her chin as another tear escaped the corner of her eye. Without a word, he leaned in closer until his lips lightly brushed her warm skin, lingering against her cheek. He kissed away her tear and drew back slowly. His heartbeat pounded in his ears.

"You are shivering," he whispered.

Kate nodded, leaning closer. Her breath teased his lips. Calisto closed the distance between them, his lips finally meeting hers, brushing and caressing. He wrapped his arms around her, drawing her in close, crushing her breasts against his broad chest. He could hear her heart racing as he deepened the kiss. Every cell in his body screamed out with longing. He never wanted it to end.

No kiss had ever tasted so sweet.

Kate slid her hands up his chest, around his neck, loosening the leather tie that bound his long, dark hair. She pulled it free, tossing the tie away and running her fingers through his hair. Every touch aroused new desire inside of him, and when their lips parted and his tongue reached gently for hers, the sound of her soft moan reached into his soul, breathing life into a long dormant part of his spirit.

Calisto was lost. Lost in her arms, in her kiss, lost completely in loving her. The rapid pounding of her heartbeat and the feel of her body pressed tightly to his brought his hunger to life. But it wasn't a hunger for blood.

Without breaking the kiss, he laid her back onto the bed, covering her body with his. Her fingers tangled in the back of his hair, holding him, wanting him, and he felt alive again. He let his hands move slowly down her body, molding over every curve. Her back arched into his touch, and he growled with desire and longing.

Centuries had passed since he felt this passion, and he was quickly losing his mind with want for her.

Forcing himself to draw back from the soft warmth of her lips, Calisto looked down into Kate's eyes, his thumb brushing over her temple slowly. He wanted to tell her he loved her, wanted to remind her. But he couldn't push her like he had last time he held her.

His gaze wandered over her face, stopping at the abrasion still marring her soft cheek. He pressed a tender kiss over the scrape, carefully brushing his tongue across the tip of his sharp fang. His blood passed through his kiss, washing over the broken skin and working its magic to heal the blemish left behind from the attack.

She hummed softly. "That made my skin tingle."

Calisto caressed her newly healed cheek. "I hope I will always have that effect on you."

Her dark eyes fluttered open, and the blissful smile on her lips took his breath away. She brought her hand up to his cheek, her gaze never straying from his. The warmth of her touch intoxicated him, until his only desire was to lose himself in her arms forever.

Slowly he turned his head to place a tender kiss in her palm.

"I've never felt this way before." She brushed his hair behind his ear, her eyes wandering over his face. "I feel like I've known you forever, but I don't know anything about you."

"I feel the same," he said. "Perhaps we know each other far better than either of us suspects."

"I couldn't stop thinking about you. I had to come back."

His lips brushed hers again. "I feared I might never see you again."

Kate nodded, a soft smile teasing her lips. "I wasn't sure you'd want to see me again after what I said."

Calisto raised his head, his gaze holding hers. "There was nothing I wanted more in this world than to be near you again, Kate. I only stayed away because you told me that was what you wanted." He caressed her cheek. "If you had not come back to San Diego, I would have visited Reno again. Whether you wanted to see me or not."

She stared into his eyes and smiled, her fingers sliding slowly through his hair.

"I like your hair down," she whispered.

"You always did."

He claimed her lips before she could question his response.

When her embrace tightened around him, his worries eased. How could he have been so careless? But he already knew. The feel of her fingers in his hair, the sight of her beautiful eyes smiling up at him, she hypnotized him, taking away his rational thought and replacing it with emotions lost to him centuries ago. Tala lived again, locked away inside the body of Kate.

And he loved her more now than he ever had before.

Kate was drowning, and she didn't care. The moment his cool hand brushed the bare skin of her back, she surrendered to the passion that wrapped her in its fiery arms. Calisto's arms. Her entire body burned, engulfed in flames of desire. This was passion she'd longed for, and never experienced with anyone else.

Calisto's hand journeyed up her spine, his fingers quickly freeing her from the binds of her bra. Kate moaned when his hand slid up to cup her full breast. Her back arched into his touch, instinctively offering herself to him. His caress sent lightning arcing through her veins, making her nipples harden with need. Heat shot through the core of her body until she was breathless. This urgent, burning hunger was more than desire, a desperate yearning to feel him close to her, touching her.

Her hands moved up his chest, her tongue tangling with his. Kate's fingers worked feverishly to free the buttons of his shirt, hungry to explore every curve of his frame. The sound of his moan, the feel of it against her lips, made her tremble with longing. She wanted to touch, taste, and love every inch of him until they were both lost forever in each other.

Calisto broke the kiss just long enough to pull her shirt free of her body before once again fusing his lips to hers. The moment her breasts pressed against his bare chest, he was lost. Passion consumed them both. He tore away the rest of their clothes, surrendering to the urgent craving for closeness. No barriers remained between them.

The heat of her skin against his left him addicted and hungry for more. His body tangled with hers, so that it was impossible to tell where one of them ended and the other began. The frenzy of desperate, hungry kisses, exploring hands, touching every inch of one another, was the most delicious madness he had ever known.

Calisto held her in his arms and rolled her beneath him. He felt the softness of her inner thighs open to him, bringing him even closer to her. His hips settled between her legs, the heat of her core enticing him until his body ached to be buried inside of her.

He wanted this moment to last forever.

His lips moved down her throat to kiss the swell of her breast. Looking up at her beautiful face from under his brow, he took her hardened nipple into his mouth, sucking it gently. The sensual way her lips parted when she gasped, her eyes watching his mouth on her skin, was beyond erotic.

Unable to wait any longer, he pressed his hips forward. The moment he entered her, he froze, paralyzed with pleasure. Their bodies were one; her moans blended with his, one song, and he felt his heart finally made whole. He held her in his arms, all of his muscles tight, lost to the fire of their passion.

Kate moaned when he moved inside of her. She watched his tongue and lips tease her nipple. Her fingers tangled in his hair, holding him close. Every thrust of his hips claimed her. The passion he awoke consumed her.

She never wanted it to end.

Pulling him back up to her lips, she moaned, tasting his mouth again. Calisto's sleek hair fell loosely around them, teasing her sensitive shoulders, shielding her from the world outside of his arms. Calisto's embrace became her world.

Her skin felt hot and ached for his attention. She bent her legs, bringing them up slowly around his waist, gasping with pleasure when he penetrated even deeper. Every chiseled muscle of his chest called to her, pure masculine power. And in this moment, he was hers.

Her nails gripped his back, her body pulsing with want and at the same time yearning for release. She couldn't get close enough to him.

Calisto was alive again. His body moved into hers like a lover, not the predator he believed himself to be. She made him feel like a man again.

But while their ecstasy blossomed, so did the thirst.

It beckoned him to taste her in a purely inhuman way, and the faster her pulse raced, the closer she came to climax, the stronger the call became. Calisto fought to keep the desire for blood at bay while he covered her neck and shoulder with passionate kisses. Her pulse tempted him, so close, her body so willing.

Suddenly he felt her nails scratch down his back. She tensed under him and moaned sharply. Her body pulsed around him, as he plunged into her over and over. Gasping her name, Calisto shuddered and his release finally exploded through him, leaving him weak in her arms.

He rested his head on her chest, enjoying the sound of her deep breaths, her heart beating, and feeling her fingers stroking his hair back from his forehead slowly.

Calisto closed his eyes. Nothing would come between them ever again.

CHAPTER SIXTEEN

The sun blazed through the window when Kate finally opened her eyes. Her muscles still felt a little tight from the run-in with the mugger the night before, and her knee was definitely bruised, but none of that mattered. What mattered was Calisto.

He was gone.

Kate sat up, looked around the room, and collapsed back on her pillow with a groan. The down comforter was askew, and sunlight filtered through the shutters onto the king-sized bed where Calisto should have been. She peered over toward the bathroom, but the door hung open and the room was dark.

He left without even saying good-bye.

Maybe she'd been wrong about him after all. Last night he held her until she drifted off against his chest. It didn't seem like a one-night stand. She saw the emotion in his eyes when they made love...

Or she thought she had.

When she rolled over to get up, she noticed something on the pillow beside her. His pillow.

She smiled, gently lifting the freshly cut Romneya bloom. Taking in its sweet fragrance, she picked up a folded slip of paper beside it.

Dearest Kate,

Please forgive me for being such a terrible host. I had out-
of-town business to attend to this morning, and you looked
so peaceful that I did not wish to wake you. I left the phone
number to reach Betty. She can assist you in retrieving your
car. I hope I will find it in my driveway when I arrive home.
I am counting the minutes until I see you again.
Love eternally,
Calisto

Kate ran her finger across the words on the page, imagining
he had touched them just a couple of hours earlier. The script was
beautiful, not the chicken-scratch most men jotted down. Holding the
flower in one hand, and the note in the other, she flopped back onto
the down pillow and smiled.

She had to get a grip on herself. She was acting like a lovesick
puppy.

But she didn't care. He hoped she'd be here when he got home.
He counted the minutes until he saw her again. Laughing softly, she
rolled over in the bed. His scent still lingered on the pillows and
sheets, and she breathed him in deeply before completing her rotation
to look up at the ceiling. She opened the note, and read it one more
time, pausing at the end.

Love eternally…

An oddly romantic salutation. She'd heard of "yours forever" or
"love always," but "love eternally" seemed almost like… a promise.
Maybe the salutation meant something different in Spanish than
when he translated it into English.

She shook her head and sat up.

She was reading *way* too much into a short note. Time to get busy.
After a quick shower, Kate walked back into the bedroom wrapped
in a plush white towel and stared at the mirror. She felt like a different
person. Last night she'd experienced the most intense passion of her
life. The thought of a condom hadn't even crossed her mind. Being on
the pill made pregnancy worries nonexistent, but still…

In spite of her uncharacteristic recklessness, she had no regrets.

She leaned in closer to the mirror, examining her wounds. Her forehead had a bruise, but other than that, she didn't see any other traces of last night's attack. She touched her lower lip, and frowned. She thought she split her lip. She'd tasted the blood, but she didn't even have a scab. Strange.

She didn't want to think about the attack. As she stared down at her jeans and t-shirt lying on the floor beside the bed, she cringed. She didn't want to put those back on.

Ever.

Walking over to one of the whitewashed dressers, she decided she'd borrow something from Calisto. She'd get a clean set of clothes from home and have his put away before he ever knew they were gone.

But the drawer was empty.

Kate frowned and opened the rest of the drawers. They were all empty. She could make up a million reasons to try to explain it, but something was wrong. No one traveled so much they didn't have any clothes at home.

The closet.

She hurried to the walk-in closet and slid the mirrored door open. One sports coat hung on a single wire hanger. The rest of the closet was unused, no clothes, no shoes, no belts, no ties, nothing. There must've been a logical explanation, but it eluded her. The feeling he had never used this room came back to her full force, and she realized again that she knew nothing about this man she thought she might be falling in love with. He might be more of a stranger than she realized.

Kate put on her bra and panties and went into the bathroom to put on the chenille robe she saw hanging on the back of the door. Tying it closed around her waist, her stomach clenched tight.

Whirling around to the toilet, she wretched until she lost whatever remained of last night's dinner. Kate sat back against the wall, resting her head in her shaky hands. She hated throwing up. Even as a teen, the few times she had stayed home sick from school, her mom had been right there to hold her hand afterward.

No one was here for her now, while she sat in the house of a man she just slept with, who also might be some sort of spy or something.

She rubbed the bridge of her nose. She usually did a better job thinking through decisions when it came to intimacy. But she'd never been so swept away by passion. The need to touch him had been all-consuming.

Just thinking about it made parts of her body heat up.

Her decision-making aside, it didn't change the fact that Calisto was hiding something. What kind of man had empty dressers and closets in his own bedroom?

The kind of man you shouldn't get involved with. She heard her mother's warning in her head. Still giving her advice she didn't ask for and definitely didn't need.

Kate slowly picked herself off of the floor, fighting another wave of nausea. Maybe she had stomach flu. Food poisoning wouldn't linger like this. When her head cleared, she tightened the robe and left the master bedroom determined to explore the rest of his house.

There had to be an explanation for the lack of belongings in his bedroom.

Walking through the living room, she stopped and gazed out at the ocean through the French doors. He had an awe-inspiring view. The waves washed up the sand, and for a moment her moonlit walk down the beach with Calisto filled her mind. Holding his hand that night had awakened something inside of her that she'd never known existed, a hidden passion and an unspoken trust.

It couldn't have been a lie.

The kitchen was at the other end of the house. It offered a very open design, with a bay window that overlooked the shoreline. Large clay tiles covered the floor, and the stainless steel industrial oven was immaculate. She had a hard time believing it had ever been used. It did have a Spanish flavor to the décor that fit Calisto.

But he's never used it, she thought but immediately dismissed it. *He's just got a great maid, that's all…*

A lame explanation, but all she had at the moment. The more she looked around, the harder it was to convince herself a housekeeper could be this meticulous. She wandered around the kitchen, pulling open drawers and cupboards, searching for food or cooking utensils that might be appropriate to have in the kitchen.

She didn't find much.

The sum total of Calisto's kitchen inventory consisted of a set of dishes and silverware, twelve cans of assorted Campbell's soups, and two boxes of cereal that were two years past their "best by" date. No pans, no cooking utensils, and no sign that the large stainless steel stove had ever been used.

She opened both sides of the side-by-side upright refrigerator, revealing an empty freezer and two small Tupperware containers in an otherwise empty refrigerator. Maybe Calisto didn't live here at all. This might be a friend's house he used to impress women.

No. She didn't want to go down that path. There must be some other reason.

She closed all of the cupboards and drawers while she pondered the strange situation she found herself in. Maybe he just got back to San Diego and hadn't been to the grocery store yet. He was wealthy, so maybe he had his meals delivered and never used the kitchen. It still didn't explain his empty bedroom or why he kept cereal he obviously had no interest in eating.

He just traveled a lot. He told her so himself.

But you couldn't pack everything. Even frequent travelers left a few things behind in their dresser drawers. But Calisto didn't.

Puzzled, and more than a little concerned, Kate continued to explore his house, leaving the kitchen and going back through the living room to an adjacent hallway.

She stopped in front of the first door on her right. Hoping for answers, she turned the knob and walked into a large office.

This was the first room she'd seen that actually looked lived in. Kate smiled. Unlike the rest of the sparse interior of his house, the office was cluttered with books, folders, and pieces of mail. This room was definitely *his*, and it looked like he spent a lot of time here.

The walls were lined with oak bookcases filled from floor to ceiling. His library reflected his love of art. Her fingers traced over the leather bindings as she skimmed the titles, until something by the window caught her eye.

A small oil painting hung to the left of the arched window behind his large oak desk. Two hands, clasped together as one. She stepped closer and stared at the muted earth-toned colors, unable to take her eyes off of it.

The way the fingers intertwined, holding their palms tightly together, spoke to her. In each brush stroke, she felt the strength behind the simple gesture that connected two people. The artist captured a pure, perfect moment, and communicated the power and strength of love through the joining of one couple's hands. Love captured on canvas.

Kate looked closer for the artist's signature and found only the initials G.S. in the bottom right-hand corner. And she noticed one more minute detail. On the ring finger of the man's hand, he wore a thick gold band, flat on top where a stone might be. Or a signet?

The longer she stared at it, the more certain she became that the hand in the painting was Calisto's. She wondered who the woman might be. Calisto was a bachelor, but that didn't mean he'd always been one. Maybe he'd been married before. But if he were divorced, he wouldn't keep a painting of him holding hands with his ex-wife. It didn't make sense. You wouldn't want a reminder of her in your office.

Unless she died.

Kate looked out the window with a sigh. She felt incredibly lonely all of a sudden. Death had touched her life, too. She hoped she was wrong about her suspicion. There was no greater pain than losing a loved one.

She hoped the woman hadn't died. She shook off the thought. She didn't even know if Calisto had ever been married.

Turning back toward the desk, Kate pulled out the high-backed black leather chair and sat down. The large oak desk had a phone and fax machine at one end, and a calendar and stacking file at the other.

Slowly, she opened the drawers of the desk, relieved to find them stuffed with office supplies and hanging files. His files were labeled with color-coded tabs, alphabetically sorted by last names. She quickly searched for her mother's file, but it wasn't there.

Kate frowned, scanning the papers out on the desk. When she

poked through his stacking file, she found it. A membership form with names and phone numbers, her parents' address and the different functions they had attended were tucked inside. Written in the bottom corner was a small note saying they were deceased, and the value of the property they left to the foundation. She flipped through a couple more papers, wondering where her mother's piano might be now. The movers picked it up almost three weeks ago.

Then she had her answer. She held up a memo Calisto faxed to Betty on the day they picked up her piano.

> *Bettina-*
>
> *Please see that Martha Bradley's piano is brought to my home after six o'clock tonight.*
>
> *Thank you…*
>
> *C*

But she'd been through most of the house, and her mother's piano wasn't here. He had a grand piano in the living room, but not the one she'd grown up learning to play. Closing her parents' file, Kate got up from his chair and left the office, opening the rest of the rooms down the hallway to reveal more of the generic décor she had seen throughout the rest of his house.

Empty guestrooms with empty dressers and empty closets, and no sign of her mother's piano anywhere.

By the time she got back to the master bedroom, it was already one o'clock in the afternoon. She was hungry, slightly nauseous, frustrated and very confused. She needed to get her car and get something in her stomach.

She unfolded his note again and smiled. Men could be so clueless sometimes. Calisto honestly thought Betty would be happy to help pick up her car, but something told her Betty would be far from happy to find her wearing Calisto's bathrobe, waiting for a ride. Nope, calling Betty was not an option. Calling Lori wasn't much better. God, Lori would blow a gasket if she told her about his empty bedroom and unused kitchen.

Edie! She smiled and nodded as she reached for the phone. Edie would help her without asking too many questions.

And after a quick call, she had it all arranged. Edie would stop by Kate's parents' house to pick up her clothes for her and then meet her up in La Jolla at Calisto's to take her back to pick up her car. It was going to work out perfectly.

Then she heard the doorbell ring.

CHAPTER SEVENTEEN

The slut never came home.

Father Mentigo left her house late last night and returned this morning right before sunrise, but her car was already gone. Kate never came home.

He wasn't sure why he felt betrayed by her actions, but it didn't really matter. It was her fault. Her doing. She would pay penance for her lust in due time. He would see to that. They would both be punished.

Severely.

Father Mentigo cranked the wheel to drive away when a white midsize sedan caught his eye. It pulled into Kate's driveway and stopped. Yanking his binoculars from their case, he watched a blonde woman with a ponytail get out of her car and hurry to the front door. She plucked a red square-shaped rock from the flowerbed to the right of the main entry, turned it over, and slid a hidden key from the back.

Father Mentigo observed her every move, noting the exact location she returned the rock with the key hidden safely inside. His heart thumped with anticipation. He waited for the blonde woman to leave.

He would have a key to come and go as he pleased. Perfect.

After what seemed like an eternity, the blonde finally reappeared, locking the door and pulling it shut. She had a backpack hooked over her shoulder, and an overnight bag in her hand, leaving him to wonder if she might be picking up Kate's things.

The white sedan drove away, and he stowed his binoculars back in their case. Dressed in his plain khaki shorts and matching button-up shirt, Father Mentigo made his way down her driveway. Picking up the red rock, he turned it over and slipped the key into his pocket. Kate could return at anytime. He had to work fast.

Within the hour, he returned, parking his car across the street, and walked down her driveway. Replacing the key inside the red rock, he put it back into the flowerbed, leaving no clue he had ever been there. He glanced over his shoulder before removing a second key from his pocket and sliding it into the lock. Relaxation filled him the moment he was safely inside of her house.

It was done. He had access to her whenever he desired, *if* she ever came home.

Patience, he reminded himself. He plotted for a chance at eternity. Nothing could be rushed.

Her scent lingered amidst her few possessions. He poked through some of the opened boxes, caressing the soft fabrics that touched her skin. Soon he would touch her skin, her soft throat.

The woman with the moon in her eyes would understand the value of immortality. In the end, she would understand why he had to hurt her. She probably wouldn't forgive him, but he wasn't seeking forgiveness.

He wanted victory. After surviving an abusive father, a suicidal mother, and the constant fear of not enough food or a place to sleep, he stood on the threshold of the ultimate victory. He would never feel death's sting. He would never feel fear or hunger or pain again.

And he would love Kate Bradley forever for sacrificing her life to help him achieve his goal. Her blood was a small price to pay for the prize he stood to gain.

A twisted smile curled his lips, as Father Mentigo imagined the scene. She would be a beautiful sacrificial lamb. A perfect tribute to the God he would soon become.

But right now he had another package to deliver to the Night Walker.

He would meet Kate face to face soon enough. He could hardly wait.

§

Kate balanced on her toes to look through the peephole in Calisto's door, cringing when she saw Betty outside, reaching to ring the bell again.

Crap! She looked down at her robe.

"Calisto?" Betty called after the second doorbell chime. "I'm going to assume you're not home and use my key."

The knob turned. Kate had nowhere to hide. She hoped she wouldn't look too much like a deer caught in headlights when Betty walked through the door. She smoothed the robe into place and lifted her chin. When the door swung open, sunlight framed Betty in her impeccable dark blue business suit and stylish heels.

"Kate?" Betty frowned. "You scared me. I didn't think anyone was... "

Her voice trailed off as her cold gaze took in Kate's ensemble. The disapproval in her eyes was painfully obvious. "What exactly are *you* doing here? Didn't you go back to Reno?"

"I did." Kate nodded with a forced smile, pulling her robe a little tighter and wishing she'd at least found a brush for her hair. "But I decided to come back here for a while."

"So I see." Betty walked past her without a second glance. "Where is Calisto?"

"I don't know." Kate turned around to follow her into the living room area. "He left me a note saying he had business all day today."

"A note. I get a lot of those from him myself."

Betty spun around to face her so quickly that Kate nearly flinched with surprise.

"So what exactly is going on here? Last time we met, you mentioned something about a job back home. But that probably doesn't matter to a woman like you."

Kate wanted to scream, but she didn't. The cool, controlled tone of Betty's voice and the way her tight ponytail made her eyes look like slits reminded Kate of a venomous viper, coiled and ready to strike.

Attempting to defuse the situation, she said, "I was mugged last night, and Calisto helped me. He let me spend the night. I'm expecting my friend here any minute with my clothes. She'll take me to pick up my car."

"Oh isn't that sweet," she said with a sarcastic grin that made Kate sick to her stomach all over again. "Is Calisto aware that his 'damsel in distress' has invited her friends to party in his house while he's away?"

Kate clenched her fists and counted to ten. Betty went into Calisto's office. What a pill.

"I said *a* friend was coming. That's hardly a party." Kate followed Betty. "We won't be staying anyway. As I said, she's taking me to pick up my car."

Betty settled into Calisto's leather chair as if it were her own and glanced up from her paperwork. "And will you be coming back?"

"That's not really any of your business."

Betty glared, aiming her pen like a weapon at Kate's chest. "Oh, but it is. Calisto is a bit eccentric and a lot reclusive. He hasn't had as much experience with gold diggers as I have. I can smell them from a mile away. As the director, it's my job to keep his assets secure."

Kate had a feeling Betty was more concerned with Calisto's ass than his assets. She turned to leave. "I really don't care what you think, Betty. Calisto's a grown man, and I'm sure he's more than capable of taking care of himself."

Kate didn't wait for an answer. Instead, she walked away from further confrontation and prayed Edie would drive up soon. She'd feel more prepared for a verbal jousting match when she had clothes on.

Kate went upstairs and made the bed while she waited. Anything to keep busy and not have to cross paths with Betty again. Finally, she heard a car drive up and went downstairs to open the door before

Edie could ring the bell.

"Oh my God, this house is gorgeous!"

"Hurry." Kate tugged Edie inside and closed the door behind her. She made a beeline for the stairs, but unfortunately she wasn't fast enough.

"And this would be your friend?"

Kate and Edie turned to find Betty standing tall in the hallway with her arms crossed and wearing a judgmental glare.

Kate sighed. "Yes it is. I didn't want to interrupt your work by bringing her in to—"

"You've already interrupted," Betty said, stepping forward and offering her hand. "I'm Betty Parker, the Director of Foundation Arts."

Edie took her hand with a tentative smile. "Nice to meet you. I'm Edna Banks, but my friends call me Edie."

Betty shook her hand with a curt smile. "Then I'll call you Edna. Please don't touch anything, and be sure not to give out this address. Mr. Terana treasures his privacy. I'm sure you understand."

Edie withdrew her hand with a nod and quietly watched Betty disappear down the hall and into the office.

"Wow. She's not very friendly is she?"

Kate chuckled, heading up the stairs with Edie. "That's a nice way of putting it."

"What's her problem?"

"She's bent out of shape about finding me here in Calisto's robe."

Edie grinned and handed her the backpack of clothes. "Oh I see... She's jealous!"

Kate took the backpack and slipped out of the robe with a shrug. "Probably, but I can't say for sure. She thinks I'm after Calisto's money, and as much as I'd like to smack her for saying that about me, more than likely there are quite a few women out there who *are* after his checkbook. She's probably just doing her job."

"She's really good at it." Edie shuddered.

Kate laughed as she tugged her jeans up over her hips. "Thanks for bringing my clothes. I really appreciate it."

"No problem. I was hoping I might catch a glimpse of him." Edie walked to the window and whistled low.

"Him?"

"Your Prince Charming." Edie winked at Kate, then returned to the view.

Kate pulled on the t-shirt. "Unfortunately he left before I woke up, but he left me this." She handed Edie the blossom and the note, watching her friend intently as she read his words.

Edie clutched the note to her chest. "Oh, Kate! He sounds wonderful!"

"He is. I still don't know him that well, but... "

"But what?" Edie grinned.

"Don't tell Lori or she'll kill me, but I might be falling in love with him."

Edie squealed and hugged her tight. Kate grinned. She'd made the right choice calling her. Edie was happy because Kate was happy, no questions asked, and right now that was exactly what Kate needed.

Because right now, she had plenty of questions of her own and not nearly enough answers.

§

Betty tried to lose herself in her work. She usually enjoyed sitting at Calisto's desk. Knowing she was the only person in the world he trusted to use his things... But she wasn't the only one anymore.

The pencil lead snapped.

"Dammit!" She cursed under her breath, jamming the tip into the electric sharpener on the corner of the desk.

It was the fourth time she'd broken it since she found Kate in that goddamned bathrobe. What else had she touched? How could Calisto have trusted her and left her alone in his house while he was away on business? Kate was practically a stranger. He'd never been so trusting of anyone before. Betty waited a year for him to present her with her own key to his house.

Yet Kate was already in his bathrobe.

She couldn't stand it. How could he have fallen for her little damsel in distress act? God, it was the oldest trick in the book. *Oh please, someone help me... Oh I'm too scared to be alone...*

She wanted to vomit.

The pencil lead snapped. Again.

"Shit!" She slammed the weak-leaded piece of crap into the wastebasket. Reaching for a new pencil, she heard a knock at the door.

She got up to answer it with a frown. Kate and her little friend left about twenty minutes ago. They couldn't be back already. With any luck, maybe they wouldn't come back at all.

She left the security chain latched and carefully opened the door. "Can I help you?"

"I hope so. I have a package here for a... Calisto Terana?" The man reminded her of one of the homeless guys in Ocean Beach with his wiry beard, but he spoke with an accent that sounded more like Nebraska than San Diego. His brown uniform looked familiar, though, and he wore designer sunglasses.

"I can sign for that. Hold on." Betty closed the door and unhooked the security chain before opening the door again.

He handed her a clipboard to sign as he glanced around. "This is a beautiful house."

Betty gave him her professionally aloof smile and handed his clipboard back. "I'm sure Mr. Terana will be glad to hear that you thought so."

She waited impatiently for the courier to give her the small brown package, but her impatience gave way to unease when she realized he was no longer checking her signature. Instead, he seemed to stare at her.

"It appears that Mr. Terana is fond of many beautiful things." His dark beard made his teeth look whiter than normal. Almost predatory. A chill slid down her spine. Maybe it was his wiry beard, or the way his sunglasses hid his eyes from view, but now he looked like a wild animal, lying in wait for his prey to come close enough for him to pounce.

Dismissing her irrational fear, she ignored his comment, cleared her throat, and held out her hand. "I'm sorry, we're very busy now.

Can I have the package?"

"We?" He peered around. "Is Mr. Terana inside?"

"That's really none of your business," she said, using her practiced, professional demeanor to cover her sudden wave of dread. "Give me the package before I call your supervisor."

He chuckled and leaned against the doorframe. "You would have a hard time reaching my supervisor. I work for a much higher power than you could imagine."

His words chilled her. When he offered the package, she snatched it from his hand and slammed the door closed, quickly locking it and sliding the security chain back in place. She leaned against the door for a moment to collect her herself. What a creepy courier.

Something about him, the way he'd looked at her, the way he tried to determine if she was alone, terrified her. She would definitely lodge a complaint to...

Betty turned the box over and frowned. Other than Calisto's name and address, there were no other markings on the box, no tracking number, nothing. It must have been a private courier service.

She peered out the window, hoping to catch a glimpse of his truck, but the only car left in the driveway was her own. Damn.

Placing the box on the corner of his desk, she jotted a note to herself to remember to call all the local couriers to find out who delivered a package to Calisto Terana. That driver had messed with the wrong woman.

CHAPTER EIGHTEEN

Calisto awoke filled with passion for the night to come. The memory of Kate sleeping in his arms, her raven hair strewn across his pillows in stark contrast to the ivory pillowcases warmed his heart.

His second chance had arrived. This time it would not end in tragedy.

He rose from his sleeping chamber and climbed the stone stairs to his room. Not the master bedroom of the main house, but *his* room. It was originally a wine cellar, but shortly after purchasing the house, he converted the cellar into a private bedroom and bathroom. His resting place during the daylight hours was far beneath his room, buried deep within the sandy soil.

He showered and dressed, pulling on his black boots and tying his dark hair back without making an effort to slow himself to human speeds. He needed to be with her again soon.

But first he needed to feed.

For a moment, he was tempted to go to the main house, just to see if she waited for him, but he thought better of it. If he saw her, he would never be able to pull himself away to feed. He couldn't take the chance that his bloodlust might overcome him if they made love before he had a chance to sate his hunger. At best, she would suspect something was wrong with him if she touched his cool skin.

She would never guess he was no longer human, but rather a Night Walker who lived only after the sun died on the horizon. He wished he could shed his immortality and be the man she deserved, the man she thought he was.

He stuffed his hands into his pockets and walked down the beach, disappearing into the night. He was lying to her. No matter how much he believed she was better off not knowing, he hid the truth from her, even denying her the chance to decide for herself.

She had no idea he would never be with her when the sun came up. Eventually he would break her heart daily by leaving her each morning. He had lived among mortals since his rebirth, but he had never loved one, never allowed anyone into his heart until now. Appearing human was simple when no one really knew him, but how long could he live a lie with the woman he loved?

At some point, she would ask him to stay.

With a frustrated growl, he ran as fast as he could, his legs propelling him toward the lights in the distance. He searched for his next meal at a shopping mall, pushing away the shadow of guilt lurking in the corners of his mind. The guilt whispered that Kate deserved a far better future than he would ever be able to provide.

§

Kate waited, trying not to watch the clock, trying not to count the minutes until Calisto walked through the door. She failed.

After Betty grudgingly left for the day, Kate took a long bath, blew her hair dry, and tried to read a book, but her thoughts kept drifting back to his note. She wished he'd told her what time he'd be back. She would have been happy to pick him up from the airport. It was the least she could do to repay him for saving her life. Or at least that's what she would have told him if he had asked. In reality, she would have been at the airport the second his plane landed because she couldn't wait to see him again.

But instead, she sat here, alone in his empty house, waiting.

And the longer she waited, the more she thought about how she might bring up the oddity of his empty master bedroom and unused kitchen. She hoped he wouldn't be angry with her for snooping around his house.

Thinking about it drove her nuts.

Kate got up from the chair in the office and replaced the leather bound copy of *A Tale of Two Cities* with a sigh, wondering where he might be. It felt like she'd already waited all night, but the clock said it was only six-thirty. Kate wandered out of the office and down the hall. When she walked into the living room, she smiled. The piano.

She sat on the bench and looked over the slick black and white keyboard. It wasn't her mother's piano, but it didn't matter. Playing took all of her concentration, exactly what she needed right now to keep her mind off of how slow the minutes crept by.

She warmed up with scales, her fingers flying up and down the keyboard in a building flurry of notes. Finally, she played a careful rendition of one of Mozart's variations on "Twinkle Little Star," starting with the simple melody in her right hand and gradually adding the harmony with her left, until the music became more complex and filled the room with its joyful song.

The act of playing, of making music and letting the chords fill the air around her, lightened her spirit. Her emotions bled through her fingertips into the keys, making every turn in the notes sound like laughter and every forte blossom with an almost tangible passion.

It was similar to the way the human voice sang. Loud and soft, crescendo and decrescendo, joy and sadness, major and minor, her fingers could convey a message words sometimes couldn't achieve.

A communication beyond anything speech could convey.

When she reached the final cadence, she slowly let the sound of the last chord fade.

Applause echoed through the room. Kate spun around with a start, and then laughed.

"God, you scared me!" She rose from the piano. "I hope you don't mind me playing your piano. I wasn't sure when you'd be home."

Calisto walked forward and took her hand, sending a familiar electricity through her bloodstream. "Not at all. What is mine is yours."

She tried not to lose her head completely when he lifted the back of her hand to his lips, but the moment he kissed her knuckles, coherent thought escaped her.

"I hope you will play for me again soon." He lowered her hand without letting it go.

Kate could feel the blush burn through her cheeks, but she shook her head and laughed. "You don't have to flatter me. I've got a degree in music. I'm well aware my abilities as a pianist are lacking."

"You are too hard on yourself. This fine instrument has never been introduced to such a beautiful rendition of 'Twinkle, Twinkle Little Star.' "

Kate's heart fluttered. He made even the juvenile title sound sexy. Seeing he had no idea how sensual he sounded made him even more irresistible. He made no effort to be seductive. He just was.

Calisto sat with her. "You enjoy Mozart?"

Kate ran her fingertips over the keys. "Very much. I wish I could play well enough to do his work justice."

He stared into her eyes for a moment with a crooked smile. Without a word, Calisto turned toward the keyboard and pulsed the steady tempo with his left hand while his right played the simple turns. Gradually it built into a faster, more complex work, his fingers teasing the keyboard until Kate thought she might never be able to wipe the smile off her face.

He played the third movement of Mozart's piano concerto in E-flat perfectly. Every trill, every turn, every frenzied scale. She'd never heard anything like it before. He wove a web of music around them, leaving her breathless.

Mozart himself couldn't have performed it with more fervor and precise intonation. Calisto played chord after chord leading up to the final cadence, urgent intensity masking his features. A lock of his dark hair dipped over his brow. He played with pure abandon and passion. Kate's heart raced at breakneck speed, watching his body move with the melody. He didn't hold back to find the right keys as she did. He felt them.

And she'd never witnessed anything so sensual.

The piece of hair dangled on his forehead, bobbing to the music with every beat he played, and the sight made her chest ache with emotion. If she didn't love him before, she did now.

Nothing in the world spoke to her the way music did, and no one had ever given her such a beautiful gift as the one he offered her now. The concentration and passion pouring out of his body and into the piano spoke volumes about his emotions.

He loved her. It seemed crazy, but she *knew* he did. He told her with every note he played.

Calisto thundered through the finale of the third movement, and when the final chord sounded, he held the keys down, his foot on the sustain pedal, allowing the strings inside the grand piano to continue to sing as if he weren't ready to give up the music yet.

When the music finally faded into oblivion, he lifted his fingers from the keys and slowly turned toward her.

He frowned. "You did not enjoy it?" He brought his hand up to cup her face, wiping away a tear.

"I loved it," Kate whispered, nuzzling gently into his touch.

"But you are crying."

"Happy tears. I've never heard anyone play like that before. You chose my favorite piano sonata."

His thumb caressed her cheek. "I am glad it pleased you. For the first time in many, many years, I feel the joy in Mozart's music. You gave me that gift, and I wanted to share it with you."

Kate stared into his dark eyes, bringing her hand up to brush the stray lock of hair back from his forehead. There were so many things she wanted to tell him, and yet words seemed incapable of capturing the magic of his music.

Instead, she leaned closer, her lips meeting his in a tender kiss that made words unnecessary. A soft moan escaped her when his fingers slid into her hair, cradling the back of her head as he deepened the kiss. She pressed closer to him on the piano bench, her hands moving up his muscled chest. Kate's pulse already raced. Just kissing him left her breathless. No man had ever had this effect on her before, which only furthered her belief he was the one.

Calisto was the missing part of her heart, her other half, but she still didn't know him. Not really.

He pulled back from her lips, resting his forehead against hers. "If there had been any way for me to stay with you this morning, I would have. I was glad to find you here when I returned."

"I was a little blue when I first woke up, but I found your note."

"I hope you can forgive me." His lips brushed hers, stealing a tender kiss. "Last night meant more to me than you could ever know."

Kate's heart skipped a beat. Between the way he looked at her, and the words he spoke, she lost her train of thought. "There's nothing to forgive. But the next time you have to leave before the sun comes up, I hope you'll at least wake me up to give me a kiss good-bye."

"Any excuse to kiss you." He leaned closer to brush his lips against hers and scooped her into his arms.

Kate's breath caught in her throat when he carried her through the room. She lost herself in the kiss, her tongue tangling hungrily with his. She struggled to silence her inner voice from reminding her that the bedroom they were entering was virtually empty. Reminding her she might not know this man as well as she should.

He laid her down on the bed, covering her body with his, their lips never parting. Her fingers worked quickly to unfasten the buttons and open his shirt. She wanted him, needed him, now.

But deep inside, she wondered if fear fed her urgent hunger for him. She pressed hot kisses down his neck, her hands sliding his shirt off of his broad shoulders. With every hungry touch of her lips to his skin, she told herself she wasn't afraid of anything. This was passion, and she was simply surrendering to it.

Or was it really fear, and she was running away from it?

Kate lifted her arms so he could tear the shirt from her body, moaned as his lips caressed the swell of her breast. The feel of his weight over her, seeing his dark hair fall over his shoulders, teasing her sensitive skin, drove her insane with desire. She couldn't resist the passion his lips offered.

Or was she just afraid she wouldn't like his answer if she stopped to ask him why his bedroom was so empty?

"Calisto, stop," she whispered, pulling him up to meet her eyes.

He lifted his head, looking up at her with dark eyes that gazed directly into her soul. God, he made it hard to concentrate. She couldn't help but watch the muscles in his chest and shoulders tense and he slowly pushed himself up, resting his elbows on either side of her head.

"Is something wrong?" His thumb gently caressed her temple, brushing her hair back.

"No... Yes." Kate sighed and shook her head. "I don't know."

Calisto frowned.

"I need to talk to you about something before this goes any further and I lose my nerve."

"Have I done something to upset you?"

She brought her hand up to cup his cheek. Touching him, knowing he was real, that he cared about her, eased her tension. Why couldn't that be enough? "I need to know you, Calisto. The real you." She stared into his eyes, watching for any sign he hid something from her. "I know this room, most of this house, is *not* you."

Calisto's smile faded, and he shook his head slowly. "I do not understand."

Kate pressed her lips together, gathering her courage. She hoped he wouldn't be angry with her for snooping through his home, peeking in his drawers and cupboards and closets. She didn't want to lose him. Not ever.

But she'd ignored her doubts to love Tom, and look how that turned out.

If Calisto lived a double life, she decided she'd rather know now. She couldn't risk getting too attached to another man with secrets. "This isn't your bedroom, Calisto. It can't be."

He raised a brow and glanced around the room before meeting her gaze again. "I assure you I own this house, as well as this bedroom."

"But it isn't *yours*. All the drawers and closets are empty. There isn't a single picture here, or anything that reminds me of you. The only room in this house that seems to have any of *you* in it is the office. The rest of this place is just an empty shell."

She brushed his hair back with her fingers. "I want to know Calisto, not the founder of Foundation Arts, or some man from an eligible bachelor list. This house and this bedroom aren't you."

Calisto rose from the bed and offered her his hand. "Come with me, I want to show you something."

Kate allowed him to help her from the bed and pulled her shirt back on. He slid his arms into his shirt but didn't bother to button it. He held her hand and led her downstairs.

"Where are we going?" she asked.

Calisto smiled, lifting their joined hands to kiss her knuckle. "To *my* bedroom."

CHAPTER NINETEEN

Calisto led Kate onto the deck and down the stairs. The sight of her smile in the moonlight encouraged him that he'd made the right decision. He loved her, and she had a right to know him, more than anyone else ever would, even if he couldn't share all of his secrets. He was stunned, not only by her perception, but by his own desire to open up to her. Mortals were often in his home and no one had ever found reason to doubt him before.

But Kate wasn't like everyone else. He wanted to tell her everything. He wanted to share his soul with her, or as much of it as he could.

"Your room is outside?"

"You ask far too many questions."

"And you still manage not to answer them."

Calisto laughed. "Perhaps."

Once they reached the sand, he took her around to the back of the house where the foundation met the sandy cliff. After he unlocked the double doors to the wine cellar, he froze.

He couldn't let Kate go inside. Not yet.

On the wall of his private bedroom hung a large canvas that he'd painted lifetimes ago, after the mission burned to the ground. His last portrait.

He used to love using his brushes and oils, creating a new world of color and life on an otherwise dull canvas, bringing light and life out of nothingness. As a mortal man in Spain, he apprenticed with a Church artist, learning to depict the face of Christ or the Blessed Virgin. His artistic talent led to his selection to sail to the New World with Father Serra. He was a priest, and also an artist, responsible for many murals on the Mission de Alcala's sanctuary walls to honor the Lord he served.

But this portrait was not of Christ.

The painting adorning the wall of his room was of his Tala. She wore his signet ring tied around her neck, and she had a Romneya bloom tucked behind her ear. He even captured the tiny crescent in her right iris, along with the secret smile she saved for him alone.

Until the night they took her from him forever.

He couldn't let Kate see it. She would recognize herself, and he had no explanation for it. Maybe he should have waited to bring her here.

"Is this it?"

Kate's voice jarred him from his worries and Calisto nodded. "Yes."

He hesitated to open the door. Kate looked up at him. "Is something wrong?"

"I have never had a visitor to my room. May I have a minute to be sure everything is as it should be?"

"Of course."

He bent to taste her lips, then straightened and locked his gaze on hers. "Wait for me."

He slipped through the door and into his room. Lifting the painting from the hook, he stared at the portrait and smiled. He didn't need it anymore. She was alive again and waiting for him right outside. Carefully, he wrapped the canvas inside the sheet and slid it underneath his bed and into hiding.

He glanced around his room and, satisfied, stepped outside.

"Can I see it now?" She smiled.

Calisto nodded with a crooked grin. "That is why I brought you here, no?"

§

He held the door open for her, and Kate stepped inside. She stared at the piano that now sat in the center of his room. Her mother's piano.

She turned, smiling up at Calisto. "I wondered where it went." She ran her fingertips along the lid of the baby grand piano. "I'm so glad it found a good home."

"Your fingers have graced its keys." He crossed his arms with a shrug. "I could not allow anyone else to touch it."

"Have you played it?" she asked, looking back at him.

"Every night."

"Really?"

"Of course." He nodded. "It made me feel closer to you."

"No wonder I couldn't stop thinking about you." She smiled. "You were thinking about me too."

"I feared I might never see you again." He caressed her cheek. She nuzzled into his touch. "I couldn't stay away."

"Good," Calisto replied, his voice just above a whisper.

"Is it?"

"*Si.*"

"Why?" She tilted her chin up toward him.

Calisto took a step closer. "Because." He kissed her tenderly, whispering against her lips. "I love you, Kate."

His lips fused with hers, and he lifted her into his arms, carrying her to his bed. Calisto lowered her slowly without breaking the kiss, his body covering hers. He slid his hands underneath her t-shirt, pushing the fabric up. Her skin felt soft in his hands, and the way her body writhed beneath him sent his desire soaring.

He needed her. Now.

He kissed her mouth, chin, down her neck, his lips and tongue tasting every inch of her skin, exploring every curve. She pulled his shirt down from his shoulders and he shrugged it off. Her warm hands ran up his back and into his hair, her nails massaging his scalp while he freed himself from his pants.

He looked into her eyes, and she saw silent passion that spoken words could never hope to communicate. Lying in his arms, she lived simply to love him. Her fingers tangled in his dark mane, pulling him closer until their lips met in a hungry kiss. His hips pressed forward, joining them, one in a passionate struggle for pleasure and closeness.

Kate rolled on top of him without breaking the kiss. His hands slid down the arch of her back to grip her waist. Gradually she softened the kiss, drawing back until she sat up, staring down at him. Calisto filled her perfectly, completely. His eyes burned with carnal desire. She felt sensual watching his gaze moving over her curves.

She savored the feel of him inside of her, grinding against his slow thrusts. She dropped her head back, moaning his name. Calisto pushed up, kissing his way along her neck. His lips fused with hers in a hungry kiss as he held her tight in his arms, her breasts crushed against his chest. Kate wrapped her legs around his waist. She couldn't get close enough. As her body reached its peak, she trembled in his arms, and gasped against his lips. "I love you, too."

§

He was sick of hiding.

Time to push the battle forward.

Even though it appeared Kate was staying with the Night Walker, as long as she remained mortal, he had the upper hand. She held the key to his plan's success. If he let her slip through his fingers now, the Night Walker had already won.

An unacceptable scenario. He had waited far too long for this. His ambition would never accept failure.

Father Mentigo combed through his thick black hair, focusing his attention on his dark eyes in the mirror. He would make an imposing immortal. His tall stature already forced most people to look up to him. The sharp angles of his face and his hawk-like nose made his cold stares even more piercing and threatening.

Replacing the comb, he picked up his silver shears and clipped his hair, cutting until it rested at least an inch above his collar. He took a moment to admire his transformation, and then reached for the ivory-handled straight razor. With a steady hand, he slid the blade along the edge of his jaw, shaving off most of his beard. Every deliberate swipe of the blade carved out a new identity, leaving behind a thin, angular goatee that gave him more defined features. He felt his bare skin and inspected his new look.

Facial hair wasn't tolerated in the monastery, but he was far from their reach now. He wouldn't be a pious monk much longer anyway.

A twisted grin curled over his lips, causing the razor blade to slice into his now-uneven jawline. He smirked, watching his blood pool around the cut and slowly drip from his face.

He'd never been very pious. But he was an excellent actor.

He finished shaving, allowing his wound to remain open, bleeding. Soon his body would be immortal, and wounds would heal almost the instant they were sustained. He dipped his index finger into the small puddle of blood pooling on the sink and held it up at eye level, marveling at the rich crimson color, the thick consistency, and the earthy scent.

Slowly, he brought his fingertip to his lips, sucking the blood from his skin, drinking in his own life. In the near future, it would be the blood of others that sustained him. The thought sent heat through his loins.

Bending lower, he licked the blood from the surface of the sink, savoring the coppery flavor of the last remaining traces of his blood. How sweet it would taste when it flowed past his lips, still warmed by his victim's pounding heart. Soon, he would have the strength he thirsted for. Very soon.

He tended to his cut before stepping out for the evening. His palms were clammy as he gripped the steering wheel of his car, the Latin chant repeating itself endlessly in the back of his mind, cloaking his true thoughts from any beings who might try to listen. His senses were on the alert, his eyes shifting from one side to the other, knowing that any shadow might hide the Night Walker. He had to be careful. It wasn't time for them to meet face to face.

Not yet.

Tonight, he would meet someone else.

Checking the address again, he pulled to a stop outside of the gated condominiums. He spotted her car inside the wrought iron fence and took a cigarette out of the glove compartment. He waited for almost an hour.

The blonde walked around the corner before he got out of his car to follow. It wasn't hard to find her on the crowded streets. She had an air about her that commanded attention, and with her blonde hair falling past her shoulders, and her tight leather skirt, attention was exactly what she got. Men and women stepped out of her way, their eyes following her as she passed.

He wet his lips in anticipation. He could taste her already.

Her stiletto heels clicked out a confident pace ahead of him, then she disappeared into a dimly lit club. He followed, making his way through the masses of undulating bodies toward the bar. Once his eyes adjusted to the shadowy surroundings, he scanned the room. His head pounded from the blaring techno music. He struggled to maintain the constant chant running in the back of his mind.

Until his plan came to fruition, he remained vulnerable. He couldn't let the Night Walker find him. He would face the immortal when he was ready.

It couldn't be the other way around.

He turned to the bar when the bartender delivered his drink. Out of the corner of his eye, he watched her. She sat alone at a small table just to the right of him. Taking a swallow of his drink, he made his approach.

§

Betty sipped her margarita and glared at the dancing couples from over the salty rim of her glass. Even the blasting music and alcohol didn't dull the anger that festered inside of her. She'd been pissed off since she opened Calisto's door and found Kate Bradley standing there in nothing but his bathrobe. The bitch was probably in his bed at this very moment, planning to screw him stupid until he married her and wrote her into his will.

She drummed her perfectly manicured acrylic nails on the table, trying to stop picturing Calisto touching another woman. She needed to find a gorgeous guy to take her mind off of him, but so far she was still alone.

"Good evening."

A nice pair of black slacks suddenly obscured Betty's view of the club. She gave him her sultriest smile and allowed her gaze to wander up his body. "Hello."

His voice was deep and rich, with an accent very similar to Calisto's. He was over six feet tall, with dark eyes and hair. His thin, well-groomed goatee only added to the overall look of sophistication radiating around him. He looked like a man who usually got what he wanted.

Nothing on earth turned Betty on more.

She took another long, slow sip of her margarita, her eyes on his, making it plain that he now had her undivided attention.

"I hope that I'm not intruding, but a woman as beautiful as you should be dancing, not sitting."

Something about the way he said beautiful sounded familiar, but she didn't take the time to try to place it.

"Are you asking me to dance?"

He nodded with a hint of a smile and offered his hand.

She followed him onto the floor. Betty sensed the stares from the other dancers and loved it. She enjoyed knowing they were drawing attention, knowing people watched their bodies move in harmony with the beat, their hips driving with carnal desire. She smiled at him with bedroom eyes and got a jolt by the heated stare he gave her in return.

Her night was finally showing some potential.

She wasn't sure how long they danced. Heavy, unspoken flirtation made it easy to lose track of time, but she needed a break. The last thing she wanted was to start sweating.

They applauded as the band left the stage for a break, and Betty took his hand, leading him back to her table. "You were pretty good out there."

"Only when I have the right partner." He gave her a sensual, almost dangerous stare.

She sat but leaned forward to ensure he had a good view. "Thank you. You know, I don't even know your name."

"Jose. Jose Mentigo."

§

Calisto didn't need to read Kate's mind to know she was elated and completely exhausted. By the time they pulled into his driveway, it was nearly three in the morning, but her face glowed, her eyes shone, and she wore a perpetual grin.

She followed Calisto into his office and sat in one of the large chairs opposite his desk. He still had some work to finish up, and she told him she wanted to read. Exhaustion set in, and within twenty minutes, her eyes drifted closed and the book in her hand fell to her lap.

Calisto smiled. Words couldn't describe how much he enjoyed spending time with her, loving her. She was his perfect mate, just as she had been lifetimes ago. In fact, Kate shared much more in common with him now than she had when he had known her as Tala.

After tonight, he was certain he loved her for the woman she was today, not the memory of who she had been.

He shook his head, forcing himself to get back to work. Looking over the notes and receipts Betty left for him, he noticed an unopened package sitting on the corner of his desk. He tore open one end, frowning when he withdrew the contents. More pictures.

This time they were pictures of Kate.

Calisto flipped through the photos of Kate getting into her little yellow car, fighting the rage brewing inside of him. The monk watched her too.

But his rage gave way to cold fear when the pictures ended with a short note.

I know you cannot protect her during the day.

Unlike the recent warnings, it didn't threaten to expose his true identity. This threat aimed squarely at Kate.

He couldn't ignore the Fraternidad any longer. He needed to find the monk who stalked him. He should have found him already. Being with Kate made everything else in the world seem insignificant.

It also made him careless.

Calisto looked over at her snoozing figure on his chair and pulled his hair back from his forehead in frustration. It was nearly sunrise, too late for him to hunt for the man who left the photos. He should have already corrected the situation, but he'd been too distracted, too wrapped up in loving her to think about hunting down the nameless monk stalking him.

Until he dealt with the priest, Kate's safety during the day was in jeopardy. He dreaded leaving her alone and vulnerable during the day. He wouldn't let them hurt her again. Not in this lifetime.

He rose from his desk and went to her side, lifting her into his arms. When she moaned and snuggled in closer to his chest, she looked like an angel sleeping in his arms. His angel.

And he needed to protect her, even during the day.

He rushed her safely inside his secret chamber below the main house. He lowered her onto the bed and lay down next to her, stroking her hair back from her forehead.

She opened her eyes and gave him a drowsy smile. "You aren't going to leave me again, are you?"

"Not yet," Calisto whispered. "I need you to do something for me in the morning while I am away."

"What's that?" Kate caressed his chest. Then she yawned.

"Call your friend again, and move your things here. Stay with me, Kate."

She sat up. "You want me to move in?"

He nodded. "Very much so."

"Are you sure?"

"If I was not, I would not have asked."

Kate hesitated for a moment, her eyes searching his. "Ok... I'll call Edie and Lori in the morning."

"Good. I will have Bettina work here in my office to keep you company."

"If you haven't noticed yet, Betty is less than thrilled that I'm here. I don't think she's going to want to stay with me. Besides, I'd much rather go with you."

"If only such a thing were possible." He kissed her forehead. "But I do want someone here with you. You should not be alone while I am away."

"I'm a big girl." She fluttered her fingers over his stomach. "I know how to look after myself."

She didn't understand, and he couldn't tell her the truth, but he knew she was in danger. He grasped her hand and held it still. "For me. Please, I do not want you left alone."

She sighed with a resigned smile and laid back. "Ok, you win. Have Betty work over here. But I'm telling you, she's not going to be happy about it."

"Perhaps not, but she *will* do as I ask." He kissed her forehead and pulled away.

Kate frowned. "Do you have to go?"

"If I did not, I would stay with you."

"Then at least hold me until I fall asleep again..."

"Happily."

And within a few minutes, Kate drifted off to sleep. Calisto smiled and rose from the bed. He had arrangements to make before the sun came up.

CHAPTER TWENTY

A few days later, with a little help from Edie and Lori, Kate had all of her things moved into Calisto's house. In no time, she had his kitchen filled with food and was thrilled when he encouraged her to hang some pictures and put some of her things around his home. It warmed her heart to know he wanted this to feel like their home, together. Every night it became more real.

But the days were lonely.

Calisto was never home while the sun was up. Even on the weekends he worked until nightfall. Kate tried not to let it bother her, but the schedule drained her. At times she didn't recognize herself. Clingy and needy were never words she would have used to describe herself.

Betty continued to work out of the home office so Kate wouldn't be alone. Not that she was awake much during the day anymore anyway. Since she moved in with Calisto, her inner clock turned upside down. She fought to keep from sleeping at night because that was their only time together. She wasn't falling asleep until after four a.m. most nights.

She had no idea how Calisto could function on so little sleep. He went to bed with her in the wee hours of the morning and was up and gone before sunrise. Maybe he slept on the airplanes? She didn't know, but each day she slept more of it away, usually only waking up when her stomach felt queasy, which still affected her off and on. It wasn't bad enough to see a doctor, but it also wasn't going away.

On the bright side, even though they were into winter, her nightmare wasn't haunting her as much. Usually, fall and winter guaranteed her restless nights of fitful sleep filled with the nightmare of the woman being chased.

Since she moved in with Calisto, the dreams changed. The woman in the leather dress with the pendant tied around her neck still haunted her, but instead of the echo of hoof beats, she saw rocky beaches with waves breaking against the shore, secret kisses and warm breezes.

She still couldn't see their faces, but she didn't care. Anything was better than the running, and the woman begging for her life and the life of her unborn baby. For the first time in years, Kate slept soundly.

Except for nights like this one.

She had fallen asleep just after midnight, early for her new sleeping schedule. Around three in the morning, she woke up with an ache in her belly that demanded attention. With a soft sigh, Kate slipped from their bed, careful not to wake Calisto, and disappeared into the bathroom to purge whatever disagreed with her.

When she stopped retching, Kate wiped the perspiration from her brow. She felt like hell, but the wave of nausea finally receded. Yawning, Kate turned to go back to bed and nearly ran into Calisto's chest.

"You scared me," she said with a gasp, letting her eyes take in his naked body. Even just rolling out of bed in the middle of the night, he was stunning. His dark hair fell loosely around his muscular shoulders, and he leaned against the doorframe. The way he looked at her made her heart pound in spite of how sour her stomach felt. "Did I wake you?"

He gently hooked his fingers under her chin and tipped her head back until she looked him in the eye. "You are still sick... "

Kate shrugged. "It comes and goes. I feel much better now."

"You should see a doctor." He lifted her into his arms and carried her back to bed. "You have been sick for the past three weeks."

She nodded, sinking into the bed and closing her eyes as he laid her back down. "I will... It's just a pain since my doctor is in Reno. I need to figure out what to do about my job, too. School starts next week and I haven't told them if I'm taking a leave of absence." She sighed at his look of concern. "Okay, okay, no more changing the subject. Tomorrow I'll figure out a way to see a doctor here."

§

Calisto settled beside her in the bed, stroking her hair as she drifted off to sleep again, but his head ached with worry. She had been sick frequently during the past few weeks. He let her believe he was sleeping, since she had obviously been trying not to bother him when she got up.

But he listened, and he was concerned. The few times Kate had been ill while they were both awake at night, she made excuses about the food she ate, but it was more serious now. In the last week, he had heard her getting sick nearly every night before he left to go to his underground shelter. Mild concern grew into worry and fear.

If he could taste her blood he might be able to discern her malady. Whatever cancer or disease she carried would taint her bloodstream.

But he couldn't bite her. He couldn't risk exposing his immortal nature, or the chance that once he tasted her blood he would thirst for more. Protecting her from the truth of his existence, the truth about her past, and the monk who stalked them both, was difficult, but he couldn't protect her from her own body.

He shook off the thought as best he could, but he couldn't help wondering if souls were doomed to repeat their fate. Was a human soul's destiny predetermined?

The Old One promised that she would live again. He did not promise a long life. Did he know she would be destined to die young again?

Calisto clenched his jaw. He wouldn't allow destiny to repeat itself, stealing her from his arms before he was prepared to let her go.

Not this time.

He rubbed his forehead, wishing he could squeeze the thoughts out of his head. He looked down at her sleeping face and found resolve in his heart. She would see a doctor and whatever ailed her would be treated.

She would be well again. Kate was a fighter—she always had been—and they would get through whatever this was together.

He kissed her tenderly and rose from the bed without rousing her from her slumber. He had work to do before the night ended.

The face of the monk stalking him remained a mystery, and his frustration mounted. His only solace came from knowing Kate was never alone while he slept. Things were working out well with Betty running the foundation from his office. Kate told him they were even talking more.

Betty also had a new man in her life, Jose, and Calisto was relieved to hear it. She was a driven woman with career goals that sometimes made men shy away from her. It was good to hear she had finally found a man who respected her ambition instead of being intimidated by it.

But recently Kate mentioned Jose's company as well, a confession that made Calisto's hackles rise.

Betty hadn't told him she was bringing her new beau to his house. Calisto immediately ordered a background check on the man. Until he stopped the monk from the Fraternidad, he needed to stay alert.

Or at least that was the excuse he gave himself.

Deep down he felt the thorn of jealousy stabbing him whenever Kate talked about playing cards and walking down the beach with Jose. He should be glad she wasn't alone while he slept hidden deep in the earth. It was his burden to walk under the moon's light. It shouldn't be hers as well.

But he didn't have to like it.

After placing the final signature on the stack of paperwork Betty left for him to sign, Calisto opened the envelope marked confidential and pulled out Jose Mentigo's background check. He glanced over all of the information, looking for any inconsistencies, but he didn't find anything.

Jose had a bachelor's degree in business management and spent the last ten years in facilities management for the Marriott Corporation. No misdemeanors or felonies, and his credit was spotless. Calisto shredded the contents of the envelope. He didn't want Betty to think he was spying on her, but allowing mortals into his life was risky.

Background checks were a necessary precaution.

Calisto retired to his daylight sleeping chambers far beneath the sand. He cursed himself for being complacent about the threats he continued to receive from the monk he had yet to find. The last threat he received prompted him to search every chance he had. It was hard to leave Kate alone at night after he was away all day, but she fell asleep earlier each night.

He had to focus on her safety. She was his world now, but he couldn't keep ignoring the risk that existed for them both while the Fraternidad watched them. He needed to remedy the problem so they could share their lives together without the shadow of danger looming around them like a heavy fog.

Calisto laid down in the darkness, and as the sunlight stole the life from his body, he made the decision to hunt down the priest that stalked them.

It was time to end the game.

CHAPTER TWENTY-ONE

The drive from Torrey Pines to La Jolla passed by in a blur. Kate pulled into Calisto's driveway and turned off her car, but instead of going inside the main house, she walked around the side until she reached the sand.

She didn't want to see Betty and Jose yet. Right now, being alone was what she wanted. No, that wasn't completely true. What she wanted right now was Calisto.

Looking up at the lazy afternoon sun, she tried to put the test results out of her mind. Her life had changed so much over the span of a few weeks, and the visit to the doctor left her reeling.

He didn't prescribe any medication for her nausea, and he assured her that she wasn't dying. Kate was pregnant.

"Pregnant," she whispered into the soft sea breeze.

She still couldn't believe it. She knew she'd missed a couple of periods, but her menstrual cycle had never been anything close to regular. The thought hadn't even crossed her mind that her bouts of nausea could be a sign of pregnancy. Besides, she was on the pill.

Even birth control pills aren't a hundred percent. The doctor's voice echoed in her mind.

Obviously he was right, and now she was living proof of that slim statistic. Instead of a prescription to settle her stomach, the doctor sent her home with prenatal vitamins and a lot to think about.

Kate loved children. Less than two months ago, she thought she would have a family with Tom. But her relationship with Calisto was still new. They hadn't even discussed marriage, let alone a family. At this point, she wasn't sure he wanted children.

But sure or not, she was having a baby.

And it wasn't his.

Tears glistened on her cheeks while the strong breeze whipped her hair. For the first time since she met Calisto, that empty feeling welled up inside her again, washing over like the waves caressing the sand.

It felt like she'd already lost him. Kate wiped her tears away and stared at the horizon, waiting for the sun to set. It was crazy to feel this way. She knew Calisto well enough to know he would never blame her for this. She hadn't been unfaithful to anyone.

Maybe he'd be happy about raising a child with her.

She clung to the thought like a life preserver to keep from drowning in the sea of doubt. She wanted to be excited for the baby and impending motherhood, but somewhere inside a dark shadow lurked that she couldn't seem to shake. Until nightfall when Calisto came home, she was alone.

Alone and afraid.

§

Jose stood on the balcony, watching the wind slide its invisible fingers through Kate's hair, envying the softness it caressed. She looked like a fragile flower, small and alone on the sand, and yet she was so much more. Kate was his sacrificial lamb, his means to immortality. She would make his dream possible, and he supposed in some small way, he loved her for that. Maybe he would tell her later while he made her cry out in pain.

A cold grin curled his thin lips at the thought.

But he wasn't ready for the final battle yet. He had crafted a false identity, infiltrated Calisto's home and his closest confidants without any of them ever suspecting his true desires. He shared Betty's bed at night and Kate's company during the day, all the while leaving threats to keep Calisto distracted and defensive. Anything to keep his mind off of making Kate a Night Walker.

But he wasn't sure the threats were necessary anymore.

Kate talked about Calisto incessantly. It was painfully obvious she had no idea about his true nature. Perhaps the Church had been wrong all these years.

Maybe the Night Walker had no intention of making her a blood-drinker. Not that it mattered. The concerns of the Church had never really mattered to him in the slightest. What did matter was keeping her mortal long enough for him to gain victory over death.

Eternity would be his to claim.

Ever since he learned of the Night Walker's existence, when the Fraternidad del Fuego Santo took him into their fold, he dreamed of the day they would meet face to face. And tonight his dream would become reality. Betty had arranged for the four of them to go to dinner together. He already counted down the minutes until he looked Calisto Terana in the eyes.

With a smug smile, Jose disappeared inside the house. He retrieved his leather attaché case and pulled out a small package.

He entered the office. "Someone just dropped this off for Calisto."

Betty looked up from her paperwork with a smile. "You can leave it here on the desk. Calisto will find it when he gets home."

He laid the box on the corner of the desk with an inward grin. He wished he could see the Night Walker's face when he opened it.

"Who delivered this?"

The sound of Betty's voice shook him from his thoughts. His eyes cut up to meet her gaze.

He shrugged. "A delivery man."

Betty eyed the box. "Did you notice what he looked like?"

"No. Why? Is there something wrong?"

Betty glared at the box before looking up at him. "Not really, it's just that I signed for a little box like this a couple weeks ago and the courier was... I don't know how to describe it, really. He just seemed creepy, like he was a stalker or something. I tried to track down where the package came from so I could complain, but no one in town had record of making a delivery here."

"That is strange. I'm glad he hasn't been back," he said, masking his features with a look of mild concern, but inside he laughed. Betty considered herself a shrewd businesswoman, someone who could spot a fraud in a heartbeat. Yet she was fucking the creepy deliveryman, and she hadn't the slightest idea.

All he had to do was cut his hair, shave, and speak without a faked accent. Of course it wasn't really her fault. Betty had never met a man of his caliber before.

"Me, too." Betty glanced at the clock on the desk. "We'd better get going. I want to grab a shower and change before we meet Calisto and Kate for dinner."

He pulled Betty into his arms. "She doesn't hold a candle to your beauty."

"I don't know what you're talking about." Betty beamed at him.

"Yes, you do," he whispered, nipping at her bottom lip when he kissed her. "Not to worry, tonight will be perfect."

§

Kate was in the shower when Calisto returned. He smiled, holding a Romneya as he crossed the room. He tapped his knuckles against the door before entering.

"I missed you."

"You're home... " Kate called from inside the shower.

"*Si*. How was your day?"

Silence.

Calisto frowned, staring at her through the frosted glass of the shower door. "Kate?"

"I'm fine."

"Did you go to the doctor?"

She turned off the water and grabbed the towel. She wrapped herself before she opened the shower door.

"Yup. But I don't want to get into that right now. I've got to get ready. We're supposed to meet Betty and Jose for dinner in an hour."

Calisto watched her move from one place to another, dressing and brushing her hair and searching for shoes... And never once looking up at him.

Something was wrong.

As she passed by again, he pulled her into his arms, lifting her chin to meet his eyes. "Talk to me, Kate. Please... What did the doctor say?"

Her eyes welled with tears, and she shook her head, blinking them back. "I can't talk about it right now. If I do, we'll never make it to the restaurant in time." Her eyes searched his, pleading with him silently. "Please, Calisto. Just let it go for now."

His chest tightened with worry, but he found himself nodding and releasing her from his arms. He couldn't force her to tell him, and as much as he longed to search her mind for answers, he fought the temptation. He had to trust her judgment. Surely if her condition was serious the doctor would have admitted her to the hospital.

It was impossible not to watch her and wonder what her secret might be. He looked over her body for any outward sign of whatever might ail her. Her eyes looked red against her pale skin. She had been crying, and it stabbed at his heart. But for now she wanted space, so he would do his best to honor her wishes.

He went to his closet, quietly changing his clothes, listening to her brush her hair in the bathroom, his inhuman senses registering her every breath. He was no longer sure he would be able to maintain his precarious control over his emotions during dinner.

"We should cancel the dinner tonight." He buttoned the cuffs of his long-sleeved shirt.

"It's too late to cancel now," Kate said, still searching for her shoes. "Besides we need to eat."

"Whatever it is, we can face it together."

Her shoe search halted for a moment, and he could see a sigh escape her.

"I hope so." She looked over at him with a weak smile. "Let's just try to forget about it for now and have a nice dinner together, okay?"

"I will do my best." Calisto turned back to slide his jacket off of the hanger. "That is all I can offer you."

He adjusted his coat. "I am going to check my desk upstairs while you finish getting ready." He leaned in close and kissed her cheek tenderly. "I love you, Kate."

And with that he left. He needed to clear his head and think. Allowing himself to move quickly, he went up the stairs and entered the main house. When he reached his office, he froze. An unmarked package sat on the edge of his desk.

Yet another reason he should skip the infernal dinner date, but Kate had made it clear she wanted to go. As much as he wanted to cancel, he could refuse her nothing.

He went to his desk, tearing open the plain brown box and reaching inside. What he pulled out of the box made his heart stop. Dangling at the end of Calisto's fingertips was a pair of Kate's white silk panties, stained and reeking of semen. Red ink covered the fabric. On the front it read simply, *Soon she will know me.* The rest of the fabric was covered inside and out with the words *Again and again and again* scrawled all over the silk in a frenzied script of red ink.

He shoved the underwear back into the box. This was no monk. This was a madman. And he was after Kate.

"Are you ready to go?"

Calisto looked up as Kate walked into his office. She had the flower he brought for her tucked behind her ear, and all at once he realized he was trapped. She was just as innocent to what lay in store for her now as she had been over 200 years ago. Again her life was threatened, and not because of her own doing, but simply because she loved him.

While he wanted to find the sick monk and kill him slowly and painfully, it was clear that he couldn't leave Kate's side, not even for a second. Not now.

Fate was attempting to repeat itself, and it seemed they were once again set on a collision course with tragedy. This time he would change the end of their story, or die trying.

If dying were still an option for him anymore.

He took her hand and kissed her knuckles tenderly, masking the dread that festered inside of him. "You look incredible."

She moved into his arms, and he closed his eyes, holding her tight. It had been centuries since he'd experienced fear. He had almost forgotten what it felt like.

He remembered now.

CHAPTER TWENTY-TWO

Jose had waited for years for this moment, to confront the immortal Night Walker. Now, he sat across the table from him talking about mundane topics such as the upcoming opera season and whether or not the San Diego Symphony would be able to maintain paying union wages.

He participated in the casual conversation, while still maintaining the constant drone in the back of his mind, reciting the ancient chant that had been drilled into his memory. They had prepared him to watch the Night Walker from a distance, not to dine with him at the same table, but Jose wasn't worried.

Even if Calisto uncovered his true thoughts and identity, he felt confident he wouldn't be harmed. The public place and the women who shared their table protected him. He and Betty were lovers, and now Kate considered him a friend. Both women would think Calisto was a monster if he suddenly attacked him.

And once the sun came up, the Night Walker would be helpless to stop him.

Perfect. Tonight, everything would change.

Amidst the conversation that surrounded him, Jose analyzed Calisto's behavior and smiled inwardly. The box he left had obviously shaken the Night Walker. He seemed distant, and his gaze tracked every new patron, examining them. Each person became a suspect.

Jose chuckled at the irony playing out before him. While Calisto sat preoccupied with his search for danger, he never suspected he dined with his foe. Calisto had no idea the man he sought sat no more than three feet away from him.

And seeing the haunted gaze in the Night Walker's eyes, as though Kate was already gone, only sweetened Jose's victory.

§

Calisto watched Kate sip her water. He'd watched everything tonight. He couldn't help it. What if the monk spied on them right now, plotting to harm her? Every person who entered the restaurant drew his attention as he lightly scanned their thoughts for any sign they were looking for him, or for Kate. Paranoia threatened to take over, but it was difficult to control it when he knew someone wanted to hurt her. He couldn't concentrate on anything, and his head throbbed with worry.

"Calisto?"

He blinked when Kate's hand brushed up his thigh.

"Did you hear a word I just said?" She raised her eyebrows and smiled, but tight lines rimmed her mouth.

"Forgive me." He rested his hand over hers.

He ached to peer into her mind and know what ailed her, but he wouldn't. He had to trust her. It would be far too tempting to dig deeper into her mind, to invade her privacy on such a personal level. He would never forgive himself for such a breach of her trust.

He patted her hand. "I was too lost in your beauty to hear the words you spoke."

She laughed, and for a moment, her tense shoulders relaxed.

"You find this funny?"

"That was a fine piece of flattery to cover up the fact you weren't listening to a single word I said." Kate chuckled.

"Am I forgiven?"

"You are if you pay the bill." Kate handed the small leather binder to him with a grin. "I thanked you for dinner and said I'd never been here before."

Calisto took the check from her. "I am glad you enjoyed it."

His words died away as his gaze shifted to the man sitting across the table from him. Was Jose glaring at him?

Calisto stared at the other man as he gently reached into Jose's mind and... The chant.

The same chant the last Spanish priest had used to mask his thoughts.

Jose knew the chant.

Rage tore through Calisto. The threat he had searched for sat at his own table, and he had been too distracted with worry to notice. Calisto ground his teeth with pent-up fury, his cold stare cutting into his adversary.

This man had been in his house with Kate nearly every day. Jose's mouth curved into a hateful smirk. Calisto wanted to kill him right where he sat. He rose from his chair suddenly, fighting to keep his voice down. "Please excuse us, ladies. Jose and I need to talk."

"We do?" Jose wore a clever mask of surprise.

"*Si*," Calisto practically growled. "Come."

Jose politely smiled at Kate and placed a soft kiss to Betty's cheek. "I will be right back."

Calisto followed Jose, struggling to keep himself from ripping Jose's heart out. He needed to wait until they were alone, then he would tear the arrogant bastard apart piece by miserable piece.

Jose stopped once they reached the main entry of the restaurant. "You don't really think I would be stupid enough to be alone with you, do you?"

Calisto fought to keep his eyes from glowing red with hatred. "Do you think a crowd of people can protect you after all you have done? If so, then you have greatly underestimated who you are dealing with."

"I don't agree. In fact, you disappoint me. You're hardly the foe I dreamed you might be. I have been with *your* women, in *your* house many times. I could have raped and killed them both any time I wished."

Calisto's fists tightened at his sides as he battled to cage his fury. "If that were true, then what stopped you?"

"They are not what I want, but they do provide me with a way to get it."

"I know what you want, and the Fraternidad is wrong. I have no intention of cursing Kate with an eternal existence. I will not make her a Night Walker. There is no reason for them to interfere."

Jose laughed and shook his head. His twisted smile sent chills through Calisto. "Do you think I care what the Fraternidad wants? They were simply a means to get what I desire. The Church's limited view of what could be gained is almost as pitiful as your own. You could be a god, worshipped, have money and power, and yet you sit in your office and pretend that you're a mortal man. You live a pathetic existence when you could have the world groveling at your feet."

"You're mad." Calisto grabbed the collar of Jose's jacket, jerking him up close. A deep growl emanated from Calisto's chest. He reached out with his mind, seeking to coax Jose to come outside with him, but the constant repetitive chant kept the madman immune, blocking Calisto's silent suggestions.

"Yes, why not kill me right here in front of all these witnesses? And don't forget Betty and Kate are waiting for me to return. What will they think of you when you have my blood on your hands? I am their friend. You'll be the madman, not me." He narrowed his eyes. "Now put me down."

Calisto threw him back, sickened at how impotent he felt. "What is it you want from me?"

Jose wet his lips like a hungry wolf. "I want immortality."

Calisto clenched his hands into fists. "Impossible."

"Then you will lose her again. I will take Kate's life while you sleep. I'll kill her slowly too, enjoy every soft whimper of pain. But first I'll enjoy her moans when I taste her sweet flesh and remind her what being with a real hot-blooded man is—"

Calisto cut him off, his fingers tightening around Jose's throat. He pinned the wiry man to the wall. The monk clawed at him, struggling to break free.

He couldn't kill Jose here, with so many witnesses.

But he would kill him.

Calisto leaned in close to his ear and growled, "I will find you, Jose. I will hunt you down and slaughter you. No one will ever find your body and the women will never know. This is not a threat, it is my solemn vow."

He freed Jose from his grip, watching the other man cough as the color returned to his skin.

"You think it will be so easy to rid yourself of me?" Jose rasped, gasping for air.

A cold, deadly smile pulled at Calisto's mouth. "Yes."

Calisto spun around and made his way back to their table. He was finished listening to the madman from the Fraternidad. He needed to get Kate out of there, now. He could deal with Jose once he knew she was out of harm's reach.

"Thank you for your company tonight, Bettina," Calisto offered Kate his hand. "Forgive me, but I have some pressing business to attend to, and we really must be going."

Kate took his hand and stood, sliding her arms into her coat when Calisto held it up for her. "Goodnight Betty. Please let Jose know that we enjoyed his company."

Before she could say anything else, Calisto led her away. He considered warning Betty about Jose, but harming her would get him no closer to immortality. His assistant wasn't the monk's target. The woman on his arm was.

And he needed to get her as far away as possible.

Once they were outside, Kate tugged at his hand. "Calisto, stop." She steadied herself, catching her breath. "What's going on?"

He scanned the parking lot for Jose. "We need to talk. But not here. Far away from here."

"Is this about the doctor appointment today?"

His heart pounded with urgency. Jose's scent still lingered on the night wind.

"Yes, we do need to talk about that. I am concerned about you, for many reasons."

She smiled and stepped closer. "I know. I'm sorry I made you wait, but it's not something I wanted to drop in your lap right before dinner. Come on, let's go home. We can walk on the beach and talk."

§

The monsignor wrung his gnarled, spotted hands in front of the fire. He never got warm enough anymore. His joints ached with arthritis, and his muscles felt atrophied after so many hours on his knees in prayer.

But prayer remained essential, especially now.

Something had gone wrong with Brother Mentigo in America. He wasn't sure what happened just yet, but he would find out personally. He couldn't in good conscience send another young monk to his death.

This time, he would make the journey himself, and if his day came to meet the Lord, let it be while protecting the world from the threat of another blood-drinker.

But he hoped it would not come to that. He hoped once he arrived in San Diego, he would find Brother Mentigo alive and well, and all of the suspicion around his disappearance would be a mistake.

He hadn't received a message of any kind from Brother Mentigo in over three weeks. The monsignor contacted the Mission de Alcala and found that they hadn't seen or heard from him either. His apartment stood empty, as if he simply vanished. Or he was dead. But until they had confirmation of the monk's passing, the monsignor chose to hope for the best.

"How many more must die, Juan?"

The monsignor smiled, hearing the familiar shuffling of feet and the rhythmic thud of a cane. He turned to see his old friend Father Doñas standing in the open archway that led into his chamber.

The ailing monk had acted as the leader of the Fraternidad del Fuego Santo for nearly forty years until ten years ago, when his failing health forced him to give up some of his responsibilities. They had been friends for decades, and Father Doñas was probably the only person left in this world who still called the monsignor by his first name.

"Has word of my trip to America already reached you?"

"It has," Father Doñas said, toddling closer. "And I have come to talk you out of going."

"Then you wasted your time. This is something I must do."

"You realize that he is probably already dead. Brother Mentigo was often a slave to his own pride. He may have gotten too close to the Night Walker and paid for his arrogance with his life. Nothing you do now can bring him back."

"That may be true, but I won't send another monk from our Fraternidad to die for this cause."

"That is the first bit of wisdom to leave your lips, Juan." Father Doñas sat in a bare wooden chair against the wall. "The years have proven that we cannot control the Night Walker. Maybe it is not our place to do so."

"Are you suggesting we simply turn the other cheek and knowingly allow him to unleash another abomination into the world?"

"I am suggesting that if it is meant to be, then we have no power to change it."

"So we let Satan's minions take over the night without trying to stop them?"

Father Doñas sighed. "You know the old story as well as I do, Juan. We both know he was one of us. How can you be so certain that he now serves Satan?"

The monsignor shook his head in frustration. "Our Lord would never condone feeding on the blood of his children so that one man can achieve immortal life. He kills to live."

"As do the lions and wolves, and yet they are still creatures of God."

"But they do not answer to sin as we do."

Father Doñas shrugged. "And the Night Walker is no longer one of us. Who are we to say his race is ruled by Satan? Perhaps our Lord has a greater plan in store that we cannot see, my friend. We have done all that we can in this matter. The rest should remain in God's hands."

The monsignor shook his head, jaw tight with frustration. "I will not waste any more time debating this with you, Father. Until I know that I have done all I can to prevent this evil from spreading, I refuse to sit back and simply watch it happen." He brushed by the elder priest. "I will be in America in the morning."

CHAPTER TWENTY-THREE

The sea breeze blew through Kate's hair as they walked together hand in hand. Seeing the waves washing up and pooling around her ankles made the danger that loomed around them seem miles away. Gradually, the thick mist of the marine layer enclosed them in its heavy embrace, and Calisto could wait no longer.

In a few hours the sun would rise and he would be powerless to protect her. The more he pondered his options, the more his rage and bitterness smoldered. Fate was cruel to allow them to find one another again, only to back him into a corner that left him no happy endings.

He needed to get Kate to safety, somewhere far from Jose, before the sun came up. She wouldn't want to go, but somehow he had to convince her. And time was running out.

"We need to talk, Kate."

"I know." She shook her head. "I'm sorry I didn't tell you before, but I knew we wouldn't have time to discuss it before dinner."

"Is it serious? Are you sick?"

"No nothing like that. But it was a shock. It *is* a shock."

Calisto stopped walking and pulled her close, lifting her chin to meet his gaze. "Just tell me."

"I'm pregnant."

His strength drained from his legs and for a moment, Calisto wasn't sure he could stay on his feet. Kate was with child just as Tala had been before she was murdered.

It was happening all over again.

But this couldn't be his child. Not this time. When he gave up his humanity he also gave up his ability to reproduce as a mortal man.

Perhaps this was her one chance, a slight change in her destiny.

Then he realized what he had to do. In order to save her, he would have to hurt her.

The situation spiraled out of his control. He needed to get Kate as far away as possible while he hunted Jose. With the threat behind him, he could find her again.

Kate might hate him, but she and her child would live. He didn't want to do this, but he had no other option. "This child you are carrying. It is not mine."

She pressed her lips together and shook her head. "I wish it was. But we could raise it together. Tom doesn't have to know. We haven't talked about having a family, but I love you. We can make this work."

"I am sorry, Kate. This is asking too much."

Her eyes welled with tears, and Calisto struggled to keep himself from pulling her into his arms. He would rather walk into the sun than be forced to see her hurt.

"You should go to him," he whispered. "You deserve a family."

"I can't go back there and pretend none of this happened. Please don't do this." A tear spilled down her cheek.

Each one of her tears burned him worse than acid. Instead of walking away from him, she reached up to caress his cool cheek, making it almost impossible for him to continue. But he had to.

Let her live long enough to hate him.

Her eyes searched his and he fought the unbearable urge to hold her in his arms and comfort her. "Do not make this harder than it already is."

"I don't understand." Her voice wavered, and he steeled his heart, reminding himself that he couldn't allow history to repeat itself. "How can you just send me away like this? I don't care who the biological father is. I love you, Calisto. You can be the father of my child."

Dear God, how her words ripped at his soul. The pleading in her gaze made him loathe himself even further, especially when he lied to her. "I do not want to be the father of your child. My life has no room for a family." He bit back the emotions that churned inside of him.

"So we make room." She dropped her hand away from his face.

Calisto's jaw clenched. "I am truly sorry, Kate. I love you, but you should do what is best for your baby."

"And you think running back to Tom is best?" She wiped at her tears, her cheeks flushing with color. "I can't turn my feelings on and off like you."

"My feelings have not changed, but the situation has." He sighed and turned to lead her back toward the house.

But she didn't move. Instead, she stood her ground, staring up at him in disbelief. "So this amazing connection we had, it was all a lie?"

He stared out at the ocean. "No. But it *is* over."

He didn't want to think about Kate with another man, touching her, hearing her laugh, seeing her smile, but he saw no other way to keep her safe. The sun would rise soon, Jose would come for her, and he would be unable to protect her.

He didn't look into her eyes. He knew if he did, he would hold her and never let her go. "Go home, Kate. Tonight. Be with the father of your child. Live a happy life."

"You really expect me to be happy without you?" she whispered.

He swallowed hard. Managing a soft, controlled tone he said, "Yes, I do. You are an amazing woman, and you will be an incredible mother."

§

Kate stared at him in disbelief. He was sending her away. Just like that. Dismissing her like he never needed her around to begin with. It hurt so badly she couldn't breathe. Her heart had just been torn in two pieces.

She shook her head. "Don't patronize me, ok? If I were so amazing, I doubt you'd be so anxious to put me on the next plane out of San Diego."

She walked away, toward the house, keeping her head up and hoping he wouldn't see the tears flowing down her cheeks again. He didn't deserve her tears, but she wept just the same. It wasn't until she reached the stairs to go up to the main house that she turned around to face him, blazing with hurt and betrayal.

"You promised me that whatever it was, we'd face it together."

"Not this," he said with downcast eyes.

He reached for her hand, but she yanked it away from him. "Don't touch me."

"I am so sorry."

"No, you're not." She stifled a sob when her voice hitched. "You're far from sorry. You're just a rich bastard who wants things his own way. I should've known. But no, I'm such an idiot! I actually believed you loved me. I bought in to all your noble romantic crap right from the start. But you know what? You're not noble. You're a coward, and you're running away when I need you the most."

She could see the hurt in his eyes, and for a moment she almost regretted her harsh words. But only for a moment. She wanted him to hurt, to feel some of the pain she endured. How could he do this to her?

"I do love you."

He never saw the slap coming, and the sting it left behind went far deeper than his skin. Calisto watched her run up the steps and disappear inside of the main house. He climbed after her. He needed to make the calls to arrange for her shuttle to the airport and her plane ticket back to Reno.

Kate would be far from San Diego by the time the sun came up.

CHAPTER TWENTY-FOUR

Her hair draped all over him. He groaned. Jose despised waking up in the morning to find Betty coiled around him like some sort of living security blanket. Soon she would respect him and pay him the homage he deserved. Because soon, he would be immortal.

He would be a god.

Jose shoved Betty off of him and got out of the bed with a smug grin. Today would be his last day of sunlight. His meeting with Calisto the previous night had been a triumph. He bested the Night Walker, and the sweet taste of it still lingered in his mouth. Seeing the fury and hatred burn in Calisto's eyes, and knowing that the immortal wanted to kill him but couldn't, was the crowning moment of his victory.

And today, Kate would learn she had made friends with the wrong man.

He had no intention of leaving now. No, today their final battle would begin, and capturing Kate would be the key. Once he had a knife pressed against her soft, mortal throat, Calisto would give him whatever he wanted, even immortality, in order to save her.

Love made him weak.

Jose showered and dressed quietly, not wanting to wake the blonde on the bed. Betty had served her purpose, and pleasured him many times in the process, but her usefulness had come to an end.

Taking his bag, Jose opened the door and stepped out. The warm morning sun washed over him, bathing him in its light as he slid his sunglasses in place and went to his car. Kate Bradley would be his, and immortality would follow once the sun dipped below the horizon.

What a beautiful day.

§

Kate disembarked the plane, bleary-eyed and brokenhearted. Purse in hand, she made her way through the sea of business travelers and tourists to the baggage claim area.

She felt like hell. Mentally, physically, just completely drained. She'd cried all night, or what was left of it after she left Calisto's home. She left without a parting kiss good-bye, no "I'll miss you," nothing. And what ate at her now, was that the last time she touched Calisto had been in anger. Her slap was the last time she would ever touch him.

Don't think about it, she scolded. *Not now.*

But no matter what she did, her thoughts ended up right back on the beach with Calisto. When her luggage came around on the baggage carousel, tears slipped down her cheeks. Calisto's leather bag with wheels. He sent her with it so she wouldn't have to carry a bag in her "condition."

Why did he have to care at all? It would be so much easier to hate him if he'd been cruel.

Instead, he wished her happiness and told her she would be a good mother.

Kate unlocked the handle and slid it out to full length, wiping her tears as she pulled the suitcase behind her through the busy airport. None of this made sense. He cared about her, she could see it in his eyes, and yet he packed her up and sent her away the second she told him about the pregnancy. No discussion, end of story, she was out of his life like an unwanted discard left on the corner. She'd never known a greater pain.

Until a terrible sensation stabbed through her stomach.

Her bag fell, the metal handle clanking against the concrete terminal floor as it hit the ground. Kate sank to her knees, wincing in pain. She could hear people shouting around her, but couldn't understand the words they said.

God it hurt... Two men helped her to a nearby bench. She knew she should thank them, but she couldn't find the words.

Kate wept with her arms wrapped tightly around her middle, rocking on the bench. Would someone call an ambulance? She might need one. People gathered around her, watching like buzzards waiting for the kill, but she hardly noticed.

She didn't care about anything except making the pain stop. It felt like a knife slowly twisted into her lower abdomen, cutting through her abdominal muscles layer by layer. And then she noticed the blood trickling out from under her skirt.

"Oh God! Someone help me, please... " she cried, fearing the worst for her unborn baby.

The blood flow that started slowly down the inside of her leg quickly became a rush of fluid. It pooled around her until she had to struggle to stay alert. Sirens rang out in the distance, but they seemed so far away.

A wave of dizziness washed over her as her body hemorrhaged. Kate tried to lower her head and take deep breaths, hoping it would help to ease the lightheadedness. She pulled air into her lungs, but it wasn't helping. The sight of all the blood made her nauseous, and suddenly she lost her balance. She couldn't sit up anymore. Before she could scream, she fell.

The impact against the cold concrete floor of the airport terminal stole the air from her lungs. A loud, hollow thud echoed inside of her head, answered by a blinding burst of throbbing pain. It felt as though she'd fallen from the top of a building, but it couldn't have been far from the bench to the floor. She hoped it hadn't been enough to crack her skull.

Kate fought to stay awake, to tell them to save her baby, but the paramedics arrived and covered her face with a mask of oxygen before she could articulate a sound.

They all talked around her instead of to her, as if she weren't even there. Kate closed her eyes on the bloody scene before her, trying to block out the pain as the chorus of strange voices echoed around her.

"Please stay back... "

"Station 5 we have paramedics here with a woman down... "

"Pressure's 80 over 50... "

"Pulse is weak, 120 per minute... "

"Start an IV of saline... "

Suddenly, her blanket of darkness brightened when a paramedic with the deep voice lifted her eyelids, shining a light over each pupil. He lifted the oxygen mask and asked, "Ma'am, can you tell me your name?"

"Kate... " she gasped softly. "Kate Bradley."

"Hang in there. We're taking you to the hospital, all right?"

She nodded as he replaced the oxygen and they lifted the gurney to take her out. She watched the lights pass overhead and whispered a prayer for her unborn baby. Then her vision blurred, and Kate embraced the darkness that lured her in, promising an end to the pain.

§

Jose's heart pounded in his ears as he hurried down the stairs. Kate was gone.

He'd wasted most of the day waiting for her at Calisto's house before he finally decided to go up to the master bedroom to look for her. He found the drawers and closets empty, and now at nearly three o'clock in the afternoon, he only had two, maybe three more hours before the Night Walker would be awake and searching for him.

"Fuck," Jose said to himself.

He needed Kate to make all of the pieces of his conquest fall into place. Without her, he had nothing to force the Night Walker to give him what he wanted. Slamming his hands against the countertop, he turned and stormed out of the house.

He had to find Betty. She was his only way out of this mess now. If he stayed with her at all times, Calisto wouldn't touch him. Attacking him with Betty nearby would be too risky for the Night Walker. Jose doubted Calisto would expose his true nature to her. He had lived among mortals, masquerading as one of them for far too long to give up the charade now.

Staying in San Diego was a risk, but a calculated risk, and he could live with that. He didn't have the time, or the desire, to flee the city. He needed to wait until Kate returned, or at least until he learned where she had gone.

More than likely Calisto hid her away somewhere. Perhaps he would be a worthy adversary after all. Jose wondered how the Night Walker convinced her she was in danger without revealing too much of the past. Or had he confessed?

She had to be nearby. But where?

Jose tightened his grip on the steering wheel, fighting to keep control over his growing frustration. Tonight should have been his moment of triumph, yet now he found himself retreating into hiding. It pissed him off, and the slut would pay for forcing him to run back to Betty. When he found Kate Bradley again, he would enjoy hurting her.

That thought alone brought a smile.

Chapter Twenty-Five

Kate stood on the beach, watching the couple from her dreams walk hand in hand into the water while the waves splashed up their legs, coaxing them deeper into the salted Pacific Ocean. The sun felt warm on her skin. The pain was gone, like it had been a bad dream...

But this was the dream, wasn't it? The pain had been real... Yes, she reminded herself. This is the dream. She'd seen this beach before.

The jasmine perfume of the Romneya blossom woke her senses, teasing her to remain under the dream's spell. She smiled, watching the couple dance. The man in black taught the woman with dark hair to waltz as the tide swirled around their calves.

They spun together to the music of the sea, slowing until finally their lips met in a soft tender kiss, and as they drew back, Kate could suddenly see through the woman's eyes and hear through her ears. And what she saw jolted her from the dream back into the cold darkness of reality.

"Gregorio," she whispered.

"Kate? Can you hear me?"

Her arms and legs felt weak and heavy. She shivered, her entire body screaming for warmth. The sharp pain she'd felt at the airport had been replaced by a throbbing, empty ache. Forcing her eyes open,

Kate blinked, wincing at the light that filled her room.

"Where am I?"

"St. Mary's Hospital." The large nurse gave her an empathetic smile as she took Kate's blood pressure. "You'll be feeling better in no time, don't you worry. I'm going to call the doctor and let him know you're awake. I'll be right back."

Kate gave her a drowsy nod, looking up at the IV stand dripping clear fluid into her veins.

"Wait!" She turned her head to find the nurse standing in the doorway. "Is my baby all right?"

"The doctor will explain everything, okay? You just rest and he'll be right in."

Kate's eyes filled with tears as the swishing sound of the nurse's polyester pants legs rubbing together faded and finally died away when she turned the corner. Her hands moved down to cover her lower abdomen, over the womb she knew was empty.

She didn't need the doctor to tell her. She remembered seeing the blood, so much blood. She couldn't still be pregnant, not after that.

The nurse came back with another blanket for her, explaining that the doctor would be in soon. After jotting a few notes on her chart, she disappeared through the door again leaving Kate with the now familiar sound of swishing polyester pants.

She looked out the window, up at the moon, and sighed. Life used to be so simple. She saw no point in telling Tom about the pregnancy. What did she expect him to say?

And she couldn't go back to Calisto after the way he treated her.

She was alone. As much as she hated that word, perhaps it was for the best.

Her eyes drifted closed again, weighed down by exhaustion, when a single thought pierced through the hazy fog of her mind.

Calisto. He was the man in black. It was his face she had seen through the woman's eyes in her dream. She was sure of it. But his name was wrong. The woman had called him another name.

Kate struggled to remember, to pull the name from her tired, aching head. It didn't matter anyway. It was just a dream. Calisto's face probably showed up because she missed him.

Her breath hitched. She settled back against the sterile pillow, closing her exhausted eyes. The clinical smell of antibacterial cleanser and rubbing alcohol made her uneasy, not to mention the IV stand that resembled some sort of emaciated sentry standing at attention at the head of her bed. She just wanted to go home.

But where was home?

§

The sun sank below the horizon. Calisto's chest rose, drawing in a slow breath, while the night restored life to his ageless body. His chest felt tight, and no amount of air seemed to loosen the constriction.

Kate wouldn't be waiting for him tonight.

And Jose would pay dearly for the pain he caused.

Heaving a sigh, Calisto rose from his resting place and made his way into his small bedroom chamber below the main house. Her scent lingered everywhere, haunting him, daring him to go look for her.

Pulling his hair back from his face, he paced the room in frustration. He wasn't going after her this time. He tried to keep Tala with him centuries before, and it had ended in her rape and murder. He would not let Kate suffer the same fate. Sending her away was the only way to keep her safe.

And she was pregnant.

Kate deserved to have a family and live the life she always dreamed for herself. She wasn't Tala anymore. Kate loved teaching, and laughing, eating lunch with her girlfriends. He'd only met Lori and Edie once, but he knew from Kate's stories they were dear to her, and they loved her. She had a wonderful life full of hope and sunshine.

She didn't deserve the darkness that came with his love or his blood.

And that was exactly what his blood promised. Darkness.

Memories of the night long ago when he unknowingly made another immortal filled his head. A Russian fur trader named Lukas. Calisto could still remember the hatred in the young man's eyes when he realized he hungered for living blood.

Calisto hadn't meant to make Lukas a Night Walker. He'd tried to save his life, not damn him for eternity.

He knew very little about his own conversion. The Old One who turned him into a healer, a Night Walker, had done so after first drowning him in Peyote smoke. His mind had been so polluted with visions, he couldn't be certain what was real versus merely illusion.

He remembered drinking from a clay goblet, but he never knew what liquid the cup held. It had burned his mouth and throat, while at the same time his body ached for more. He never imagined he swallowed blood from the Old One's veins. His white-haired maker disappeared before he ever thought to ask.

Lukas' transformation was accidental, but it didn't matter. The young fur trader never forgave him. He went insane with bloodlust, and for a time Calisto had hunted him, planning to bind him to a tree to wait for the sunrise, but after the bloody slaughter of an entire family, the young man vanished.

As the years passed, Calisto assumed the other man had ended his own existence.

That night, Calisto learned his blood carried the curse of the Night Walker race. The Old One's blood filled the goblet the night he changed. He knew that now.

Since that the fur trader's disappearance, Calisto vowed he would never make another Night Walker.

The power that came with the Night Walker blood required control and heavy responsibilities too great to entrust to another. Calisto would never forgive himself if he unknowingly created a monster and unleashed it into the beautiful mortal world he cherished so deeply.

Therefore, Jose's lust for immortal blood would go forever unsatisfied.

But forever would not be long for the monk. Calisto would see to that. And he would enjoy killing him, watching the sick, bitter life fade from his hateful eyes. It would not bring Kate back into his arms, but it might help to relieve some of his pain and frustration over losing her.

He clenched his fist and stood. Silence was his only companion now. It wrapped its arms around him, suffocating him until he thought he might scream with rage. It wasn't supposed to end this way. But fate denied them happiness again, just as she had before.

Quietly, he pulled Kate's portrait from under the bed and removed the sheet. He hung it on the wall in its rightful place in his chamber. Her beauty took his breath away, even when it was only oils on a canvas.

Brushing his fingers along the bottom of the frame, his whisper seemed to echo in the thick silence of his room. "I will always love you, Kate."

Grabbing his leather jacket, Calisto disappeared into the night in search of Jose Mentigo, and revenge.

§

Jose wrapped his arm loosely around Betty's shoulder just the way she liked it. He'd kissed her ass all evening to get her to take him back after his sudden disappearance this morning, and it drove him insane.

Swallowing his pride left a dry, bitter taste in his mouth.

He glared at her, watching her giggle at the movie on the television. He wanted to knock the smile from her lips, and blacken her eyes, until she begged him for mercy. Until she learned to show him the proper respect, no, that wasn't nearly enough. He wanted to beat her until she feared him. He fought to cage the fury smoldering inside of him.

Right now, he needed Betty at all times. She stood as his human shield against his inhuman foe.

"Baby, can you get me a Diet Coke from the fridge?" She tilted her head back to smile up at him.

Jose ground his teeth together, barely controlling the urge to yank her head back and rip her throat out. And he hated being called such an asinine pet name. Baby. Fuck.

He got up with a cold nod and went into her kitchen, grinning when he saw the butcher block full of knives. Wouldn't she be surprised if he came back with one of those instead? He smirked at the thought and opened the refrigerator. He didn't imagine she would call him "Baby" if he were holding a knife to her throat.

His fingers closed around the cold aluminum can when a chill shot down his spine. He felt like he was being watched. Clutching the soda tighter, Jose slowly turned around, half-expecting to find someone right behind him. But the kitchen was empty. He stepped closer to the sink, staring out through the window into the night.

Something watched him out there, he felt it.

Jose reached for the switch and turned out the light. The instant that darkness surrounded him, he took in his surroundings. The can of Diet Coke slipped from his paralyzed fingers. Right outside the window a raven, an enormous raven, hovered in the night sky, staring at him.

Adrenaline pumped through Jose's bloodstream as he fumbled to flip the light switch back on. The thing outside was much too large for a raven. And something about its eyes, the way it glared at him through the glass, unsettled him. Jose snatched the Diet Coke from the sink where he'd dropped it and hurried back into the room with Betty.

"Thanks, baby," she murmured, taking the soda without so much as looking at him.

Jose hardly noticed. He couldn't look away from the sliding glass door, from the darkness beyond the glass. The moving shadow still hovered outside, watching him. He struggled to control the fear, telling himself it was probably some sort of large bat. But bats were rare animals in this beach community, and a bat with an eight-foot wingspan would be unheard of.

And yet, if he turned off the lights... A hissing noise and a sudden splash of cold liquid snapped him out of his thoughts.

"Jesus Christ! Damnit, Jose, did you shake this up?"

Between Betty's sudden outburst and the cold spray of the Diet Coke dousing them both when she cracked open the can, Jose leapt up from the sofa, barely stifling a gasp.

"I might have dropped it once," he shot back.

"Shit... I'm going to have to soak this blouse or it'll be ruined."

She gave him an openly irritated sigh and disappeared down the hallway.

He watched her walk away with a hateful stare, but when his gaze shot back to the sliding glass door, his pulse raced so fast he felt light-headed.

Let me in, Jose. The Night Walker whispered into his mind.

The chant. Jose fumbled, trying to get his silent mantra going as he fought the power of the Night Walker's hypnotic suggestion.

Jose shook his head slowly, reaching inside of his shirt to withdraw his gold crucifix pendant. He watched in horror as the raven landed on the balcony. The air around the bird churned, rippling with electricity while the bird mutated back into a man.

Calisto smirked at Jose and reached for the sliding glass door. Jose lunged to lock the door, but the Night Walker was too fast. The door opened and Jose jumped back, holding up his cross like a talisman.

"Did you really believe I needed an invitation to come in?" Calisto asked with a bitter, cold stare. "I can go wherever I please, and you can put your crucifix away. Nothing can protect you now."

Jose hoped he sounded more confident than he felt. "You are wrong. Betty would never forgive you for harming me. She would expose you for the blood-drinking monster that you are. You would not risk that. You enjoy your life in this world far too much to jeopardize it."

"Perhaps. But what if I showed her all of the little messages and photos you have been leaving behind for me to find over the past few weeks? Would she still care for you then, Jose?"

"I would deny it. You have no proof they're from me, and she would take my word over yours."

"Can you be certain of that? She has known me far longer than you. And I can convince her of anything I wish, if I choose to do so."

"You have not used mind control on her before. You won't use it now." Jose glanced down the hall hoping he might see Betty return.

Calisto shook his head with a cold smirk as he circled around Jose, walking with his hands clasped behind his back. "Are you really so arrogant? You know nothing of what I can and cannot do."

"I know more than most," Jose said, wrestling to bury his fear and bolster his confidence. His eyes followed the predator that circled him.

"Then you must know that I am going to kill you."

"I know you would like to, but I also know you still cling to some sort of human decency, and that is your weakness. You won't kill me here under Betty's roof, and I won't leave it, so the way I see it, I am perfectly safe."

Calisto rushed him, knocking the air from Jose's lungs as they both fell to the floor.

"Jose?" Betty called. "What's going on out there?"

Calisto's eyes glowed a dark crimson and without conscious effort, Jose found himself calling back, "Everything is fine, I'm just cleaning up."

He stared up at Calisto's smug smile, his heart pounding in his ears as the realization of what had just happened stabbed fear into his heart. He hadn't answered Betty's call of his own free will. The Night Walker's mental suggestion made him speak. And he'd been powerless to stop him.

"You have no idea of my power, Jose Mentigo. And I *will* kill you." Calisto stood, leaving Jose sprawled on the floor below him.

He bent down to yank Jose to his feet, but Betty's footsteps echoed on the hardwood floor of her hallway. "Thanks for cleaning up, baby."

Jose scrambled to his feet, looking around the now-empty room. The Night Walker was gone. Vanished.

§

Calisto flew through the night sky, once again in the form of a large raven.

He wanted to kill Jose with every breath, but he wouldn't harm Betty in the process. With Kate safely hidden, he could take his time and savor the battle. Jose couldn't be with Betty all the time. Calisto would be patient, and he would enjoy his revenge when the time finally came.

But in the end, he would still be alone.

Calisto fed voraciously, gorging himself with the blood of three
gang members, but no amount of blood could fill the emptiness inside
of him. His body ached, not for blood or revenge, but for Kate.

But she was something he couldn't allow himself to have.

Landing silently on the deserted beach, Calisto stormed into his
bedchamber. He tried not to think about Kate, to wonder if she'd told
Tom that she carried his child. Would she reconsider his proposal of
marriage?

The cheating bastard didn't deserve her.

He sat at the piano, his body tight with emotion, and played
Rachmaninoff's *Piano Concerto No. 2 in C Minor.* His fingers
pounded the ivory keys of Kate's piano, transforming the emptiness
and pain in his soul into an audible yearning; a passionate fever of
melancholy that cried out to whatever god might be listening.

A single red tear of blood made its way down his cheek and
fell onto the keyboard. The splash of color on the white keys jarred
him from the spell of pain that hypnotized him. Calisto withdrew his
fingers from the keys, staring at the red stain.

Slowly, he rose from the piano and went to the mirror. He raised
his hand to the single trail of blood that ran from the corner of his eye
down the length of his cheek. After all of the years since he wept over
Tala's grave, it still shocked him to see blood where tears should be, a
visual reminder that he was no longer a man, but a monster.

CHAPTER TWENTY-SIX

"You sure you're okay, lady?" The cab driver helped Kate from the backseat. The noise of other cars dropping off passengers at the Reno airport made it hard to hear the man. "You're awful pale."

"I'm fine." Kate reached for the black leather bag she never unpacked during her brief visit to Reno.

"At least let me get a skycap." The cabbie took off in search of help before she could stop him.

She must look like hell for a cab driver to go out of his way to help her.

She felt like hell. She ached all over and probably had no business getting on a plane to go back to San Diego, but where else could she go? The hospital discharged her, and there was nothing left for her in Reno anymore. Besides, she was finished running, even when she only left because it was expected.

Lori would pick her up at the airport, and Kate could stay with her until she felt better. She still hadn't told Lori why she went back to Reno, or why she visited the hospital. She couldn't talk about it. Not yet.

The skycap helped Kate check her bag. His unmistakable look of concern only reaffirmed that she must look exactly as crappy as she felt.

"Do you need any help getting there?" he asked, pointing her in the direction of the terminal for her flight.

"No, I'm fine, thank you."

He nodded, and Kate walked away, amazed at how heavy her legs felt. The walk to the terminal left her winded and dizzy, but she got there. With a sigh of relief, she plopped down in a chair, fighting back tears.

She'd lost her baby. Her baby was... She couldn't finish the thought. She'd failed her child. At least that's how she felt. Dabbing her eyes with a tissue, she struggled to hold herself together.

They upgraded her ticket to put her in first class. Apparently there were perks for looking like death walking. The flight attendants kept flashing her kind, I-hope-she's-not-contagious smiles and brought her a pillow and blanket.

She managed to sleep through most of the flight, groaning when the flight attendant tapped her shoulder. Grudgingly, Kate blinked her eyes open and shivered as she set the blanket aside.

"Thanks for everything," she told the flight attendant who helped her to the Jetway.

"Good luck, Kate. I hope you feel better soon."

Had she told them her name? She wasn't sure she wanted to know what else she might have mentioned in her dizzy and dazed state. Frightening to realize she couldn't remember most of the flight.

"Thank you. I'm sure I will."

"Good, and I hope you see Gregorio again very soon."

Kate's knees wobbled for a moment. "Who?"

"You told me about a man on the beach, Gregorio... Don't you remember?"

Gregorio. The name the woman in her dream had called Calisto. Gregorio...

"I hope I see him too," Kate finally answered. "Thanks again."

She turned around and slowly made her way up the Jetway. Her legs already ached when she reached the top. Somehow she made it through the terminal with only a couple of stops to rest.

"Jesus, Kate!" Lori rushed to the escalator leading to the baggage claim and helped her to a chair. "What happened?"

Lori sat down beside her and Kate tried to explain, but tears won out over her voice and instead of talking she ended up sobbing. She wasn't sure how long they sat together in the airport, but she'd never been more grateful to Lori for her company.

She didn't ask another question, just held her and stroked her hair until the tears finally passed. Kate drew back with a sniffle.

"Sorry about that. Can we leave now before I lose it again?"

Lori nodded and helped her through the airport and out to her car.

"Just wait right here," she said, taking Kate's ticket with the luggage tag stapled inside. "I'll grab your luggage and we'll get out of here, okay?"

Kate nodded in agreement, too tired to argue that she could get it herself, and watched Lori's red hair disappear into the river of travelers. The doctor discharged her earlier in the morning with strict instructions to rest, and now she found it almost funny.

Rest was inevitable. She was too wiped out to do anything else.

The drive back to Lori's house was a blur. She slept through most of it. Once they were settled inside, Lori brought mugs of hot tea and sat down beside her.

"Okay, what's going on?"

"Other than my life falling apart around me?" Kate blew gently on the surface of her tea. "Not much."

Lori frowned. "Is it Calisto? Is that why you were at the airport?"

"I went to the airport because the hospital in Reno discharged me and I didn't have anywhere else to go. I gave up my apartment when I moved back out here."

"The hospital?"

Kate nodded, taking a sip of her tea. "Yeah... I went back to tell Tom I was pregnant."

Lori leaned forward in her chair, taking Kate's hand in hers.

"But I... " Kate cleared her throat as another tear spilled over her cheek. "I lost the baby before I could tell him." Lori squeezed her hand in support. "I lost a lot of blood, but the doctor said I should be fine."

She sipped her tea, trying to avoid another wave of tears. A palpable silence settled between them. She almost hoped her friend would lecture her about jumping into a relationship with a man she hardly knew.

But she didn't.

Instead, Lori hugged her. "I'm so sorry. You're sure it was Tom's?"

"I was too far along for it to be Calisto's baby," Kate said, looking down at her mug.

"So where is Calisto now?"

Kate shrugged. "I don't know."

"Does he know you went back to Reno?"

"He sent me there," Kate sighed, finally raising her eyes to meet Lori's. "He looked like he'd seen a ghost the second I mentioned being pregnant, and immediately decided he didn't have room in his life for a family. A few minutes later he had plane tickets for me to go back to Reno to live happily ever after with Tom." She shook her head and wiped her nose. "As if I could just waltz back into his cheating arms and live happily ever after. But it doesn't matter now. The baby... " The word filled her head, blinding her with another wave of tears. "I lost the baby before I could even tell Tom I was back in town."

"Do the doctors know why it happened?"

Kate shook her head, wiping her eyes. "Something might have been wrong with the baby, but they said it's common in the first trimester. They don't know for sure what happened. I lost a lot of blood, so they kept me overnight in the hospital on antibiotics and fluids."

"Did they give you anything for the pain?"

"My heart hurts worse than my body. I lay in that hospital bed feeling more alone than I've ever felt in my life."

Lori frowned. "You were alone?"

"Yeah." Kate nodded. "Why?"

"Because on the way back from the airport you kept talking about some man in black named Gregorio."

Kate's hands trembled. She stretched forward to place her mug on the coffee table before she spilled it all over herself. Running both hands down her face, she fought for some kind of clarity. There must be a way to put the pieces together. She'd had the same dream for too long. This couldn't be a coincidence.

It had to mean something.

The dream had changed, but the woman in her dreams remained same. She wore that same pendant. And when she smiled and laughed on the beach, Calisto's face smiled down at her. But she called him Gregorio.

Where was Gregorio while the woman ran for her life with a man on a horse closing in on her? What if Gregorio was the man chasing her?

She shook her head, forcing the thought from her mind. They were just dreams. She saw Calisto's face because he sent her away and she couldn't stop thinking about him. She missed him. That felt logical.

But what if there was more to it?

"Are you all right?" Lori asked, pulling Kate back from her thoughts.

"I need to talk to Calisto."

Lori cocked her head. "After he abandoned you when you needed him most?"

"He didn't abandon me. He thought I would get back together with Tom and have a family. I'm sure he thought he did the right thing."

Lori shook her head. "You are giving him *way* too much credit. Let's face it. If he really loved you, could he just put you on a plane and send you away at the drop of a hat like that?"

"Damnit, Lori. You weren't there. You didn't see his eyes when I told him I was pregnant. He looked so sad. I don't think he wanted me to go. He did what he thought was best for me and my baby."

"Or he was sad because now you've see his true colors. Now you know once and for all that when you really need him, he won't be there for you. He can't fool you anymore."

"Enough. Please, stop it." Her eyes brimmed with tears all over again. "He's not like that. I need to talk to him, and if you won't take me, I'll get a cab."

Lori sighed. "Are you sure you're up for this, Kate? He may not be happy to see you again."

"How can you say that?"

"I'm just being honest, hon. You weren't with him very long, and even though you think you were both deeply in love, the world's a cruel place. Sounds like he used you. You told me yourself he was never around in the daytime. How do you know he's not already married with five kids?"

"All of that might be true," Kate whispered, praying otherwise. "But it doesn't change the fact that I need to see him."

"Fine." Lori sat back and crossed her arms.

"Can I use your phone? I just need to call Betty and be sure Calisto is still in town."

"No problem." Lori handed her the cordless phone.

After a quick conversation with Betty, Kate hung up with a slight frown.

"What is it?" Lori asked. "Is he in town?"

Kate shrugged. "It's nothing, I guess. She said as far as she knows he's not out of the country."

"So what's the frowning all about?"

"Nothing really. Betty said Jose was looking for me yesterday, and they were glad I got back okay."

"Isn't Jose Betty's new boyfriend? Why would he be looking for you?"

"I don't know. I hope it's nothing about Calisto. What if something happened to him?"

"Geez Kate..." Lori rolled her eyes. "Betty would have told you. Let's not forget you're the injured party here. He dropped you when you needed him most."

"Please stop saying that. He did what he thought was best."

She hoped that was all he was doing.

Lori sighed, shaking her head. "I hope you're right, for your sake. So when do you want to go?"

"I need to sleep a little first. Promise you'll wake me up at four so we can leave?"

"All right, I promise. But I really think you should rest longer than a couple of hours."

"I'll be fine," Kate said, lying down on the sofa. "Thank you."

Lori draped a soft blanket over her, and before she realized it, she fell asleep.

§

"Please wait for me," the monsignor said, exiting the taxicab. He walked down the deserted driveway toward the home of Kate Bradley.

Secrecy no longer ranked as his main concern. He worried about Brother Mentigo and Kate. The only correspondence he received from Brother Mentigo since he left the monastery included this address and mentioned that Kate had indeed met the Night Walker. However, she was still mortal at the time.

But that was weeks ago. Now he prayed he wasn't too late.

After ringing the bell twice, he peered into the front window of the house. It looked empty. Except for the sleeping bag on a big easy chair, there he saw no other sign that anyone had been inside.

He rubbed his forehead. Was he too late? With a sigh, he walked back to the taxi.

"Take me to the Mission de Alcala." He clutched his crucifix and prayed.

Chapter Twenty-Seven

Lori finally drove away. It took a lot of arguing on Kate's part, but her VW, still parked in Calisto's driveway, had been the final bargaining chip. That and her demand that Lori back off and just support her decisions. Once Kate showed her she had car keys to leave if she needed to, Lori agreed to go home. She still insisted on giving Kate a final reminder to call if she needed her, no questions asked.

Kate had to promise she would before Lori finally drove away.

Calisto trusted her to keep his private room private, so once Lori left, Kate walked around the back of the house toward his bedroom below. She didn't want to wait in the main house, but she couldn't have gone down to his room with Lori around. Hopefully, she wouldn't be alone for long.

Kate dug through her purse for her keys, walking across the sand toward the small double doors hidden under the deck. She breathed a sigh of relief when she finally heard the familiar jingle of metal and pulled her key ring free of her leather bag.

She stepped inside and closed the door behind her, blinking her eyes until they adjusted to the dim light. His scent lingered in the room, making her ache to lose herself in his arms. She glanced at her watch and took a deep breath. If Calisto were coming back home tonight, he'd probably walk through the door any minute now.

Kate went to the piano, intent on playing something while she waited, but she never made it to the piano bench.

Her feet were glued to the floor, her body frozen in place, and her eyes locked on the large canvas portrait hanging on the wall.

It was her, right down to the tiny crescent in her right eye. But there was more to it. Her hair was longer, her skin slightly more tanned, and around her neck hung the pendant from her dreams. Only now she saw it clearly. It wasn't really a pendant. It was a ring.

Calisto's ring.

Kate blinked back her tears, her head throbbing until she wasn't sure what was real anymore. She saw the woman running again, heard the hoof beats pursuing her, or was it the pounding of her head?

Her heart raced, and she couldn't catch her breath. Her entire body ached, drained of energy, and her feet stung. Every step felt like her legs were on fire, burning until she thought she might scream in pain. She was no longer *watching* the woman running through the brambles, she *was* that woman...

Her lungs heaved, her muscles were in agony, and finally she couldn't run any longer. Kate crumpled to the floor.

§

Calisto awoke in his usual fashion, but after rising from his resting place, he frowned. Someone lurked inside his private chambers a few feet above. He heard a human heartbeat, racing.

His thirst demanded his attention, but he pushed the hunger aside as he rushed to roll away the large stone that kept his resting place hidden from the rest of the cavern. Replacing the stone, he hurried out of the cave and up toward the double doors beneath the deck. They were closed. If someone had broken into his private chamber, the locks would be broken, or the doors pried apart.

Unless someone unlocked it.

Kate!

In less than a second, he stood inside, unable to believe his eyes. But his initial rush of joy vanished, replaced with worry. She lay collapsed on the floor, weeping, and the lingering unmistakable scent of blood surrounded her.

"Kate?" He kneeled at her side and searched for any sign of an injury. Thankfully, he didn't find any wounds. Stroking her hair back from her face, hoping to soothe her, Calisto leaned closer and placed a tender kiss to her hair. He stopped cold when he heard her whisper.

"Gregorio?"

Calisto sat beside her and withdrew his hand from her hair. When her dark eyes, so full of pain and confusion, finally met his, he knew.

Kate remembered.

"That's your real name isn't it?" Kate whispered.

Calisto nodded slowly.

"Oh God... " She backed away from him. "Then it's all true. My dream. It's real... It was me!"

Tears gathered in her eyes, and fear. The fear tore at his heart and made him wish he had never intruded upon her life. He offered his hand. "Please do not be afraid. I would sooner die than hurt you."

"But let me guess, you can't die, right?" Kate sniffled, making no attempt to take his hand. "What does all of this mean? How can you still be alive?"

He slowly lowered his hand, realizing she had no intention of touching him. "Does it matter?"

"Don't answer me with more questions. Not now. I need answers. Please."

Calisto sat beside her, leaning against the corner of the bed. "Where would you like me to start?"

"It's me in my dreams, and up there," she pointed. "In the painting. It's me, but it's not me." Kate paused. He watched her struggle to understand. "Who was I back then?"

"Your name was Tala," Calisto answered quietly, staring up at the canvas. "You were a member of the Kumeyaay tribe here. We met on the beach on a summer afternoon. I had never seen an angel until the moment I saw you with the wind in your hair and a Romneya behind your ear."

"Gregorio doesn't sound like a Kumeyaay name."

He stared into her eyes. "It is a Spanish name. I was Father Gregorio Salvador back then. I was a priest at the Mission de Alcala. I helped build it."

"That's why you were wearing black." Kate said.

"Black?"

"I had a new dream. Instead of the woman... " She hesitated and corrected herself. "I guess it was me. Anyway, instead of running, she learned to dance with a man dressed all in black. She called him Gregorio. I didn't see his face until last night. It was you."

Calisto's eyes brimmed with tears he wouldn't allow to fall. Knowing she remembered a precious moment they had once shared together, one of the moments he had treasured in his heart for centuries, touched him deeper than he ever could have imagined.

He nodded slowly. "You taught me the language of your people, and in trade I taught you to waltz." A soft smile warmed his features. "Learning to waltz in the waves was all your idea."

Kate smiled faintly. "We were smiling and laughing... Then we kissed."

"I fell in love with you." He paused, wishing she would look at him. "I had pledged my life to God, but I gave my heart to you."

She pressed her lips together, eyes downcast. "Were you the man chasing me in my nightmare? The man on the horse, was that you?"

Calisto froze, too stunned to speak. He had thought about this day ever since the Old One told him she would live again, but never in all his years on this earth did it occur to him she might believe he was her attacker. Why would she suspect him?

"No... I love you. I always have. Why would you think otherwise?"

"I never saw the killer's face in my dream. I always woke up before... But she... I was pregnant. It makes sense. A priest would get into big trouble for that kind of thing. Wouldn't a secret pregnancy be motive enough?"

Calisto's expression darkened. He wished he could spare her the details surrounding Tala's death, but he saw no other way. She wanted to know, and she had every right to know.

But would she ever forgive him?

"I knew about the baby. Knowing you carried my child made me happier than I had ever been. But I was also an innocent fool. I trusted Father Jayme, my superior. I believed he was my friend. I wanted to marry you and raise our family together, so I confessed my sins and told Father Jayme of my plans to give up the priesthood." His voice dropped to a whisper. "I never dreamed he would pass judgment on you for my decision."

"She... I was killed by a priest?"

"Not physically, but he ordered it."

She shook her head slowly. "How did you find out?"

"I searched for you, to share my news and ask your father to let us marry. One of the guards from the mission rode past me." He choked back the lump of emotion tightening in his throat.

Kate glanced at the portrait. Her hair, usually so vibrant, was dull and lank. Yet she was still so beautiful.

He forced out his next words quietly. "He had my signet ring, the one you used to wear around your neck. It dangled from his wrist while he rode away. Then I knew. Father Jayme had betrayed me. He had no intention of allowing me to give up the cloth or marry a native woman. Something terrible had happened, and I ran, searching everywhere for you."

He had never shared this memory with another soul, and even with the passing of lifetimes, the pain still felt fresh. "I found you lying motionless, your dress shredded, your body covered in blood. I was too late."

A tear rolled down Kate's cheek. She moved forward and wrapped her arms around him, weeping softly as they held one another on the floor. "I don't know how any of this is possible, but I love you, Calisto."

He tightened his arms around her and stroked her hair. "My beloved Kate. You should not have come back here."

Kate pulled back from his arms and stared at him. "How can you say that?"

"Because you are in danger here."

"I don't understand."

Calisto shook his head and rose from the floor. She watched him as he paced, trying to find a way to convince her to leave. "There is no time to explain. Please remember I will always love you, and go. Leave me and this place, and never look back."

She stared at him for a moment, her mouth parted and disbelief clouding her expression. She stood slowly and shook her head. "You know me better than that. I love you, and until you tell me what is going on, I'm not moving from this spot." He opened his mouth to speak, but she raised her hand. "I'm not finished yet."

Kate walked toward him and took his hand. Her brow pinched as she glanced down at their joined hands. He realized his flesh was still cold, since he had not yet fed.

She looked into his eyes, her gaze questioning him before she uttered the words. "How can you be the same man who helped build the Mission de Alcala, who loved Tala, and still be standing here holding my hand?"

"I cannot answer that." He pulled away.

Her touch felt like fire against his cool flesh. His thirst clawed its way through his strong will, aching to be quenched. He couldn't tell her the truth. Even if she believed him, he couldn't bear to see the disgust that would surely follow.

"I would rather have you hate me as a man, than fear me as a monster."

Kate sighed with exasperation. "Enough with the noble riddles you call answers. Talk to me. You tell me you love me, and then you send me away? That's not love. Trust me with the truth. I can't accept anything less."

He shook his head and turned away. "Save yourself and your baby and go."

"There is no baby. I... The baby..." Her voice trembled. "I lost the baby when I got back to Reno."

Without a word he turned and drew her into his arms. He should have realized what had happened when he caught the scent of blood around her and found no wounds. It would also explain why he'd never heard the sound of another heartbeat. Maybe the baby never had one.

Again she had needed him, and again he wasn't there for her.

Calisto closed his eyes, kissing her dark hair. He was through pushing her away. For better or worse, he would embrace her into his secret life.

He needed her.

"I am so sorry, Kate. I thought you would be safe, and have the life and the family you have always wanted."

"All I want is you."

He held her tightly, whispering into her hair. "Holding you in my arms again has made every lonely night of my existence worthwhile. I gave up my humanity to hold you again."

She frowned, shaking her head, and he pulled away to look her in the eyes. "I don't understand."

"I am a Night Walker, Kate. I live only after the sun has died."

Confusion clouded her eyes when she gazed up at him, and finally he forced himself to go on. "After I lost you, I could not face another day. I abandoned the God I served, and His church. Your tribe took me in and brought me to the Old One in the cliffs over the ocean. He was a wise healer, but even he could not mend my ailing heart. What he offered instead was a chance to stay alive until you lived again."

"But how is that possible?" Kate asked. "No one lives forever."

"I will, until the day I decide to watch the sunrise."

"Impossible. Are you telling me he cast some sort of spell on you? A hex or something?"

"No. He gave me his blood and it changed me. I was no longer a man. I became a Night Walker."

"Gave you his blood?"

"I drank it, Kate. Blood is what keeps me alive now."

"Like a vampire?" Doubt filled her eyes. "You expect me to believe vampires are real, and I'm in love with one? That's insane. All of this is crazy. It can't be true."

He took her hand in his and brought it to his cold cheek. "My flesh is cold because I have not yet fed. I was not on business trips or out of the country during the daylight hours. I slept far below this room, deep inside a cave along the cliff, safely hidden from the sun. My kitchen sat empty when you came to my home because I do not eat. Not food, anyway."

He paused, gauging her reaction before he went on. "I *am* an immortal, Kate, a Night Walker, but I am *not* a vampire. I do not kill for pleasure or sport. I do not make minions of blood-drinkers to keep for my companions. I have no fear of garlic or crucifixes." A hint of a smile sparkled in his eyes. "And I certainly do not turn myself into a bat."

She stared up at him for a moment. A soft smile warmed her lips, followed by a chuckle until it finally bloomed into laughter. She didn't believe him. He didn't blame her.

Calisto lowered her hand with a tentative smile while he waited for his words to settle in her mind. He loved the sound of her laughter. Seeing her smile and hearing her laugh was the most precious gift he would ever receive.

Sadly, it was short lived.

She lifted his hand, examining it closely. He wondered what she searched for. But he didn't ask, and he made no move to draw back from her inspection. He asked her to believe the unbelievable. The least he could do was give her time to accept it.

Her gaze moved back up to his face without making eye contact. He watched her eyes move slowly over his features until she finally met his stare. "I'm trying to understand, but it can't be true. There must be some other explanation."

"I wish there was."

§

Tears came to her eyes. She lifted her hand to caress his cool cheek. None of this could be real, just part of a twisted nightmare. But deep inside she knew she wasn't sleeping. Her thumb brushed over his skin and a tear rolled down her cheek.

"I can't accept this, Calisto."

"How else can you explain that I still live?"

"Maybe you aren't as old as you think you are. You've probably been having dreams about your past life too. You just caught onto yours sooner than I did, and you remembered me."

He shook his head, taking her hand to walk her closer to the painting on his wall. "I painted this picture of you, Kate. The G.S. in the corner is for Gregorio Salvador."

She didn't want to believe it. Believing his story would mean accepting the world around her held much more than she ever realized. Beings she only dreamed of might be real, lurking in the shadows. She looked up at him, searching for some other explanation.

Calisto cupped her cheek in his hand. "I am telling you the truth. I helped build the Mission in 1769, and I led the attack and burned it down in 1775. I fell in love with you when I was a man on this beach, and I have loved you as an immortal ever since."

"Stop it," Kate stammered. "Just stop it. I don't want to hear anymore. I don't want to believe this. It can't be true."

She looked up at the painting again, warring with herself. He knew too many details, and when he told her about his time with Tala, the memories played out in his eyes. He had been there. But if she accepted that much to be true, then she had to accept his entire story.

Calisto wasn't a man at all.

Not anymore.

Her heart raced, and her fingertips tingled. It felt like her lungs couldn't find any air in the room. She swallowed the lump in her throat and started for the door. "I can't handle this right now. I need some time to think."

"Wait, there is more you should know." He reached for her, but Kate kept walking.

"I've heard more than I can believe already, Calisto. Just give me some time to think, okay? I won't tell anyone if that's what you're worried about. Everyone would think I'm insane anyway. Maybe I am."

Before he said another word, she walked out the door. He went after her, catching her arm as she reached the steps to the main house.

"You are in danger, Kate."

"Don't." She pulled away. "You can't scare me into staying with you. This is *my* life. I'd like to have some control over it. Just let me think all of this through. I'll be back tomorrow night. If you've really loved me for over two centuries, then what's one more night?" She bit back her tears and turned away. "Now leave me alone."

Chapter Twenty-Eight

Jose had searched Kate's house as well as Calisto's home, and still hadn't found any sign of her. After spending another day searching for her, his frustration level peaked. He had no choice but to return to Betty's condo and wait until tomorrow. The risk of being without her once the sun went down and the Night Walker awoke was far too great. His life insurance rested on Betty's shoulders for now.

However, if she called him baby or asked him to rub her back one more time, he thought he might entertain canceling his insurance policy by ripping her throat out. He daydreamed about kissing her cold, dead lips good-bye and never looking back.

He wanted to make that dream a reality.

Instead, he sat at her glass dining table, choking down her pathetic attempt at Spanish Gazpacho soup. He had grown up on gazpacho as a boy in Spain. The last thing he wanted to eat while in America was food he could get back home.

To make the soup even worse, she heated it.

"How is it?" Betty asked.

Jose looked up from his steaming spoon. "It's hot."

"It's soup."

He raised a brow. "It's gazpacho."

"I know that." Betty made a face. "Eating cold soup is disgusting. I improved it by serving it heated."

Jose dropped his spoon back into the bowl and shoved his chair away from the table.

"Where are you going?"

"Out." He grabbed his jacket.

He felt her glare burning into the back of his head and smiled. He couldn't kill her, but it brought him some solace to know he pissed her off.

"I tried to do something nice for you," she said.

Jose reached for the door and turned around with a sarcastic smirk. "Then I guess you failed. I'm going out to get something I can actually eat. I'll be back before sunset."

The hurt in her eyes satisfied him and eased the growing rage inside of him. She wouldn't cry. He knew her well enough to know she'd never give him the satisfaction of tears, but he had wounded her. It would suffice for now.

Jose closed the door and looked up at the sky. Twilight. Shit.

Calisto might already be alert.

Rubbing his hands down his face in frustration, he cursed himself inwardly for his carelessness. He should've checked the time before insulting Betty and storming out. He couldn't wander back in now and keep his pride intact.

But if he ran into the Night Walker without Betty, he would have much more to worry about than his pride.

He took a deep breath and turned back, forcing himself to open the door and step inside. He pasted a look of contrition on his face. "I couldn't leave knowing I hurt you. Forgive me?"

"You were an asshole."

God, he hated her. He'd been a jerk intentionally. Did she think he didn't notice his own behavior? Of course she did, because Betty knew everything. She thought she did, anyway.

"I am very particular about food from my homeland," he said.

"At least I tried." She sipped her mineral water. "You didn't even say thank you."

His fists balled up at his sides while he fought to hold back the fury lurking far too close to the surface. He refused to play her game and thank her for anything, least of all the slop she called gazpacho.

Closing the door behind him, Jose walked through the sterile interior of her condominium and around the glass dining table. He brought his hands up to her shoulders and kneaded them firmly, imagining his fingers gripped her throat instead of her shoulders.

Betty hummed, dropping her head forward. "Mmm, feels good."

He nodded, closing his eyes and working his hands in closer and closer to the base of her neck, his fingers pressing harder, gripping tighter. As the fantasy grew in his mind, he saw her eyes light with terror when she realized she had made a fatal error in judgment. It was a sweet victory, even if it was only in his imagination. Soon it would be real. Soon he would choose who lived or died.

He would have the ultimate power, even over death itself.

Betty's hands reached up to cover his own, moving them farther out on her shoulders, but in his mind, he strangled her, slowly watching the life drain from her icy blue eyes. He pressed his hips against the back of her chair, his member aching for satisfaction.

Jose's fingers slid down from her shoulders until his hands cupped her breasts, kneading them forcefully. Her back arched, responding to his aggressive touch.

He opened his eyes, looking down at her, watching his hands corrupt her body, his fingers sliding in between the buttons of her blouse to tease her hungry flesh. Gripping either side, he suddenly ripped it open. Buttons clattered around them, and his hands invaded her black lace bra, pinching her nipples until she gasped.

Dominating her was a sinful pleasure that he enjoyed immensely. And he intended to enjoy her, right here, right now.

With a sweep of his arm, he cleared the table of the soup, as well as everything else. Plates and bowls shattered against the marble floor, glasses spilled, and what remained of their dinner smeared red across the glass dining table. He yanked Betty into his arms, his lips claiming hers in a demanding kiss that would accept nothing less than complete surrender. He unclasped her bra, yanking it fiercely from her body.

Her fingers searched for the buttons on his shirt, but Jose caught her hands, bringing them down and behind her waist. He held her wrists behind her back with one hand, and suddenly broke the kiss, turned her away from him, and shoved her facedown onto the glass table. Yanking up her skirt, he tore her thong underwear and kicked her feet further apart. Her hips tilted slightly, hungering for his entry as he opened his pants.

He stroked himself for a moment with his free hand. Watching her lie there in front of him, pressed facedown, topless on the dirty table, her skirt lifted to expose her most private areas, and the remnants of her torn underwear still clinging to her upper thigh, made his erection rock hard.

He was in control. He had the power.

Jose thrust himself inside of her, violating her over and over, imagining she resisted instead of working her hips into his. He envisioned her moans of pleasure were cries of mercy, and her nails were digging into his wrists out of fear instead of pleasure. When he finally spent himself inside of her, he wished he could just walk away.

Jose stepped back as Betty stood up with a blissful, sexy smile. "You're forgiven. God, that was incredible."

It would have been even better if she could no longer speak. He tucked himself back inside his pants and zipped them up.

"Come on, I need a shower now. If you wash my back, I'll wash yours," she said with a purposefully seductive tone, re-igniting Jose's urge to choke her to death.

He forced a smile and nodded, following her back to the master bedroom. He watched her take off what remained of her clothes and undressed while she started the water in the shower.

Betty stepped inside with a smile. "Oh I almost forgot, Kate called today while you were out. She was looking for Calisto. I guess she's back in town."

Jose froze. "She is here, in San Diego?"

"Yes. She's probably with Calisto right now."

His heart pounded in his chest, making his pulse throb in his ears.

He lost himself in his thoughts as Betty washed his hair. Her constant petting usually annoyed him to no end, but right now he hardly noticed.

He needed a plan.

He squeezed shampoo into the palm of his hand, working it through Betty's long blonde hair, and weighed his options. If Kate was calling Betty to find out Calisto's whereabouts, then she obviously had no idea of her lover's daylight sleeping habits. Jose felt fairly certain Kate had no idea about Calisto's true nature.

"That feels so good, baby."

Jose's jaw clenched when Betty's voice interrupted his chain of thought. He didn't answer her, just pulled her back into the water, rinsing out the shampoo and letting his mind wander back to his plans.

If Calisto hadn't revealed he was a blood-drinker, then what made Kate leave? Had they fought, or did Calisto send her away for her own safety without explanation? He supposed he would know soon enough.

The first step would be finding Kate. He couldn't risk going to Calisto's home tonight. Then it came to him.

Kate's house.

He still had a key. He could wait for her there until daylight, and even if she didn't come home, once the sun came up, he'd be free to go to the Night Walker's house and meet her there while Calisto slept.

Quickly rinsing off the soap, Jose stepped out of the shower and toweled off. The bathroom tiles were cool against his feet.

"Where are you going?"

He gave Betty a dismissive glance. "To find Kate."

"What?"

He could already hear her anger rising to the surface. Jose learned early on Betty had an unmistakable cold sarcasm to her voice when something displeased her, and he heard it now.

"I said I am going to find Kate."

"Now? You can't be serious." She added with a sultry smile, "I had plans for you."

"I'm not interested in your plans. In fact, I have plans of my own."

She stepped out of the shower, her eyes blazing. "You're not going anywhere."

"I disagree." He pulled on his jeans.

"I don't believe this." Her cheeks flushed with color. She grabbed his wrist. "You can't be serious. You're really going out right after we had sex to see Kate?"

"Yes." Jose jerked his arm free and pulled on his shirt. The moment his head popped through the opening, her hand connected with his cheek. The slap echoed through the bathroom.

"Over my dead body."

Jose looked at her with a cold, hateful sneer, lifting her hand to kiss it. "As you wish."

Before she had a chance to react, he shoved her against the wall, and his hands closed around her throat to prevent her from screaming.

Finally, after weeks of enduring her company, he saw the fear he had hungered for burning in her eyes. Her hands flailed, slapping and scratching at his face. Her struggles satisfied him far more than he imagined. Her body glistened, still damp from the shower, her breasts heaving as she fought to breathe.

Beautiful.

Once again his jeans became uncomfortable as his arousal grew. Wedging his shoulder against her flailing body, he removed one hand from her throat to open his pants.

A whimper escaped her crushed windpipe, and he laughed as her vain attempts to escape increased. Before he pulled himself free from the confines of his jeans, Betty's knee jammed up into his groin, hard.

He lost his grip on her, doubling over in pain.

Betty wrestled free of him and ran for the door. Rage shot through him as Jose reached out and caught a handful of her hair.

"You whore!" He growled, still grimacing in pain.

He yanked her back to him, striking her across the face with his free hand, his ring biting into the soft flesh of her lip as she fell to the floor.

He pinned her to the ground, gripping her throat until she choked for air. "You said you had plans for me. Well, I have plans of my own." He freed himself from his jeans.

Jose's hips surged forward, and he plunged back into the moist warmth of her body. He loosened his hold on her throat just enough to hear her gasp and cry. Such an exquisite sound. He licked away the blood on her lip, laughing as she tried to slap him away from her.

"I like it when you fight."

He ran his hand up her curvaceous body to grip her breasts, pinching them viciously until he saw the pain register in her eyes. He bent forward to kiss her swollen lips, biting at them as he whispered, "I'm only giving you what you wanted... "

His words trailed off as he brought both hands to her throat, squeezing and clenching her neck. Her struggles weakened and the life faded from her eyes. Within minutes, she stared blankly at the ceiling. He continued thrusting his hips into her, enjoying every seizure of her muscles. He withdrew from her dead body, leaving her on the floor in a heap.

He stared down at her lifeless form for a moment. He had fantasized for years about taking a life. He never realized it would be so empowering.

Tucking himself back inside his jeans, he knelt down to kiss her temple, gently stroking her wet hair back from her battered, lifeless face. "I will never forget you, Betty."

He straightened, kicking her onto her stomach, and walked out without a second look.

CHAPTER TWENTY-NINE

Calisto watched Kate go, unsure of how he should react. He wanted to chase after her and keep her safe, but he also knew she deserved time to think about the ramifications of what he had revealed.

If she chose to love him, they would never have a normal life. No children, no picnics in the afternoon. Her life with him would be confined to the night. He would never be able to give her a family. She needed to consider the truth of what their future would be like, without him hovering nearby.

However, her safety still had to come first.

He ran into the darkness, his body transforming into a raven as he took flight. Time to finish his battle with Jose. For good.

Calisto landed silently on the balcony of Betty's condominium and looked through the sliding glass door for any sign of Jose. With Kate back in San Diego, he couldn't risk allowing the madman to live any longer. If he had to mesmerize Betty to complete his mission, then so be it.

It had to end now.

He didn't bother to knock, but reached for the door handle. It wasn't locked. Calisto stepped inside and frowned. It was quiet, too quiet. Could they be sleeping already?

Calisto found her taste in contemporary design unbearably stark and sleek, but right now, it wasn't the coldness of her interior design that had his attention.

It was the mess. Uneasiness washed over him when he saw Betty's dining room table.

In the years he'd known Betty, she'd never left a mess behind. In fact, on occasion she had tidied up his office when he'd left papers strewn across his desk, or his wastebasket sat precariously on the brink of overflowing. So seeing her dining room in such a state of disarray worried him.

Puddles of soup dried on her glass dining table, and broken glass and shattered bowls littered the marble tiled floor. Silverware lay strewn all the way across the room. Betty never would have allowed a mess like this to linger so long.

He hurried down the hallway toward her bedroom, his pulse racing. If Betty and Jose weren't here, then where were they? He couldn't risk allowing the deranged monk to find Kate. He opened the bedroom door, hoping he'd see Betty and Jose inside sleeping.

When Calisto entered her room, preparing to call her name, the scent of blood assaulted his nose, bringing his thirst to life again. A moment later he found her naked body lying in a heap on the floor of her bathroom.

His heart sank.

"Bettina," he whispered, kneeling beside her as he carefully turned her over.

His eyes glowed when he saw her lifeless stare, her swollen bloodied lip, and the black and blue bruising around her throat. He reached out to close her dead eyes, whispering the last rites he thought he had forgotten centuries ago.

Jose had done this to her, Calisto had no doubt. He should have warned her. Guilt stung him. He knew Jose was dangerous, but he thought Kate was the target.

He needed to find her. Now.

"Forgive me, Bettina," he whispered, as he covered her body with a towel. Calisto vanished.

§

Kate left the top down on her convertible as she drove down Interstate 5 toward Point Loma. The cold wind stung her cheeks while more tears slid down her face and wet her skin. Her brain felt overloaded. She wasn't sure whether she felt heartbroken, terrified, or just insane. Maybe a combination of all three.

She wished she could believe Calisto was crazy and write off his story about drinking blood and past lives as delusional nonsense, but she couldn't. Too much of what he said made sense.

"God, maybe I'm the crazy one!" She laughed sadly, pulling off the freeway.

How could vampires or Night Walkers—wasn't that what he called them—really exist? They couldn't. They were myths. But if Calisto wasn't really what he said, then how else could she explain that she'd known him for nearly two months and had never caught a glimpse of him during daylight? And how many philanthropists had private bedroom suites underground?

He also knew about her dream, and had the painting of her on his wall with G.S. in the corner. Gregorio Salvador. The man from her dream. And Calisto's signet ring with the dove gliding over the flames matched the pendant she'd seen in her dreams.

Too much to chalk it up to coincidence.

The longer she thought about her past life with him, the more she remembered. Memories of secret meetings on the beach under the cover of night filled her head. She used to untie his hair and run her fingers through it. She always loved seeing his hair loose and free.

She still did. She guessed some things never changed.

She could remember picking Romneya flowers and wearing them in her hair. She'd always loved the smell and the stark contrast of the white petals like crushed silk against the ebony color of her hair.

Calisto told her the truth. As impossible as it seemed, nothing else made sense. If he planned to lie to her, surely he would've come up with a more believable story than *I am an immortal Night Walker.*

But assuming he told her the truth, then what kind of future could they have together?

She always pictured herself getting married and having a family. She loved Calisto more than she realized she could love another person, but this was too much. He drank blood from living, breathing people.

Could she love a man who killed to live?

If she stayed with him, there would never be a big wedding and no family gatherings. In fact, they wouldn't have a family at all.

And what about her work?

She couldn't teach choir all day and then stay up all night with him. Eventually she needed to sleep. She would end up giving up her days so they could be together at night. She'd already started down that road when she lived with him before the pregnancy.

She'd made the choice to give up the sun without even realizing it, but she also hadn't known the schedule would never change. In the back of her mind, she thought at some point he would stop traveling so much and they could be together during the day, too. But it would never happen. She knew that now.

There was so much they would never share together.

She wiped her eyes, driving aimlessly through her hometown. Point Loma was fairly deserted at this time of the night, or very early morning. The quiet was a relief. The last thing she needed was people staring at her, wondering why she was upset.

They'd never believe it even if she told them.

It's nothing really, just that the man I love with all my heart and soul is a blood-drinking immortal.

Oh yeah, she'd be in a padded room in no time.

She pulled into the driveway of her parents' empty house and rested her head against the steering wheel. She knew she'd never love another man as much or as deeply as she loved Calisto. When he smiled at her, she felt whole. He was the other half of her soul.

Her heart had found him again even after lifetimes apart.

She couldn't walk away. She wouldn't, not now, not ever. But if she stayed, would love be enough to sustain them? Would he still love her when she turned eighty and he still looked like a gorgeous man in the prime of his life? Kate wondered if she might grow to resent him as the years stole away her health and beauty and left him untouched.

With a sigh, she heaved her exhausted body out of the car. She still hadn't recovered from losing so much blood during the miscarriage, and the lack of sleep wasn't helping. She needed to rest and face all of this with a clear head.

Grabbing her purse, she went to the door, wishing she had a bed to sleep in. At this point, even her sleeping bag in her dad's easy chair sounded like heaven. Kate stepped into the dark house and closed the door behind her.

The second the deadbolt latch engaged, pain shot through her, stealing her voice before she had a chance to scream. A blade pressed against her throat, and blood oozed from a new opening in her shoulder.

"Welcome home."

CHAPTER THIRTY

The monsignor awoke with a start. His ailing heart raced, his brow perspired, but the vision remained clear in his mind. Blood. So much blood.

The vivid dreams weren't a new phenomenon for him. Dreams were what led him to the Fraternidad as a young man. He'd dreamt of fire and a man who fed off the life of others. The monsignor spent his life learning about the Night Walker and searching for a way to stop him.

His wrinkled hands shook when his feet touched the floor and he rose to dress. He had to go back to Kate Bradley's house. Her address had come to him twice during his dream. Brother Mentigo stood covered in blood. The final snapshot of his vision included a bloody handprint marking the window of the house he visited yesterday.

Kate Bradley's house. He didn't know what the dream meant, but it couldn't be good.

His arthritic fingers slid back through the wisps of his gray hair, taming them as best he could before he reached for the phone to call a taxi. He would be at her house within twenty minutes.

He hoped he wouldn't be too late.

§

Kate stumbled up the stairs backward as her attacker tugged and pulled her up with him, the blade of his knife still pressed against the soft skin of her throat. The darkness was a palpable creature now, and every step she took made the pain in her shoulder throb throughout the rest of her body. Her whole shirt felt wet and sticky with her warm blood.

She tried to calm herself, but terror won out, and her heart raced. Blood pumped through her veins and out of her wound at an alarming rate. She fought to stay alert, knowing if she fainted now she might never wake up.

At the top of the stairs, he yanked her into the master bedroom that used to belong to her parents and closed the door. He grabbed her shoulders and turned her around, his fingers digging into the stab wound until she felt nauseous from the overwhelming pain.

Moonlight cut through the darkness, making shapes out of the shadows. She tried to focus on the half-moon through the window and distance her mind from her attacker. He could hurt her body, but she would keep her spirit.

She would live through this.

"I thought I had lost you, Kate."

She recognized the voice, and it broke her concentration. "Jose?" She gasped, blinking to try and clear her vision. She couldn't believe her eyes. "Why are you doing this?"

He smiled and slid the blade up her arm. Only now she realized it wasn't a knife. Jose held an ivory handled razor, the old style the barbers used, and ran it slowly down the front of her shirt, slicing the fabric open.

Oh God, he's going to rape me...

She brought her hand up to her shoulder, pressing her fingers over the wound in a weak attempt to slow the bleeding as she took a step back.

"Calisto will be here any minute," she lied, praying she sounded more confident than she felt.

Jose stepped forward, reaching up to grab a handful of her hair and drew her in close to him. "I am counting on it."

Scratches covered his face and arms, and her heart sank. Were they from Betty?

She winced as he leaned in even closer. Jose pulled her hand away from her wound, and she watched in horror as his tongue reached out to lick her blood. She whimpered, trying to push him away.

With a cold, calculated chuckle, he drew back to meet her eyes. "Forgive me for injuring your soft skin, but I needed the scent of your blood to draw him in."

"You're insane!" Kate spat at him.

She tried to turn her head away when his breath blew across her face. "I am a visionary. And you are my sacrificial lamb. Through you, I will gain immortality."

She struggled to break free, but the more she fought, the tighter his hold became until she couldn't resist any longer. Jose brought his bloody fingers to her face. He stroked her cheek, his lips brushing hers as he whispered, "I know you don't want to die for this cause, but I will always love you for your sacrifice on my behalf."

§

Calisto flew toward Point Loma, his heart pounding in his ears as his large raven wings beat against the cold night air. Betty's body had still been warm and it wasn't rigid yet. Jose couldn't have been gone for too long. He prayed now that Kate hadn't gotten home. Maybe she went to one of her friends' homes. He had to find her before Jose did.

He opened his mind as he glided past the Cabrillo monument, flying inland toward Kate's house. When he landed on her street, his form once again that of a man, he ground his teeth together. The scent of Kate's blood called to him.

His hands shook with fury and hunger. He hadn't fed, and with the sunrise so near, his immortal body already slowed and weakened. He wouldn't have much time, and the intoxicating scent of her blood distracted him.

His thirst, like a primal animal, roared with temptation.

He threw open the front door, splintering the wood frame as the deadbolt ripped through it. Her blood left a trail up the stairs. Calisto followed, bursting through the bedroom door a moment later.

"Let her go."

Jose slowly broke the bloody kiss, turning around to smile at Calisto as he pressed his razor blade against Kate's throat. "You are not in a position to demand anything."

Calisto locked eyes with Kate for a moment, his jaw clenching when he saw her wounds. Blood pooled at her feet, staining the beige carpet. Kate's anemic complexion panicked him. His eyes cut to Jose's face again as he stepped forward. "She has nothing to do with this. Let her go and we can talk."

"I don't want to talk." He tightened his grip on the blade. "You know exactly what I want, and if you don't give it to me, Kate dies."

She winced in pain, and a drop of blood trickled down her neck.

Calisto narrowed his eyes, masking the dread brewing in his gut. "You will have nothing until she is safe."

He reached out to the madman with his mind, trying to control him, to convince him to let Kate go. The Latin chant repeated, and regardless of Calisto's focus of his power, Jose blocked his mental connection.

Jose laughed. "Do you really believe I am that stupid? If I let her go, I am a dead man. There will be no talking. I can see the hunger in your eyes... " His words trailed off as he bent forward to lick the drop of blood from Kate's throat, his eyes never leaving Calisto's. "Have you tasted her blood yet, Night Walker? I can see why you want her for yourself... So sweet and rich... "

"Leave her alone!" Calisto shouted, sickened at how deeply he longed to taste the blood draining from the wound in her shoulder.

Jose jammed his finger into the cut, and Kate squealed in pain. "Stay back, or I'll do more than just hurt her!"

Calisto clenched his fists at his sides, restraining himself from moving any closer. Jose glanced out the window and then back to Calisto with a twisted smile.

"The sun is coming, Night Walker. Stop wasting time."

Calisto struggled to think of a plan. His thirst demanded satisfaction, his body grew weak with hunger, and soon it would be morning. He was running out of options. He couldn't give Jose his blood, but he wouldn't allow him to kill Kate either.

The sound of her scream jarred him from his thoughts. Jose had opened her shirt and slid his blade across her abdomen, opening another deep wound.

"How much more will you make her suffer?"

She cried out, trembling, bleeding, and in pain, and Calisto couldn't take anymore. "Let her go! Just let her go and my blood is yours."

"No, Calisto don't... " Kate cried, but her words were cut off by Jose's blade moving back up to her throat.

"Shut up, whore!"

"Let her go!"

This time the command didn't come from Calisto. He turned to find an elderly priest standing in the doorway.

The robed man held up a hand and enunciated each word. "Brother Mentigo, in the name of God. Let her go."

"God?" Jose laughed. "Monsignor, I will *be* a god. Why should I fear Him? You have no power over me. Soon, no one will."

Calisto stepped to the right, moving out of the path between the old priest and his deranged missionary. His eyes locked on Kate's. He could get to her faster than Jose could see, but he wouldn't chance it, not with Jose's blade pressed against her jugular vein.

"God has power over us all, Brother Mentigo. He will forgive you if you repent. Come, I will pray with you." The monsignor took a step forward, offering his hand.

Jose pressed his fingers into the long cut along her abdomen. Kate gasped, her legs buckling.

"Both of you stay back!" Jose shouted.

Calisto froze where he stood, and the monsignor slowly lowered his hand.

"This is not your fault, Brother Mentigo," the old priest said. "I never should have sent you here. The Night Walker has clouded your mind and lured you to thirst for his dark power. Give up this dream. God has a higher plan in store for you, my son."

"You know nothing! You're just an old man praying that God will welcome you into his heavenly gates. You knew about the Night Walker's power and you chose to let it slip through your fingers. I will not make that same mistake."

Calisto watched Jose's hand tighten on the blade at Kate's throat. Staring into her eyes, Calisto finally allowed himself to peer into her mind. Her thoughts were clear.

I don't want to die.

He lunged at Jose with inhuman speed, knocking him to the ground, and punched him so hard that he felt Jose's jaw crumble with the force of the blow. Kate fell, gasping, and the pungent scent of blood exploded through him.

Calisto, help me!

Turning around, he lifted Kate into his arms. Blood pumped out of her severed artery at an alarming rate. Her battered body broke his heart. The stab wounds and the cut on her abdomen could be mended with his blood, but he feared the damage to her neck, her jugular vein, might be too severe. What if she still bled internally?

If he offered his blood into her body to heal the internal injuries, she would be changed forever.

"Call 9-1-1!" he screamed at the monsignor.

The old man disappeared down the stairs as Calisto stared back into her eyes, blood-filled tears sliding down his cheeks. "I cannot lose you again, Kate."

"I love you," she whispered. Her hand rose to touch his cool cheek, wiping away his tear before falling back to her chest again.

He bent to kiss her forehead, and a searing pain shot through the back of his left shoulder. Calisto turned to see Jose's hand draw back again before his blade bit into Calisto's arm. He held Kate in one arm and shoved Jose with the other, sending the man flying back into the other wall.

Calisto wished he had fed. His strength dwindled and his wounds healed much slower than they should. And now he was losing blood. Carefully he put Kate down, resting her back against the closet. Her eyes widened, and Calisto spun around just as Jose rushed him, knocking him to the floor.

Jose sliced into Calisto's chest viciously with his razor blade, but it wasn't the razor that Calisto fought to keep away. It was Jose's disfigured, gaping mouth.

The more Calisto bled, the more the monk struggled to drink the blood. And the more blood loss he suffered, the weaker Calisto became. Finally, Jose managed to close his mouth around a wound in Calisto's wrist. Grabbing Jose's hair, he yanked him back. How much had he taken? Was it enough to change him?

He couldn't take that risk.

Summoning up the last of his strength, Calisto rolled over, pinning Jose on the floor underneath him. With his eyes glowing crimson, he plunged his hand through Jose's ribcage and tore out his still-beating heart. The madman gurgled beneath him, his hands dropping to the floor. Calisto watched the life drain from his crazed eyes before he turned his attention to the still pulsing organ in his hand. Did it any of his immortal blood hide within its chambers?

With his back to Kate, Calisto lifted Jose's heart to his lips and drank, emptying it of what little blood remained in the chambers before dropping it back onto Jose's lifeless chest. Surely the immortal Night Walker blood couldn't change Jose's body without a heart to pump it through his veins.

Calisto heard a weak moan and spun around, hurrying back to Kate's side. Her chest rose and fell with shallow, raspy breaths. She looked deathly pale. Blood still oozed from her wounds, painting the white closet door a vicious red.

He was losing her.

"No!" he screamed, lifting her into his arms and cradling her. "Please Kate... Stay with me. Please. Do not leave me."

He wept and opened his mind to hers. She barely clung to consciousness as he whispered into her mind. *I love you.*

I don't want to die. Please, Calisto, don't let me die.

He drew back to meet her eyes, searching them for answers. "Do you understand what you are asking, my love? If I do this, you will no longer be human. You will be a Night Walker."

Fate brought us together. It was supposed to be different this time.
Her eyes pleaded with him. *I don't want to leave you. Not again.*

He opened the collar of his shirt, his heart heavy with guilt and
sorrow. He never wanted this dark life for her. Would she grow to
resent him for stealing the sunshine from her life? Did she really
understand how this would change her?

He was too selfish to hesitate.

Using Jose's blade, he made a deep cut into his shoulder and
cradled her head close to him. He placed a tender kiss to her ear and
whispered, "Drink, and live forever."

Her lips felt like heaven on his skin, but he didn't feel a pull at his
veins. Was she already unconscious?

He held her tighter, closing his eyes, praying she would drink.
Suddenly he felt her mouth come alive, sucking, drinking him into her
injured body. Calisto fell to his knees, feeling her blood soak through
his pants as he held her tight. His body screamed with hunger the
more she drank from him. He stroked her hair tenderly, and watched
as his blood mended her mortal wounds.

He prayed that her mind and heart would remain unchanged. He
couldn't bear to see the madness in her eyes that had haunted Lukas
centuries before.

Drink from me, she whispered into his mind.

Calisto kissed her shoulder, trembling with temptation. *Not yet.*

He felt her strength returning, her body clinging to his, no longer
weighing heavily in his arms, and finally Calisto's heart rate calmed.
Fate would not steal her from him this time. Her destiny had changed.
Forever.

§

The pain faded away, and she realized Calisto held her in his arms
while she drank. She never imagined she could be so thirsty. His blood
made her feel warm all over, her skin tingled, and her lips ached for
more.

She wasn't sure how, but she communicated with him without
speaking. She only thought her words and he seemed to hear them
and answer directly back into her mind. There weren't words to tell

him how much she loved him, but she thought if he drank from her, maybe the feelings in her heart would pass through to him.

But he wouldn't drink, and now she felt him trembling. Was she making him weak? Kate pulled away, but he held her close, his voice echoing in her mind.

Do not worry for me, Kate. Drink deeply and be strong.

She nodded against him, taking more of his blood into her body, making him part of her. Her arms slid around his waist, clinging to him as his blood filled her mouth again and again.

"In the name of God, what have you done?"

Kate turned to see the old priest, the one Jose had called a monsignor, standing in the doorway. Without a word, Calisto rose to his feet, still cradling her in his arms. She rested her hand over his heart, amazed to find the wound she had just drunk from already healing.

"What I have done has nothing to do with God."

"Does Kate know she has sold her soul to the Devil himself?"

Calisto laughed, shaking his head. "Is that what you believe?"

The monsignor looked at Jose's dead body and back to Calisto, raising the cross around his neck. Calisto glared at the leader of the Fraternidad as he carried Kate past the priest.

"Your cross has no power over me, Monsignor. And I am no one's servant, least of all Satan's." He stopped and turned back to face the priest once more. "If you wish to blame someone for what has happened here tonight, I suggest you reflect on your own actions."

"I was trying to save her from this fate," the monsignor said.

"I had no intention of making Kate a Night Walker. My only wish was to love her for all of her life. I never would have stolen the sunlight from her. You and the madman you sent made this necessary. Because of your effort to meddle in my affairs, innocent blood has been spilled again, and for what purpose? Is my existence worth so much to you and your church? Perhaps now you will finally leave me in peace."

Calisto started down the stairs. Kate heard his heart pounding in his chest and felt his strength ebbing, but he didn't allow it to show.

I can walk, Calisto.

Rest, he whispered into her mind. *I need to get you away from here.*

The monsignor called after him, "If I am to blame, then why have I not met the same fate as Brother Mentigo and Brother De Cardina before him? Why am I still alive?"

Calisto glared over his shoulder at the monsignor and growled. "Because there are worse punishments than death. Live with your guilt, old man. May it rot in your heart and kill you slowly for many years to come."

§

Calisto didn't stop again. Every step made his body ache, and the sunrise threatened to steal what remained of his strength. He struggled and forced himself to keep moving, clutching Kate close to his chest. Once he reached the beach, he stopped and lowered her to the ground.

She looked up at him with concern in her eyes. "You're weak."

Calisto nodded. "There is much I need to tell you, but the sunrise is too close. We have to take shelter."

"Will you be all right?"

"I need to rest and then I will feed," he said, hoping he masked the true depth of his exhaustion. He wasn't sure he had the strength to move the rock face to get them inside his underground resting place.

Kate nodded. "Where do we go to rest?"

Calisto raised a shaky hand and pointed at the entrance to a small cave in the side of the sandy face of the cliff. He took her hand and led her into the darkness. When they reached the back of the cave, Calisto leaned against the wall, resting. Kate felt the rock that barricaded their entrance, exploring it as if she were looking for some kind of secret handle. He stumbled beside her.

"There is no key or latch and it is too heavy for humans to lift without a crane."

"Then how do we get inside?"

"I will roll it aside," he said, moving to the right side of the boulder. He wasn't at all sure he could budge the stone in his weakened state, but he had to try.

"Can't we just stay in your bedroom below the house?"

"No. The monsignor knows where I live. If he comes to search for us he will eventually find the room and us, and if the sun is still in the sky, I am not sure you would survive being exposed to it. I will not take that risk."

What usually seemed easy was now practically impossible. Finally he managed to shove the rock aside far enough for them to crawl through.

Kate moved through the opening first, before he followed her into the darkness. Panic seized him for a moment when he tried to replace the boulder across the mouth of the cave. He didn't have the strength to move it.

Then Kate stood beside him, digging her feet in the sandy soil as she pushed with him. He didn't have to ask. She was simply there for him. He no longer walked alone in this world. The realization stunned him. Never again. Gradually, with her help, they rolled the boulder back into place.

Calisto sank to his knees, no longer able to stand. He couldn't remember a time when he had ever been so exhausted. He felt Kate take his hand and slowly forced his exhausted eyes to open.

"Just leave me. There is a bed at the end of the cavern."

"I'm not spending another day without you," she whispered, hooking his arm around her shoulder. "Come on."

Calisto struggled to his feet, leaning on her to maintain his balance. They made their way through the darkness toward the dimly lit cavern. The tiny oil lamp he left burning sat on a small alcove he carved out of the cave just across from the antique bed. He saw his reflection in the mirror on the wall and grimaced. His face looked pale and gaunt, and his hair lost its inhuman luster.

"I look as dead as I feel," he whispered as Kate helped him down onto the bed.

A tender smile lit her features as she pulled his boots free. "Everyone is allowed to get tired once in a while. Even you."

He brought his hand up to caress her cheek. Her skin already felt cooler to the touch. Less human. "I am so sorry, Kate."

She lay down beside him, staring into his eyes as she spoke. "I made this choice. You don't have anything to be sorry for."

"You have no idea what I have cursed you with."

"As if sharing forever with you could be a curse." She took his hand, entwining her fingers with his.

A smile tugged at the corner of his mouth. "Do you have any idea how much I love you?"

"Now you'll have forever to tell me... " Kate kissed his lips and whispered, "Rest now. You have a lot to teach me once the sun goes down."

He opened his arms, holding her close. "While we sleep your body will die... "

He tried to warn her about the changes she would find when she awoke, but the sun rose over the earth, draining him.

"Then I'll die in your arms."

He smiled and kissed her hair, lifting his head to take one last look at her beautiful face. She was already lost to the sun, but the soft smile on her lips warmed his cold body.

"You have my heart forever, my love."

His head settled back on the pillow, his arms holding her close as the sun stole his final breath from his body.

Chapter Thirty-One

Kate shivered, her heart picking up a slow rhythm. The echo of a lone wolf's mournful howl haunted her as her eyes fluttered open. Seeing Calisto leaning up on his elbow, looking down at her with his lips curved in a sensuous smile, banished the residual loneliness of her dream.

She reached up to cup his cheek. "This is much better than waking up to a note that you had out-of-town business." She pulled him down to kiss her lips and murmured softly, "I'm going to like waking up with you."

Calisto smiled and nibbled at her lower lip. "This is the first time I have ever awakened to find a beautiful woman in my bed."

"Ever?" Kate arched her brow.

"*Sí.* When I was mortal I spent my life as a priest until I met you. We met in the shadows, but we never got the chance to drift off in each other's arms. The day I confessed and gave up my vows was the day Tala... " His words drifted off as he bent to kiss her again. "Waking to see your face is the greatest gift I have ever received."

Before she could reply, Calisto got out of bed and slid one arm under her neck and the other under her knees. Kate shivered, wrapping her arms around his neck. "Where are we going?"

Calisto smiled, carrying her from the room. "I have a hot bath ready for you."

Kate peered around behind them and cringed, closing her eyes. The bed was a mess, the white sheets stained and rumpled. Calisto hadn't been kidding the night before when he told her that her body would die while they slept. No wonder she'd felt wet and cold when she woke up.

"I did all that last night?"

Calisto kissed her forehead as he lowered her feet to the floor of his large marble bathroom. "It wasn't you, my love. The Night Walker blood banishes all of the remains of your humanity while your body is transformed."

She wanted to crawl under a rock. Instead, she stepped down into the sunken tub. The hot water felt good on her cool skin. "I'll clean it up. I don't want you to have to."

"Look at me." She met his eyes and he lowered his voice. "Please do not be embarrassed by this change. It is like being born again to the night. Nothing more." He kissed her. "Rest here while I clean up and feed."

Kate settled into the steaming water, watching Calisto's naked form disappear into their bedroom.

Their room.

She rested her head back against the marble tub and lifted one hand out of the lavender scented bubbles. Her skin didn't look any different. She spread her fingers, turning her hand back and forth before letting it slide back into the warm water. Last night seemed like a bad dream. Under the water, her fingertips slid along her abdomen, searching for the deep cut Jose had made, but her skin felt smooth. She reached up to her shoulder for the place he'd stabbed her, but again, the wound wasn't even tender.

Was she really immortal now? It seemed impossible. She closed her eyes, drifting off in the warm bathwater.

She sat up when Calisto returned. He stripped the sheets from the bed and bagged them. She tried not to remember the death she'd seen in the bed. Blood, vomit, and she didn't even want to think about what else. Her wounds were healed, and the fact that she could hear something as soft as sheets sliding off the mattress was evidence that her hearing was enhanced now too.

What else could she do?

Calisto?

Instantly, he leaned against the doorway. His hair hung loose around his face, and the view only got better as her eyes slid down his muscular frame. He wore a pair of jeans and nothing else.

"You heard me." Kate slid a little lower in the tub.

He nodded, the corner of his mouth curving into a smile. "Of course I did. Your mind reached out to mine."

Kate gnawed at her bottom lip. "Could you hear everything else I was thinking?"

"I could, but I have always respected your privacy." Calisto stripped off his jeans and stepped into the spacious bathtub behind her. He lifted her onto his lap, sliding his arms around her waist. "Unless your mind reaches for mine, your thoughts are your own."

Tipping her head back to look at him, she smiled. "That's probably a good thing. I had some pretty impure thoughts going."

He held her tighter and kissed along her shoulder. "Sounds very... intriguing."

She turned around to face him, her legs straddling his waist. Calisto claimed her lips, and she moaned into the kiss. His tongue tangled with hers, teasing her with the faint taste of blood. Something foreign stirred inside of her, animalistic and urgent.

Kate broke the kiss, gasping for breath as she rested her forehead against his. She wet her lips. "I'm really thirsty. I think I need some water."

He held her a little tighter, kissing her hair. "It is not water you thirst for."

She looked up at him with a crease in her brow. "What are you saying?"

Calisto caressed her cheek. "You are a Night Walker now. To live you must feed on life."

She pulled back from his arms. "You make it sound noble, but what you're really trying to tell me is that I need to drink people's blood. That I'm… thirsty for it." She shook her head, her eyes downcast. "I don't think I could bite someone. I can't imagine drinking… " She shuddered, her voice fading away.

He grasped her chin, tilting her head so their gazes met. "I am sorry, Kate. I wish there had been some other way. I never wanted this life for you."

Guilt and worry filled his gaze.

"This isn't your fault. I didn't want to leave you. I understood what you were doing, and I'll deal with all of this. I will." Somehow. She pressed her lips together, fighting the hunger brewing inside of her. Though she tried to imagine biting someone, she could only envision herself in a cape with fangs. Ridiculous. She grinned. "I don't think I'm ready for blood-sucking vampire lessons just yet."

Calisto rolled his eyes and laughed. When he relaxed against her, she traced his chest muscles. "We are not blood-sucking vampires," he said.

"I know." She rubbed her pelvis against his and kissed him. "I just wanted to see you smile again."

Calisto bit her lower lip lightly, teasing her new heightened senses. "How did I live so long without your kisses?"

She parted her lips, and her tongue tangled with his. He cupped the back of her head and moaned into the kiss. She shifted her hips, and he pressed against her opening.

He thrust up, sinking himself deep inside of her. She dropped her head back with a gasp. Calisto bent to take her exposed breast into his mouth, enjoying the way her fingernails dug into his shoulders.

He licked over her nipple slowly, slid his hands down her wet body, gripped her waist, ground against her, and claimed her.

The candlelight flickered around them, bathing them in a warm glow as the water teased her cool, sensitive skin. All of her senses seemed more acute, more intense. She could feel every sensation, every curve, every inch of his body caressing hers. He thrust into her, slowly at first, his eyes locked with hers.

Staring into his eyes, she felt her mind instinctively slip into his. She felt his heated desire and love for her, his concern over her transformation, and finally...

Before she could identify the emotion, his mind was closed to hers.

Kate brought her hands up from his shoulders to cup his face. "No more secrets. Please, Calisto."

His thrusts slowed and his eyes sparkled. Something was happening with his eyes. They were changing. Her heart pounded. His dark eyes now glowed crimson. She'd never seen anything like it, but she wasn't afraid.

"What's wrong?"

He wet his lips. "Nothing is wrong."

"But your eyes." She searched his face for any other changes.

He brought a hand up from her hip, trailing a wet finger along the curve of her neck. "Your blood calls to me."

She turned to kiss his finger before meeting his eyes again. "Is it because I'm a Night Walker now?"

He shook his head slowly. "No. Your blood has been a temptation for me every time we made love."

"But your eyes never changed before."

"I was careful, hiding my true nature as best I could." Calisto slid his hand back into her hair as he kissed her lips, and Kate couldn't help but wonder if he had fangs now. Calisto met her eyes again. "Do I frighten you now?"

"No." She hesitated. "Are my eyes glowing too?"

"Not yet." Calisto wrapped his arms around her, his kiss demanding her submission. She moaned as his tongue claimed hers. His hips worked slow and deep, rendering her incapable of coherent thought. Tilting her head, she deepened the kiss until she tasted blood.

She jerked back from the kiss, shocked to feel her pulse race at the sight of blood coloring Calisto's lips. He reached up to wipe it away, but she caught his hand. This was the blood that saved her life and changed every part of her. She leaned forward and kissed him, her tongue tasting his lower lip.

"Did I cut you?" She whispered against his lips.

"Yes."

She shivered at the desire in his voice. "You liked it?"

He nodded, meeting her eyes. "Very much." His lips curved into a dangerous, sexy smile. "I have never made love with another Night Walker."

Kate wet her lips, feeling truly desirable for the first time ever. She didn't know if it was because she was a Night Walker, or knowing that she'd loved Calisto for lifetimes.

At the moment, she didn't care.

Kate smiled and leaned in close, her lips brushing against his ear. "I have." She drew back and rested her forehead against his with a satisfied grin. "I'll be gentle with you."

Calisto smiled and wrapped his arms around her, fusing their lips together. Kate clung to him, no longer sure where her body ended and Calisto's began. Her mind slipped into his once more, and in that moment she'd never felt closer to another soul. They were one.

Almost, my love. Calisto's voice whispered through her mind. *Drink from me.*

Kate's heart fluttered, but he responded, slamming into her harder and faster, driving conscious thought from her mind as he kissed and nibbled his way down her neck to her shoulder. She felt his sharp teeth brush over her skin, but instead of tensing, her pulse quickened. Her skin felt hot, hungry. His lips caressed her shoulder and his mind reached out to her again.

Please Kate. Be one with me.

Kissing along the muscle of his shoulder, she surrendered herself to the passion. She sucked at his skin, her teeth teasing his flesh. One of his hands sank lower in the water, between them, stroking her and urging her even closer to the edge. With her body on fire, aching for release, she sank her teeth into his shoulder.

Lightning shot through Calisto's body the moment Kate burst through the final barrier between their souls. The pull at his veins as she drank him into herself sent waves of hot, erotic pleasure through his entire body. He kissed along her perfect ivory shoulder until he could no longer fight the temptation.

He moaned against her skin when he tasted her blood on his tongue. Making love to her, sharing her body, her blood, her soul, he'd never felt passion like this before. He could feel her love for him, her acceptance of their new destiny and life together. Her hunger and desire for him.

The water splashed around them, out onto the floor, but he didn't care. He needed her now. All of her.

I'm yours. She gasped into his mind as her body clenched around him, taking him over the edge with her. He didn't loosen his hold on her as he kissed over his bite, watching the pinpricks close on her skin.

"And I am yours, my love." He drew back just enough to meet her eyes. "I love you."

She smiled, and he felt his spirit soar. "I love you too." Kate kissed him and whispered against his lips. "Always."

EPILOGUE

The moonlight sparkled on the water. Calisto lay on the beach, leaning back on his elbows, laughing as he watched Kate practice calling fish onto the shore.

"You could help me, you know." She grinned over her shoulder, struggling to catch the jumping fish before the tide pulled them back into the water.

"I could, but watching is much more fun." He smiled.

She amazed him more with each passing night. Over the past two weeks she had already embraced so many changes, in her body and her mind. He tried to introduce her new powers slowly, to ease the transition, but Kate took to her newfound talents and abilities with a natural grace that astonished him.

What pleased him most, in spite of all of the changes she faced, deep down she remained the same spirit, his mortal love, Kate. The moon still shone in her eyes, and she never missed an opportunity to laugh.

And as impossible as it seemed, he loved her more with each passing night.

Kate splashed through the water, groaning as the last fish got away. "I give up!" She walked up and plopped down onto the sand beside him. "What good is using telepathy to call the fish to me if I can't get them to stay still once they're up on the sand?"

Calisto shook his head with a smile. "I never did like fish anyway."

"I was just practicing. I'm new to this Night Walker thing, remember?" She smiled and kissed him. "Ready to dance with me?"

He raised a brow. "Are you finished calling the fish?"

"Would you stop that?"

"Stop what?" He struggled to keep from smiling.

"Answering my questions with another question."

"Will this do instead?" Calisto sat up, kissing her deeply as he rose from the sand and pulled her up into his arms. Slowly he drew back, lost in the dark beauty of the moonlight shining in her eyes.

"You can answer me with kisses anytime," she whispered with a smile.

"Good." He took her hand, walking out into the waves. He hadn't waltzed in centuries, but with Kate in his arms, it was easy. Her laughter, her smile, just hearing her say his name made his heart soar.

Eternity was theirs to share.

The marine layer floated in from the ocean tide, surrounding them until the moonlight became an iridescent glow. The waves lapped at their ankles while they turned in each other's arms, laughing together. Calisto smiled down at her, stealing a kiss.

The lifetimes he spent waiting for her spirit to enter this world were worth every second.

§

Overhead, wings glided silently on the night breeze. A white-headed eagle with intelligent eyes soared above them, watching from a distance.

Finally, his plan had begun to unfold. She was immortal. Again. He had waited thousands of years for this night, had been the instrument of fate to ensure they would come together. The world would be his once more. But he had to be patient. Tonight, he would only watch them. Watch and wait.

For now.

Acknowledgements

There are so many people I want to thank that I'm not sure where to start. I'd like to thank the entire crew at Entangled Publishing for welcoming me into the family. Liz Pelletier, who invited me to submit my book, and Heather Howland, for making me the perfect cover and capturing the heart of the book in the tagline, I can't thank you two enough.

I also want to thank Kelley Armstrong and Barbara Vey, who encouraged me to join RWA and pursue my publishing dream. Your encouragement has meant the world to me!

I also owe the last chapter to Angie Fox, who thought Calisto and Kate deserved it. Thanks for all your valuable feedback and guidance!

To my fabulous editor KL Grady, thank you so much for coming on this journey with me! It's still surreal to me that we ended up working together again on my first novel! How cool is that?

Thanks to my wonderful publicist, Roxanne Rhoads, for helping me to get the word out about the book, and keeping the schedule organized for me.

I could not have pulled off the medical references in the book without the input of Dr. D.P. Lyle.

Lastly, I have to thank my husband, Ken Kessler, and my mom, Ally Benbrook, who have read *Night Walker* in all its versions and never complained. Thanks for always making the time to read and give me your feedback! Through all the ups and downs on this publishing journey, you never stopped supporting me and believing this book would be published. I couldn't have done this without you.

About the Author

Lisa lives in San Diego with her husband, two teens, three dogs and a cat. She loves hearing from readers: LdyDisney@aol.com. Visit her at: http://Lisa-Kessler.com.

Made in the USA
Charleston, SC
24 October 2011